Raid on the Bremerton

Raid on the Bremerton

Irv Eachus

THE VIKING PRESS / NEW YORK

Copyright © Irving A. Eachus, 1980
All rights reserved
First published in 1980 by The Viking Press
625 Madison Avenue, New York, N.Y. 10022
Published simultaneously in Canada by
Penguin Books Canada Limited

LIBRARY OF CONGRESS CATALOGING IN PUBLICATION DATA
Eachus, Irv
  Raid on the Bremerton.
  I. Title.
PZ4.E115RA   [PS3555.A25]   813'.54   80-14635
ISBN 0-670-58912-8

Printed in the United States of America
Set in CRT Gael

To Susan Odbert Eachus, with love

AUTHOR'S NOTE

This is a work of fiction. The incidents, technical details and specifications, and major characters are imagined. Where real-life public figures are portrayed, their words and actions are strictly my own invention.

The vessel, reactor plant, shipboard organization, and procedures depicted here are based on fact, and the naval base at Long Beach, California, is generally as it is described in the story. However, there is no nuclear-powered cruiser named *USS Bremerton*, and there are no nuclear-powered ships presently home-ported at the Long Beach facility.

Only when my characters exhibit dedication, resourcefulness, loyalty, and humanity do they even generally resemble the men of the U.S. nuclear navy with whom I served.

I.E.
Davis, California
November, 1979

Thursday, January 10

1

They moved among the abandoned warehouses like a pair of wary rats, scurrying from shadow to shadow, pausing repeatedly to test the damp night for any hint of danger.

Stay low, the German had taught them; move fast, stop often. If they spot you, run like hell, and never turn to fight unless there is no place else to go.

Of the two the woman was the better at it. Her young body was strong and nimble, her balance superb, her rhythm smooth and easy so that the parts of her body seemed to flow in a single motion. She virtually danced along the broken asphalt, neatly dodging the tall clumps of brittle brown grass that pushed up through the cracks. After four hundred yards she was hardly panting.

The man lumbered along after her. He was huge, a full head taller than the woman, so big through the chest and shoulders that he appeared top-heavy, as though he would topple over if he ever stopped, if he could stop at all. His shoes crunched on the loose surface, sending showers of stones scattering into the darkness, making more than enough noise for both of them.

The woman led. She chose their course through the shadows and decided when they would pause to survey the broken ground. And she carried the closest thing they had to a weapon: an ordinary buck knife taped to the inside of her left calf. The man followed a few yards behind, effortlessly toting a black canvas satchel football fashion in the crook of his right arm, though it was packed with more than forty pounds of tools and equipment.

They were dressed identically—blue Levi's, black turtle-neck sweaters, black gloves, black running shoes, blue navy-style watch caps pulled down over their ears—but the effect was markedly different. In the clinging outfit she became panther-like, sleek and taut. He looked like nothing less than a Black Angus bull, a mass of charging muscle.

They stopped at the corner of the last building and crouched together in the shadows, close to the wall, careful not to rub against the peeling beige paint. The night was calm and overcast, cold by Southern California standards even for January. By morning the fog would be on the ground, cutting visibility to a few yards, but for the time being it swirled several hundred feet overhead, aglow with the light of the nearby city so that it diffused a faint gray luminescence over the landscape like a counterfeit dawn.

Before them was a large open field covered with weeds that had been mowed down to ankle-high stubble. In the center, amid heaps of discarded gravel and dirt, less than a hundred yards from their hiding place, they could see the transformer within its high-fenced enclosure, illuminated by a single overhead floodlight.

The man checked his watch. It showed 11:08. Immediately he opened the satchel and began to unpack.

The woman touched his wrist. "Wait until the jitney goes by," she whispered. She had been well taught; her voice was barely audible.

"What for? They ain't gonna see us."

"Just wait," she ordered.

A flicker of annoyance showed on his face, but he shrugged and settled back on his haunches.

Their hiding place was situated almost a half mile from the mainland on a low, manmade peninsula known as "the Mole," a massive, three-mile-long jetty that hooked out into San Pedro Bay to form a large, well-protected harbor. To their left was the Pacific Ocean, an oily black expanse that merged into the overcast with no distinguishable horizon. To their right, beyond the building and narrow road, was the inner harbor, its calm surface mirroring the lights of the mainland.

Few sounds reached them, and those that did were muted by the absorbing cloud cover. There was the steady slosh of the surf and a faint tinkle of music from across the harbor and a faraway creaking of ships against their moorings, but all those were rendered flat and lifeless, like cheap sound effects. Only the constant, powerful hum of the nearby transformer seemed real and immediate. The two sat listening to it until the jitney appeared, a pair of flickering headlights far down the road.

"A minute early," the woman announced, checking her watch.

The man looked up just in time to catch a glimpse of the vehicle, half the size of a normal bus, dirty, faded gray, bouncing and grinding its way toward the docks, carrying no more than five or six passengers. The noise allowed them to follow its progress as it stopped at the piers, made the big turn at the end of the Mole, and headed back past them toward the mainland. Only when the sound had died away completely was he permitted to unpack.

While the satchel's contents were being unwrapped and sorted, the woman stood and surveyed the route to the transformer. Their movements up to this point had been hidden by the buildings and a nearly total darkness, but on the final approach they would come within the glare of the floodlight. This was the part that would depend least on skill and most on luck—on the chance that no one would be walking along the ocean or driving up the road or watching too closely from one of the buildings across the harbor. It was not a moment she was looking forward to.

She picked up a bag of tools and whispered to the man, "You ready?"

He nodded.

"Okay, let's go!"

Stealth was now pointless. She went at a dead run, covering the distance in thirteen seconds and sliding feet-first into the base of the fence. Immediately she scrambled to the corner of the enclosure and peered around for a quick check of the road. Nothing. She signaled to her partner.

He came more slowly, the gear flapping from his shoulders, one loose line skittering along the ground behind him. He skidded to a stop, showering her with a hail of small rocks and dirt, grinning.

The woman ignored him and turned to study their target. The fence was constructed of heavy galvanized chain link, over eight feet high. The only gate was on the harbor side, secured with a heavy chain and a brass padlock that would have taken a half pound of explosives to blow. At eye level on all four sides were warning signs, metal rectangles with enormous faded-red letters that warned:

DANGER—EXTREME HIGH VOLTAGE

and in smaller print beneath:

Authorized Personnel Only

And, as if the signs and lock were not enough, five strands of rusty barbed wire encircled the top of the fence.

Inside stood the transformer, over thirty tons of humming copper and steel, truly monstrous at close range. Its casing alone stood six feet tall. On top, like three ribbed horns, were the five-foot-tall, oil-filled insulators connecting it to the thirteen-kilovolt input from the overhead powerlines. Long vertical metal bars, ten to a side, were welded to the casing to increase the cooling surface. The entire assembly was bolted to a twenty-by-twenty-foot slab of ten-inch-thick concrete. Everything, including the pole that supported the floodlight, was painted a chalky gray.

The woman looked up at the top of the fence and scowled. "The barbed wire we practiced on was a lot tighter. Can you handle this?"

"No sweat," the man said. "Just stand back and watch."

He unrolled a long, narrow piece of canvas and with a

quick throw flipped it neatly over the top. Next he took a carefully coiled rope ladder made of nylon lines and wooden crossbars and, twirling it like a lariat, tossed it so that it lay on the canvas, creating a lightweight but very serviceable ladder on both sides of the fence.

The two moved with even greater haste now that their equipment lay in plain view. The ends of the ropes had hardly touched the ground inside the enclosure before the woman had them secured to the bottom of the fence and was urging him to get going. He tested the ladder, showed her where to steady it, and started up. In a few seconds he was at the top and ready to turn, but then he heard her sharp warning.

"Car coming! Get down!"

For an instant he was caught squarely in the glare of the approaching headlights. Then he jumped, leaping sideways to avoid hitting her, landing with a thud and rolling onto his belly. The woman went flat, too, sprawled face-down in the dirt. They were hidden by the transformer, but above them their climbing gear hung unfurled like a banner.

The woman crawled to the end of the fence and looked around. "It's going awful damn slow," she hissed. "It could be Security."

"Maybe," the man answered, clearly skeptical. His doubts seemed justified as the car continued past slowly, but suddenly the brake lights flashed and it jerked to a stop.

"Shit, they've spotted us!" Her tone was tense but not panicky.

"No," the man whispered, moving up beside her, "I don't think so. Let's wait a minute."

They looked on intently as the passenger door flew open and the sound of male laughter poured out. "If you puke in here I'll kill you!" somebody yelled. And then, amid more laughter, a figure stumbled from the car and began retching at the side of the road. The insults from inside the car continued, countered by a barrage of groans and obscenities from the sick man. After three or four minutes, two men clambered out of the back seat and began dragging the protesting sufferer back toward the car. "Let the sonofabitch walk," the driver called out, but they somehow managed to load him in and shut the door. The arguing continued for another long minute, and then, with a squeal of tires, the car was gone.

The man stood up and wiped off the gravel imbedded in his palms. "Whew!" he said, grinning. "We barely escaped that time."

The woman answered his sarcasm with a glare. "Let's get to it."

He moved obediently toward the ladder, but his chuckling continued.

The second time he made it over without incident, using the awesome strength of his arms to haul himself up and over, then dropping the last six feet to the ground. In a few seconds he was standing inside, waiting to catch the bag of equipment.

He unpacked quickly, arranging the contents in precise order along the base of the fence. When everything was ready he pulled on a pair of surgical gloves and turned toward the machine. He had read the technical manual several times and forgotten most of it, but he was an expert on one particular component, the cooling oil drain, a common half-inch valve hidden between two support girders at the base of the casing. It was to that component that he now directed his attention.

He worked efficiently, following a procedure he had memorized during endless rehearsals. The valve was located under the bottom lip of the casing, out of reach of the floodlight, so he operated entirely by touch as he had during the blindfolded trial runs, identifying his tools by notches etched into the handles and measuring dimensions by the width of his thumb. A small flashlight was fastened to a chain around his neck for use if it was needed. It never was.

The woman waited outside the fence, glancing from him to her watch to the deserted road in an anxious cycle. She could only see his crouching figure and hear the click of metal tools and his occasional grunts. Every once in a while he would straighten up and flex the stiffness out of his back, but immediately he would bend down again and resume his work. He said nothing to indicate how well he was progressing. Then, suddenly, she heard a heavy splattering sound and saw a river of dark amber begin flowing toward the edge of the concrete slab. She knew this was the oil used to cool the transformer, and with the valve cranked wide open, it was gushing out in a violent hemorrhage that held her spellbound.

Meanwhile the man was in constant motion, climbing to the top of the casing to adjust the vent, then to his cache of tools, then back to the valve to check on the flow. The first trickle of oil had been only slightly warm to the touch, but as it spilled out, gallon after gallon, reducing the cooling capacity by a third, then a half, it began to smoke like motor oil on a hot manifold, and a sweet burning smell filled the air.

When two-thirds of the coolant had been bled off, he stopped the flow by closing the vent and began working on the valve. Despite the slippery gloves and the awkwardness of having to balance on a support strut to keep from stepping in the spreading pool of oil, it took him only six minutes to disassemble the valve, install a faulty disk in place of the good one, and reassemble it. When he was finished, he noted with satisfaction that a small trickle of coolant continued to seep from the outlet.

There was nothing left for him to do but clean up and get out. And quickly, too, for the hum was already beginning to build into an angry buzz.

He threw the tools and parts and finally the rubber gloves into a spare plastic bag and tossed it to the woman. The lake of oil had spread to the bottom of the ladder, forcing him to leap for the second rung, but he made it easily and joined the woman as she finished packing for their escape. The rope ladder was hauled down and coiled over his shoulder. There was a moment of concern when the canvas snagged on the barbed wire, but he was finally able to jerk it free and wad it into a spare bag. Together they swept the ground clean of tracks, turned for a final check of their work, and picked up the gear.

By 11:45, slightly ahead of schedule, they were gone.

2

Karl Schmidt sat on the balcony of his Ocean Boulevard apartment, gazing toward the sea and wondering if the fog would settle in before the explosion occurred. So far it had held off, and the view of the coastline was clear: from Orange County, with its glittering lights, north to the Point Fermin beacon, and as far out as the fourth offshore oil platform camouflaged with concrete facades and colored floodlights. But his apartment was on the twelfth floor, and the fog seemed to be hovering just inches overhead, threatening to engulf his perch at any moment. Not that he particularly cared, but he knew that Andrea would care very much.

He slouched in a big, high-backed wicker chair, seemingly relaxed, his feet propped up on the middle rung of the wrought-iron railing. He was supposed to be on watch, but only occasionally did he pick up the pair of precision German-made binoculars and scan the naval base three miles away. For the most part he was satisfied just to sit and wait.

He was a tall, handsome man in his mid-forties, strong and lean, with angular features and an abundance of dark wavy hair salted with gray. He was dressed in worn brown cords, a plaid flannel shirt, and a pair of well-polished soft leather boots. To ward off the night chill he had put on a quilted nylon jacket, which he wore unzipped with the collar turned up to pillow his head. In his left hand he held a pipe, in his right a small tumbler which he frequently refilled from a fifth of Scotch on the table beside him.

The pipe was there out of habit and a genuine taste for the sweet, biting smoke. The Scotch was a different matter, part of a deliberate effort to drink himself out of a serious and persistent depression. Karl Schmidt was worried. He was worried about the operation, about his new and sometimes bizarre colleagues, even about himself. Worry was something that had never before plagued him in twenty years as an operative; nervousness and fear, yes, many times, but not worry, not the nagging, brooding anxiety that ate at his ease of mind like a malignant tumor. In the old days, in places behind the Wall, it would have been called Defeatism with a capital D, a crime for which one could be sent to prison, to an asylum, or even shot. Whether or not it was a crime, he knew it was undisciplined, counterproductive, and possibly dangerous. People who worried should not get into this business, and those who did got out quickly, one way or another.

He also knew it was damn useless. The clock had started, as Andrea was fond of saying; the operation was already under way. Most of his belongings were gathered together, ready to be shipped out of the country the following morning. The things he would need over the next few days had been set aside, innocent things like his razor and toothbrush that would be of no use to the swarms of investigators who would inevitably come. Those special items that he was taking were already packed beneath the false bottom of the toolbox: a packet of German marks and Swiss francs, a legitimate Austrian passport, and, as always, the big .45 automatic, carried so long that the bluing was worn from the barrel. Even the special report was done, except for the final entry. In his usual meticulous fashion he had completed everything, and yet he continued to fret. So he continued to fill the glass.

When the telephone rang at five minutes to midnight the bottle was nearly half empty.

"They're off the base," a man's voice said. It was the Arab.

"Good," Schmidt answered, noting the time. "They are right on schedule. It must have gone well." His voice was deep and his enunciation crisp, as it often is with someone who has studied the language long and carefully. There was a very faint, unidentifiable accent.

"So it would seem," the other man said flatly.

"You do not sound very enthusiastic."

"I think you are foolish to go through with this. These people are amateurs, and crazy besides."

"As I recall, it was you who offered me this assignment."

"I was speaking then as a representative of my government. Now I am speaking as your friend. Get out, Karl. It's not going to work."

"Your concern warms my heart," Schmidt said.

The Arab chuckled. "Like smoldering cow dung."

"Something like that," Schmidt said.

The two men laughed and hung up.

Twenty minutes later Schmidt heard the front door open and close. He leaned around the back of the chair and saw Andrea in the living room, bending over the coffee table and lighting one of her thin brown cigarettes. She had shed the woolen cap and unpinned her long black hair so that it hung in disarray; otherwise she was attired just as she had been an hour earlier out on the Mole.

"I'll be out in a second," she said, and disappeared toward the bedroom. But a few minutes later she called out to him, asking for a shirt. He stepped inside to find her standing in the hallway, nude from the waist up, holding the black turtleneck in her hand.

"It itches," she said by way of an explanation, indicating the sweater. "I tried to find a shirt but everything's packed."

"In the big suitcase on the bed," he said, hardly glancing at her. He had seen her like this many times: the small white breasts with their budlike nipples that jiggled provocatively when she moved, the flat, tanned belly, the slender neck and smooth shoulders. In fact, he had seen all there was to see; she had a habit of walking around with nothing on at all. He thought she was a brazen, probably compulsive exhibitionist, no doubt quite delighted by the reactions she evoked, for all her nonchalance. It was something he had long ago accepted as a harmless eccentricity, if not a pleasant distraction. Only his women friends had ever objected.

She soon reappeared wearing one of his blue long-sleeved dress shirts which, true to form, she had not bothered to button. She lit another cigarette and playfully blew a cloud of smoke in his direction.

"Well?" she asked impatiently.

"Well what?"

"Aren't you going to ask me how it went?"

Schmidt studied her with fascination as though he had never seen her before, which in a sense he had not. She sat coiled on the edge of the couch, flicking her tongue nervously over her lips. The hand that held the cigarette was actually trembling. An ash fell on the table, and she brushed it off without thinking. It was not her usual style. Cold and calculating was all he had known for the months they had been together. Cold and calculating and brilliant and tough and unflappable. He had come to regard her as a kind of emotional celibate, practicing the same discipline and self-control that she preached. But there was nothing cold or calculating about her now. She was as excited as a child just off a roller coaster, watching him expectantly, looking as if she would burst.

"Okay," he said finally. "How did it go?"

"It was a piece of cake! A fucking piece of cake!" Her intensity was extraordinary. Her face was flushed, her dark eyes glittering with delight; even her nipples, revealed as she flung her arms wide in jubilation, were erect with excitement. "You should have been there. My God, it was beautiful, absolutely beautiful. We were in and out again before they even knew we were there. Forty minutes, just like we planned it. And that idiot at the gate, I swear it, Karl, he saluted us on the way out."

She danced across to the bar and splashed a glass full of bourbon, then flung herself onto a stool and swiveled around to face him. Her expression was triumphant. "A piece of cake," she repeated. "And the rest of it will be, too." She raised her glass in a mock toast. "Watch out, you goddamn fascists, here we come."

Her outburst left Schmidt feeling uneasy. He had seen her act tempestuously in the presence of the others, but that was acting in the performance sense. Right now she seemed to be genuinely out of control.

He spoke calmly. "Where's Givens?"

"Getting rid of the van." she answered.

13

"Where?"

"Where? Downtown, of course. That was the plan." An edge of annoyance had crept into her voice; she wanted to celebrate, not be quizzed.

"I thought you were supposed to go with him."

For an instant she was genuinely confused, but then a change came over her. Her gaze hardened into a glare, and her tone became cool and deliberate. "So I changed my mind," she said sharply. "Who the hell's running this operation, me or you?"

Schmidt suddenly felt better. That last line had come from the Andrea he had known all along—a nice bit of indignation, well timed and neatly executed. So was the next one, which she delivered a few beats later.

"I'm sorry, Karl, I didn't mean to snap. But sometimes you're just too goddamn negative."

"I suppose I am," he said, wondering if she suspected how negative he actually felt.

"Even after tonight?"

He avoided her question, moving out onto the balcony instead. But she followed him.

"Come on, Karl, tell me the truth, don't you feel more confident after tonight?"

He leaned back against the railing and looked directly at her. "If you want the truth, Andrea, I will tell you. You have every right to be pleased about tonight. It was an important mission, and apparently you carried it out flawlessly. But it was also a relatively simple operation and a safe one, nothing like what is ahead of us." His tone was gentle but direct. "Besides, at this point we know only that you got out safely. We do not yet know that your effort was successful, or, if it was, that it will be accepted as an accident, or if it is accepted as an accident, that it will produce the necessary results." His smile was soft. "You see, even in this first step there are so many uncertainties."

She laughed bitterly. "You're some optimist."

"You wanted the truth."

She lapsed into a long silence, gazing in the direction of the base. Finally she spoke. "Will we be able to see it from here?"

"See what?"

"When the transformer goes."

"Yes, if the fog stays up."

There was another long silence, then she spoke again, this time with forced confidence. "It *will* work, Karl."

"Your sabotage?"

"The whole operation."

"I hope so, but we must be careful never to underestimate the opposition. If they suspect anything at all they will wipe us out."

"They won't suspect."

"Perhaps. But maybe they already do and are just waiting for us to move before they fold us up. I have known it to happen before."

"It won't this time. I know we'll succeed," she said.

He found her smugness irritating. She was like the proverbial ostrich. "How can you be so certain?"

"I just know."

He fought a flash of anger. "What if one of your young men panics?"

"Impossible," she said. "I have them both under control."

If she had acknowledged even the remote possibility of failure he would not have replied as he did, but her complacency finally got the better of him. "So you are that good a lay?"

"Yes, I am," she snapped, and slumped into the chair. "Now I don't want to talk about it any more."

Schmidt cursed himself for his lapse. All the excitement had left her, replaced by a distant look of depression. She sat shivering in the cold night air, the shirt now wrapped tightly around her and pinned beneath her arms, her knees drawn up and locked together.

The German gazed out at the night and sighed wearily. "You may be right about our chances. Certainly there is nothing we can do about it now."

"Unless we call the whole thing off," she mumbled.

He looked at her, astonished. "You are joking?"

"Well, you're so damn convinced it's going to fail—why not? Should we commit suicide?"

"I am only saying, as I have said all along, that the risks are very great."

"But do you think we have a reasonable chance? Not certain, just reasonable?"

She had trapped him nicely. He could either acquiesce or trigger a bitter and doubtlessly futile argument, one that would force him to examine the basis of his gnawing anxiety much closer than he cared to.

"It is a good plan," he said finally, not quite answering her question.

She accepted the evasion and rewarded him with a wonderful smile. "Yes it is, isn't it?" she said with the pride of authorship.

There was another encounter between them that night, one of a very different sort. Andrea had gone inside, leaving him alone with his thoughts. But a few minutes later she returned, stark naked.

"You interested in getting it on?" she asked, as though she were offering to fix him a sandwich.

"I beg your pardon?"

"Do you want to get it on? That's American for 'do you wanna fuck?' " She was grinning at him, obviously enjoying herself.

"I understand the meaning," he said with annoyance.

"Well then?"

"I understood that ours was to be a purely professional relationship."

"So I've changed my mind."

"Depression therapy for a troubled old man?"

"Maybe. Or maybe I'm just turned on. What difference does it make? It's a hell of a lot better than just sitting around."

"Such romance."

"Answer the question, yes or no?"

"I may not be up to your standards."

She laughed. "That's not what I hear. Literally. Some of your girlfriends are real screamers."

He shook his head. "You astound me."

"Would you please make up your mind—it's cold out here."

He looked at her thoughtfully. "You would have me believe that you want to make love to pass the time?"

"Sure, why not? Besides, it would resolve one of your major concerns."

"Which is?"

"Whether or not I'm that good a lay."

He had to smile. "Yes, I suppose it would."

He found a certain charm in the absurdity of her argument as well as in the sight of her nude body. He was too sober to accept that she would engage in gratuitous lovemaking, not after her lectures on the manipulative possibilities of tactical sex, but he was a bit too drunk to care much about her real motives. Without further reflection he picked up the bottle and followed her through the curtains.

◂ 3

Schmidt had calculated that it would take two hours for the transformer to be destroyed by overheating. He was wrong.

The fault was not with his computations, which were correct based on design specifications taken from the technical manual; the problem was that those specifications only represented the minimum performance levels the machine was expected to meet. The reality was something else again. For whatever reason, whether overdesign, production-line tolerances, or simple pride of workmanship, the builders had produced a machine that exceeded its specifications by something over fifty percent. In fact, so tenacious was the huge transformer that for a period of nearly three hours it seemed that it might actually survive.

This was not the case, however, during the first twenty minutes, when the temperatures in the center windings soared past the design limit, and the normal hum rose to a scream. But amazingly, just as the temperature edged over the 150-degree centigrade mark, the critical parameters began to stabilize. Somehow the small amount of remaining coolant had combined with direct radiant transfer to balance the complex equation of heat gain and loss. At temperature levels far exceeding those it was designed to withstand, the machine endured.

Then, at 2:52 a.m., it happened. The faulty valve disk inserted by the saboteur disintegrated under the enormous pressure, and the last precious gallons of boiling coolant sprayed out. It was an intolerable loss. The transformer was doomed. Within milliseconds the coil temperature shot above 200 degrees centigrade, and the remaining trace of oil exceeded its flashpoint. The initial explosion would not have seemed particularly awesome to anyone watching, simply a brief, shuddering thud like a muffled cannon shot, but the internal damage was tremendous. The force of the blast twisted the huge copper coils out of position and slammed them together violently, shorting ten thousand volts directly to ground in a blinding blue arc. Simultaneously, the weakest of the casing welds ruptured, admitting the cold night air and triggering a series of shattering secondary blasts.

The up-line disconnects began to vibrate as the current running through them surged into the thousands of amps, the red paint seared black, and the wires that fed the position sensors simply vaporized. But before the disconnects could melt open, the oil-filled insulators atop the transformer burst, and the primary supply lines snapped free to whip above the enclosure like three angry snakes.

Sparks and molten copper flew everywhere, some of it splattering to earth a hundred feet or more beyond the fence. The stench of melting plastic mingled with the pungent odor of ozone, and fragments of red-hot metal fell like rain. It was

18

only a matter of time before one of them landed in the pool of spilled oil and the entire enclosure was engulfed in flames. Minutes after the floodlight flickered out, the area was reilluminated by the glare of a growing inferno.

✓4

The distant burst of flames brought Schmidt out of a pleasant reverie. He was back in the wicker chair, barefoot and shirtless, warmed by Andrea, who was asleep on his lap wearing only the nylon coat. When he saw the explosion he gently shifted her head on his shoulder and reached for the binoculars.

The movement jolted her awake. "What is it?" she asked.

He told her.

"It's happening?" she cried, leaping to her feet, fully alert. She grabbed the glasses away and leaned far over the railing, oblivious to the cold metal bar pressed against her flesh. "Look at that!" she shouted. "Jesus Christ, look at that! The whole damn place is going up, Karl. It's the most beautiful thing I've ever seen!"

She offered him the glasses, but he declined. He didn't need them to see the spreading red glow or the black funnel of smoke that was billowing toward the overcast. "You look," he said. "It's your doing."

She watched the destruction, quivering, oohing and ahing, and even crying out to him at moments of particular violence, until he sternly had to remind her that others might be listening. Her passion in the bedroom had been exhilarating, if not altogether convincing, but it paled in comparison to the real thing.

Five minutes after the fire began a dozen emergency vehicles appeared on the road leading from the mainland, a parade of flashing red and blue lights seeming to glide across the water. Ten minutes after that a helicopter appeared to illuminate the chaotic scene with its spotlight. And throughout it all the woman stood enthralled at the railing, the binoculars pressed to her eyes.

Schmidt grew cold and left the balcony to fetch a shirt, only to be recalled by Andrea's urgent voice.

"The lights," she said worriedly. "Why are the ships' lights still on?"

He peered through the glasses at the spot where the few ships that were in port stood beside their moorings. Against the glow of the fire their masts were a forest of steel spires and strange, weblike antennas. Atop each, as the woman had noticed, a standard white light showed clearly.

"Emergency generators," he reassured her. "Each ship has at least one that comes on automatically when line voltage is lost." She seemed satisfied with the explanation and went back to her watching.

It took an hour and a half for the flames to be beaten down into a smoldering glow. Not once during that time did she leave the balcony, though she sent Schmidt for cigarettes and a pair of pants. Ninety minutes of consuming rapture. She should have been exhausted by the time it was over, but instead she was more excited than ever.

"I wish we could go in tonight," she said breathlessly.

"It will come soon enough," he answered. His voice was weary.

"I'm ready right now."

He felt her intensity and knew that he would never be that ready.

Friday, January 11

5

Fifty miles off the coast of Southern California the nuclear-powered cruiser *USS Bremerton* steamed in circles through choppy seas, part of a nine-ship task force engaged in a fifth and final day of antisubmarine warfare exercises. At the moment, Commander Howard Jones, the Bremerton's engineering officer, was engaging in an exercise of his own. He was being officially indignant, which meant he was acting angry whether he was actually angry or not. His lead reactor technician, Hal Maurer, was quite familiar with the act, since he was usually the one on the receiving end of it. As these performances went, the engineer wasn't doing too badly; there was a nice crimson flush creeping above the collar of his khaki shirt and a few beads of sweat glistening on his boyish face, but his heart wasn't in it. For an all-out effort Jones required an audience, and this time it was only the two of them in the privacy of the engineer's stateroom.

"This one is from the captain," he said, waving the green memo in the air. "It's not just me this time, it's from the Old Man himself. So listen up."

Maurer tipped back his metal chair and let it rock on its two back legs to the slow, steady roll of the ship. He was trying to concentrate, but he was finding it difficult. The distraction was the room; he was always fascinated to be in one of *their* rooms. It was not like the junior officers' compartments, which were merely miniature versions of typical college dorm rooms done in steel, a pair of beds built into the bulkhead, two lockers and two tiny metal desks, and maybe a tape player with speakers hung in the corners. This one was actually a *state*room, almost like something from the real world—which was Maurer's term for anything civilian. This desk was reasonably large and made of wood, as were the two floor-to-ceiling bookcases. There was a small couch, a wooden end table with a lamp, and a full-sized stereo with reel-to-reel tape-deck and speakers mounted permanently on the bulkhead. There was also an electronic organ which, according to rumor, the engineer played with a certain amount of flair. There were even two original paintings: a ramshackle farmhouse by Earl Thollander and a yacht harbor scene by Noal Betts, hung with a sense of irony above a huge, minutely detailed wooden model of the *Bremerton*. And most fascinating of all, there was a porthole, a circle of glass and brilliantly polished brass set into the port bulkhead, less than a foot in diameter but a window nevertheless, looking out at the constantly moving horizon. It was that view that Maurer reluctantly abandoned to focus on the official Word.

Jones stood to read the memo, seeming to lean to and fro, although in fact he was standing essentially in place and the room itself was tilting. " 'Petty Officer Maurer will'—notice the captain said *will*, not could or should, or might—'Petty Officer Maurer *will* apologize personally to Messrs. Johnston and Kramer for his inappropriate remark. Further, he *will* draft, for your review and approval, a letter to the membership of Local 426 of the International Brotherhood of Electrical Workers recanting his comment and exonerating the Navy of all responsibility. Your immediate attention to this matter is appreciated. Respectfully, John L. Reynolds, Commanding Officer.' " He put down the memo and looked squarely at Maurer. "Any questions?"

Maurer pursed his lips thoughtfully. "May I smoke, sir?"

"No, you may not!" Jones said. "Now stop screwing around and just tell me when this is going to be taken care of."

"It isn't," Maurer said without rancor.

"You're being insubordinate."

"No, I'm not. I'm being honest."

"You'll wind up at captain's mast."

"Which will prove interesting. I'm betting that demanding my apology to a bunch of yardbirds is not a legal order. And I think you know it."

Jones didn't blink. "You're probably right there, but what they'll get you for is the original offense—conduct unbecoming . . ."

"What was unbecoming about it?" Maurer asked.

"For God's sake, man, you called the IBEW a bunch of commies."

"A figure of speech."

"The wrong figure."

"But I also called them fascists, so it's a wash."

"Huh?" the engineer said, looking bewildered.

"Calling someone a fascist-commie, which is what I did, is like mixing an acid and a base: it comes out water."

Jones puffed up until Maurer thought he would pop the buttons off his shirt. "Water, Mr. Maurer, is what you've gotten yourself into. Hot water! Right up to your goddamn chin. I think you had better square away."

Maurer was unimpressed. "You call kissing a yardbird's ass being squared away? The Navy really is going to hell."

"Jesus Christ," Jones moaned, slumping onto the couch and letting his head fall back so that he was staring up at the overhead. "Why does my best nuke have to be my worst sailor."

"Life's a bitch."

The engineer shot him a stern look. "Watch yourself."

Maurer was close to overstepping the limit and he knew it. "Sorry," he said quickly. "Just philosophizing."

Jones reflected for a moment and then shrugged it off. Chief engineers are not particularly loved as a species, and nuke engineers even less so. Their only purpose in life is to make sure that when the captain says "go," the ship goes. To accomplish that they have to stay on top of their men every second, including keeping them out of the rack when everyone else is sound asleep and keeping their men on board when everyone else is on the beach. It is not a job that brings much popularity with it, especially when the young division officers, eager to stay in good with their men, are quick to shift all the blame right back upstairs. In the *Bremerton's* engineering department there were probably a half dozen men who thought that Jones was anything other than a rotten son of a bitch. Maurer was one of the few.

The engineer pulled two good-quality cigars out of his shirt pocket and offered one to Maurer. "Let's go off the record."

Maurer nodded and took the cigar.

"And let's be serious," Jones added.

"Okay, let's."

The engineer lit up and settled back, resting both elbows on the back of the couch so that his ample gut strained against the confining shirt until Maurer thought it would surely fail this time. "Look, Maurer, we both know this isn't your first run-in with the unions. I'm still taking crap for your wisecrack about them needing two foremen for every worker."

"Two foremen *and* an inspector."

"Whatever. The point is I know the captain isn't going to back down this time. You're going to wind up with your ass in a sling, and that's not something you really want, or me either. Now how about being cool just for once? It's not going to kill you to apologize."

"To them? It just might." He shook his head. "You know, I don't understand this outfit. I'm probably just about the worst sailor there ever was. I never polish my shoes, I let my hair grow three inches too long, and I don't even own a dress uniform. I call officers by their first names, and I'm religious about never saluting anyone. During the Vietnam war I wore a peace symbol on my hat, and after the Three Mile Island accident I went around the plant pasting up stickers that said 'Stop Nuclear Power Before It Stops You.' But do I get any shit for it? Hell, no. I get 4.0 quarterly marks, leave-time whenever I want it, and whatever position I want on the watchbill. Yet let me make one bad joke to a pair of clowns in hardhats, and the whole place comes unglued. Does that make sense?"

Jones kept the cigar clinched between his teeth and spoke between puffs. "What you're saying is that you're a pain in the butt, which I won't argue with. But you get away with it because you're also the best damn reactor technician in the fleet. Only this time you went too far."

"Too far?" Maurer said with annoyance. "Come on, Jones, it was only a joke. Hell, that's just my word. You know that. I use it ten times a day; I say fascist-commie-puke like some people say turkey or clown. Can I help it if those two union-types haven't got a sense of humor?" He sighed wearily. "Besides, these yardbirds piss on us every chance they get; it's about time they caught some of it themselves."

"You come on, Maurer, don't give me that aw-shucks routine. You're such a great student of history, are you trying to tell me you can't understand why a shop steward from a major international union would be sensitive about having his organization referred to as a bunch of commies? Be serious."

"I guess you have a point," Maurer said. He chewed thoughtfully on his cigar for several minutes. Finally, when a roll of the ship momentarily righted his chair, he stood up. "Okay," he grumbled, "I'll make you a deal. I'll take care of your union problem if you'll take care of mine."

"You have *another* union problem?"

"Musicians."

"Musicians?"

"Well, it's not exactly my problem," Maurer explained. "It's McGurk's problem, but he's my friend."

"You have strange friends," Jones muttered.

"Yeah, well, he isn't too crazy about you either. But whatever you may think of him as a nuke, he plays a mean guitar."

"So I've heard."

"For the last few months he's been doing some gigs around Long Beach—piano bar kind of stuff. He's good, he really is."

"So other than the fact that he isn't supposed to be moonlighting, what's the problem?"

"The moonlighting issue is part of it. Ever since he started working, the musicians' union has been on his back to join. Last week they wrote a letter to the captain calling attention to the fact that a member of his command is working as a civilian, etcetera, etcetera."

"Why doesn't he join?"

"He'd like to, but the dues are more than he could make playing in a month."

"And you want me to keep the captain out of it?"

"You've got it, boss. You bail out McGurk, and I'll *join* the damn IBEW."

Jones had to rub his double chin to keep from smiling. "I wouldn't be surprised if you had set this whole thing up just to swing this deal."

"Me?" Maurer asked.

"Never mind, I don't want to know. Let me think about it for a minute. Blackmail is a very complicated business." He puffed several times on the cigar, watching Maurer through the resulting cloud of smoke. "Okay, you apologize to the two hardhats and write the letter, and I'll go to bat for your buddy . . ."

"Thanks," Maurer said happily. "You're a real gentleman."

"Except," the engineer continued, halting Maurer on his way toward the door, "there is one small thing."

Maurer sighed.

"Admiral Spencer, the Long Beach base commander, is aboard today and—"

"Oh, no," Maurer interrupted. "I know what you're going to say, sir, and I've just got too much work to be a tour guide." He rattled off a half dozen priority items, making up most of them as he went along.

Jones flashed a self-satisfied grin. "Do give him your top-of-the-line tour, Maurer, V.I.P. all the way. I'll arrange for some flashy little drill in the forward plant for about fourteen hundred. Okay?"

Maurer crushed out his cigar brutally. "Off the record, sir," he grumbled, "this is bullshit."

"On the record, Maurer, it is also an order. A very legal order."

Maurer shook his head and opened the door. "Can I opt for the captain's mast instead?"

The engineer laughed and then told him to get out.

⌁6

Rear Admiral Richard W. Spencer turned out to be a bespectacled little man with thinning gray hair and a self-conscious grin who listened carefully and asked intelligent questions. He arrived at the training office on the 0-2 level aft at precisely 1300. To Maurer's surprise there was no entourage, just the admiral in his blue *Bremerton* baseball cap with the appropriate amount of gold on the bill and two stars on the open collar of his shirt, and a seaman guide who scurried away when Maurer opened the door.

The officer extended his hand. "I'm Admiral Spencer. Thank you for taking time out of a busy schedule to talk to me."

Maurer returned the firm handshake and then watched, amused, as his visitor looked around with frank amazement.

"What is this place?"

Maurer followed his gaze. Warm sunshine flooded into the room through two doors that opened directly to the outside. Beyond them the Pacific slid by the port side of the ship, an expanse of choppy blue water glistening in the white glare of the reflected winter sun. A pair of birds floated by, outriders of the escort of gulls and albatross that dipped and soared around the fantail waiting for the garbage from the noon meal to be delivered into the sea. A half mile away a destroyer steamed on a parallel course. Much further out, just visible on the bright horizon, was an aircraft carrier.

"Nice, isn't it?" the technician said.

"That's something of an understatement."

"When the *Bremerton* had its own meteorology station, the weather balloons were filled and rigged here. And launched from here," he said, as he led the Admiral to a narrow landing just outside the open doors. "Now we call it the patio." He caught the admiral eyeing the chairs that lined the railing and quickly added, "For studying, of course."

"Of course," the admiral said, smiling.

Maurer led him back inside and through a watertight door into a room furnished with rows of tables and chairs. "This was the mapping room. As you can see we've converted it into a classroom. The trainees spend the morning here in formal lectures and the afternoons down in the plant qualifying." He pointed toward a door across the room. "There's a small space in there that used to hold the teletype machines. We use it now for test-taking."

The admiral shook his head. "I've never seen anything like it. Three spaces big enough to hold a blimp, a goddamn picture window, and a sundeck, all just for the training division. You nukes really rate."

Maurer grinned. "Well, sir, I guess they figure it pays to be good to the people who give you your power and lights."

"They may have a point."

Maurer sat on the nearest table. "All right, Admiral, what would you like to know?"

"I understand you're going to brief me before we tour the plant."

"Right. Pick a briefing. There's the Fossil Fuel Special, where we consider the reactor as nothing more than a ten-million-dollar boiler and concentrate on the steam side. I'm not real heavy on turbines and condensers, but that's what most people are comfortable with. Then there's the Politician Version—how much everything costs, how long it took to build, how long it will run, and how fast it will go. Finally, there's the Super Deluxe—in a half hour I make you a nuclear engineer."

The admiral laughed. "Since I've had enough of turbines and condensers to last a lifetime, and God knows I won't ever be a politician, I guess it will have to be option C." He tilted his head and gazed at the technician over the top of his gold-rimmed glasses. "Seriously, I've got five nuke ships coming into Long Beach over the next six months, not counting the *Bremerton*. I need to get some kind of handle on how they work."

Maurer hopped down from the table. "All right, then," he said. "Let's do it!"

The half-hour briefing stretched into ninety minutes, interrupted only once when Maurer called down to postpone the drill. They graduated quickly from the elementary diagrams in the propulsion plant manuals to the detailed tech manuals and even to a huge, dusty chart of the nuclides. Before long the tables were cluttered with reference materials of every sort, and the air was filled with chalk dust from Maurer's quick, crude drawings.

By the time they were done, the technician had covered everything from basic nuclear physics to core design and safety analysis, and as fast as he could explain one concept, the admiral was off onto something else. Using an old nuclear engineering textbook by Glasstone and Sesonski, Maurer explained the processes involved in the fission of uranium-235 and how the heat energy of hundreds of billions of fissions was transferred to the cooling water passing between the fuel plates. On mechanical schematics he showed how the coolant carried that heat in a loop to the steam generators, where it heated an entirely different water system to produce steam for the turbines, and then returned to the core through the huge reactor coolant pumps to be reheated.

He drew sketches to explain how the neutron-absorbing control rods were inserted between the fuel plates to alter the rate of fission and how, when the rods were driven all the way down into the core, the reactor was shut down.

"Is that what is meant by a 'scram' of the plant?" the admiral asked.

"Almost," Maurer said. "If the control rods are driven in using the rod motors—at a rate of about two inches per minute—that's a normal shutdown. If they are made to literally drop into the core, that's an emergency shutdown or scram, which can be initiated manually or as a result of an automatic signal." He went on to describe the automatic emergency shutdown systems that constantly monitored pressures, temperatures, flow rates, and power levels to assure the safe condition of the core.

"Have you ever seen a scram?"

Maurer smiled. "Not counting drills, I've manually scrammed twenty-one times. I've had probably twice that many automatic scrams."

Spencer's expression was a mixture of surprise and concern. "So it's that common?"

"It's certainly not uncommon," Maurer said. "Of course, most scrams are for what you might call technical reasons, faulty indicators, things like that, but once in a while it does get crazy down there."

"For instance?"

"Well, for instance, on one memorable occasion I had what amounted to a secondary side steam rupture. At the reactor control panel it was like every damn meter was going in a different direction at once. Reactor power was increasing at close to five percent per second, and when you're at eighty percent to begin with, that's scary. I scrammed it mostly because I didn't know what the hell was going on."

"Five percent per second. That means you were at one hundred percent in four seconds."

"Yep, that's exactly what it meant. As I recall, the meter showed a hundred and three percent when I dumped the plant."

The admiral pursed his lips. "What would have happened if you hadn't scrammed?"

"If I hadn't manually scrammed it it would have scrammed automatically from a high power shutdown signal."

"And if that failed to work?"

"That's a hypothetical question."

"Okay, hypothetically."

Maurer thought for a moment. "There'd be an excessive temperature increase, from five hundred to a couple thousand degrees in a few seconds. The water in the coolant channels would flash to steam. The fuel plates would begin to buckle and burst. Eventually the core would be destroyed." He indicated the seventeen thick volumes of propulsion plant manuals stacked on the desk. "Basically that's what those books are all about. How to prevent something like that from ever happening. Reactor safety essentially comes down to a pair of simple rules: Never have more reactor power than you have capacity to cool the core, and conversely, never have less capacity to cool the core than you have power."

"Do you think those two conditions will always be met?" the admiral asked.

"You're asking me if nuclear reactors are safe?"

"I am."

Maurer spent a moment toying with a piece of chalk before answering. "The kind of catastrophic accident we're talking about would require that the equipment and the operator failed simultaneously. The odds against that happening are extremely high."

"So reactors are safe."

"Yes," Maurer said. "In my opinion they're safe."

Maurer closed the briefing with an explanation of negative temperature coefficient, the complex interaction of coolant temperature and reactivity that permits the reactor to respond automatically to changes in power demand.

The last point caught the admiral by surprise. "You're telling me the reactor automatically adjusts to steam demand? I thought that's what the control rods were for, and you operators."

Maurer shook his head. "The control rods are used only for starting up, shutting down, and compensating for some nuclear changes that occur during operation. Once we get the turkey started up and on the line, about all we do is sit and take readings."

"I'll be damned," the admiral said, chuckling. "Then what good are you?"

"None at all." Maurer said, "At least not until everything goes to shit."

If it didn't look simple on paper, it at least looked comprehensible. There it was in crisp black on white, straight-edged, neat, parallel lines running in formation across page after page and always bending in precise 90-degree turns; a great many symbols—check valves, disk valves, D/P cells, venturies, reliefs, vents, and drains—but perfectly uniform and arrayed with an eye for graphic balance. Even the electronics of it, presented on countless foldout sheets, flowed in systematically bundled lines from one box to another. But down in the control room of the number-one reactor neither the illusion of simplicity nor the hope of comprehension could survive amid the confusion of meters and switches and counters and indicator lights of every color and shape.

The admiral, tailing in behind Maurer, looked around with honest astonishment. "Impressive," he said quietly. "Truly impressive."

Maurer smiled; it *was* impressive. He thought so every time he saw it. Forward control, officially designated the Number One Enclosed Operating Space, or EOS, was small even by shipboard standards, a mere thirty feet abeam and half that wide, yet it held virtually all the controls and instrumentation contained in the enormous control rooms of commercial landbound reactors.

Along the aft bulkhead were the three main operating consoles, manned by operators seated in high swivel chairs bolted to the linoleum deck, with padded backs and arms and seatbelts for use during heavy seas. Each console was designed in three sections: a sloping lower board, a vertical middle section at eye level, and a top section tilted down, so that the operators seemed engulfed by the instrumentation like a pilot in a cockpit.

From the right-hand console the electrical operator controlled the two forward plant turbine-generators, power to the reactor coolant pumps, and the main switchgears. The center console was the throttle board for the port main turbine, with its chrome ahead and astern wheels, turns counter, and old-fashioned engine order telegraph.

The reactor control panel was on the left, a marvel of compact instrumentation. By Maurer's count, there were 27 rotary switches; 63 toggle switches; 106 green, red, amber, and white indicator lights; two rod group position counters; two power level meters; two power rate meters; two multichannel pressure meters; four temperature meters; a pressurizer level indicator; an ESI tank level indicator; a primary coolant flow meter; a steam flow meter; and, dominating the center of the lower section, a big pistol-grip control rod in-and-out switch—all jammed within a space so small that the operator could view all of them without so much as tilting his head.

The major controls and indicators were arranged on the vertical section in a pattern that represented an overhead view of the reactor primary system; in fact, a stylized diagram of that system was actually etched into the panel surface. A large circle in the center represented the core itself; four lines extending out toward the corners of the panel represented the four primary loops, with appropriate symbols to indicate the positions of the outlet and inlet valves, reactor coolant pumps, and steam generators. For each set of loop stop valves there was a control switch and a set of indicator lights—an amber bar for "shut" and a green circle for "open." At each pump symbol there was an on-off switch and speed controller. On the lower center of the panel, directly at eye level, were the master power and temperature meters, and below these, in a row, were the twelve most important alarm lights monitoring reactor pressure, temperature, coolant flow, and power. And in the very center of the center circle, protected by a plastic shield, was the reactor scram switch which, if turned either way, would shut down the plant by sending the control rods hurtling to the bottom of the core.

Although the aft bulkhead was the main operating arena, the other three were hardly less crowded with equipment and instrumentation. At one end of the room, beside the doorway, was the panel which monitored the water levels in the four steam generators. Stacked at the other end were a dozen flat, gray contactor boards and a special set of panels which permitted the independent monitoring of vital core temperatures.

The forward bulkhead was a maze of cable runs and junction boxes. There most of the communications equipment was located, including a loudspeaker system that allowed the occupants to monitor any one of the dozen intercom systems aboard the ship.

The desk of the engineering officer of the watch stood on a raised platform in the center of the room, so that the EOOW overlooked the three operating consoles. Looking like the counter of a restaurant with two chairs identical to those of the operators—one for the EOOW and one for his messenger—the desk was noticeably free of switches and dials. Instead there were the trappings of authority—the indispensable seventeen volumes of propulsion plant operating manuals, three telephones, two push-to-talk speakerphones, and the microphone feeding the plant's p.a. system. The man on the platform never operated; he commanded.

The man on the platform when Maurer and the admiral entered forward control was Lieutenant Junior Grade John Dills, an abusive, twitchy man, known among the operators as "the Duck" because of his pigeon-toed waddle. Dills had been on the *Bremerton* less than four months and qualified as EOOW only three weeks ago, but hatred of him was already widespread, largely because as assistant training officer he had taken a special delight in restricting trainees who had fallen behind in their qualification. Even Maurer, who didn't normally subscribe to the popular biases, found it hard to suppress a grin at the anonymous quacking sounds that frequently were issued over the squawk-box during Dills's watches. He was hardly surprised when the j.g. greeted them brusquely and immediately returned to his logs.

"A real charmer," the admiral whispered.

Maurer winked. "Mr. Dills is *very* conscientious."

The officer's face remained perfectly straight. "I'm glad to hear it."

Maurer introduced his guest to each of the operators and briefly described their panels. When they reached the reactor control panel Maurer turned back to the EOOW. "Request permission to relieve the reactor operator for the purpose of training."

Dills looked at Billy White, the RO. "That all right with you?"

"No, sir," White said tersely. "I was just about to start my readings."

Maurer kept smiling, though with some difficulty. "That's okay, White, the admiral and I will be glad to get your readings. Besides, I believe Commander Collins wants to brief you on the drill."

White stared back. "After the readings, I said."

"Now, *I* said." Maurer's voice was icy, and just loud enough for White to hear.

White looked around at the other operators, who were watching with expressions that ranged from contempt to amusement. Dills himself was judiciously ignoring the confrontation. Finding no allies, White gave a helpless shrug, angrily scribbled his signature on the log, and stormed out.

The incident lasted only a few seconds, but the admiral was noticeably rankled. "Jesus," he said quietly, when they were finally seated at the panel. "I hope everyone's not being so nice just on my account."

Maurer shifted uncomfortably. "Sorry, sir, I don't mean to make excuses—God knows that White's no charmer under the best of conditions—but in his defense I've got to say that twelve hours of watch a day in this pressure cooker would drive a saint to shit."

The Admiral looked startled. "Three watches a day, at sea?"

"At sea and in port. This division has been on port 'n' starboard duty since Thanksgiving, and we only make it in port by cutting five stations and putting one reactor technician on watch. If we have to keep one of the plants up, we go to two-on and one-off."

"I hope that's just on the *Bremerton*."

"It's that way everywhere in the nuclear program," Maurer said. "We've got a manpower shortage that makes the rest of the military look downright flush. I don't know how true it is but I've heard rumors of nuke subs that couldn't get underway because they were so short on operators."

"Do you know the reason?"

"Which one do you want? Six-year minimum enlistment, private sector competition, rotten shore duty rotation, rigid entrance requirements, a bitch of a training program. Take all those things and add them to the shortages caused by the end of the draft and the rotten image of nuclear power in general, and you've got yourself a very big problem."

Maurer paused to sign the log, then continued. "And that's only part of it. This program is constantly being raided by the civilian nuclear industry. If you go to any commercial reactor you'll find that better than half the operators are ex-Navy. Not retired Navy, mind you, but recruited in mid-career. It's a vicious circle: the worse the manpower shortage, the rougher it gets to live with the program, the higher the bailout rate. Between the 'push' of rotten working conditions and the 'pull' of attractive jobs in the civilian sector, the retention rate of the program is going right down the tubes."

"So why are you here?"

"Because I love it," Maurer said, then pushed the log sheets toward the officer. "Now how about giving me a hand with the readings?"

The process took nearly fifteen minutes with Maurer reading and explaining each indicator and the admiral carefully recording it on the twelve-page log. Soon after that White returned, and Maurer and his guest retreated to the back of the room.

"What happens now?" the admiral asked. He could not help but notice the sudden mood of expectancy that pervaded the room. Dills had closed his log and was watching the panels attentively. The messenger had left his chair on the platform, conferred briefly with someone just outside the door, and then returned to take up a position behind the electrical operator. Two trainees, qualification cards in hand, had stationed themselves in the entryway and were talking in whispers.

"Clearly there's a plot afoot," the technician answered. "The khaki-clad gentleman you saw talking to the messenger is Lieutenant Commander Collins, the electrical officer. As drill supervisor he is briefing the key operators on their roles. I know that White's in on it, and the messenger. Probably others, too."

"Hardly a surprise drill."

"Oh, we have those, too, but surprise drills don't have very much training value. This way the trainees can be on station and ready to go."

"Does the EOOW know?"

"Only that there will be one. But as to exactly what it will be, I doubt if he knows. The engineer likes to stick it to the newly qualified EOOWs."

The Admiral smiled. "Do *you* know what it will be?"

"No, sir!" Maurer said, then pursed his lips. "But if I were a betting man, I'd guess you were about to see a P.I."

"A what?"

"A Partial Insertion. It's an alternative to a scram of the reactor. Scramming the plant is the safest and most complete shutdown, but it has several drawbacks. For one thing it's a hell of a mechanical shock for those rods to drop into the core like that, which is no small consideration when you expect your plant to last fifteen years. But even more serious is the length of time required to recover from a scram. Depending on plant temperature and other factors, it can take up to a half hour, which is fine if you're sitting beside a pier somewhere but a real bitch if you're in the middle of a shipping channel or riding out a typhoon.

"The P.I. is one alternative. Instead of dropping the rods all the way to the bottom if an emergency shutdown is triggered, a special system drives them in at extremely high speed for only ten inches."

"And that shuts down the reactor?"

"Temporarily," Maurer said. "Of course, if there is a real emergency condition in the core, the reactor can be scrammed manually, but better than ninety-five percent of our automatic shutdown signals are caused by equipment malfunction, circuit noise, or, most often, good old operator error. The beauty of the P.I. is that recovery can be accomplished in anywhere from thirty seconds to five minutes."

"I see. And you think that's what we'll get?"

Maurer nodded. "The engineer tailors his drills to the importance of the visitor. The higher the rank, the flashier the drill. A P.I. is our most spectacular number, and you're an admiral."

"Do I detect a tone of disapproval?"

"Oh no, sir, I'm sure you're a great admiral."

"Of the drill." the admiral said.

"Frankly, yes. The system still has some bugs in it. I'd prefer not to tempt fate."

The admiral started to reply when a voice blared over the loudspeaker: "THIS IS A DRILL, THIS IS A DRILL. DECREASING PRESSURIZER LEVEL AND PRESSURE IN THE NUMBER-ONE PLANT."

"Here we go," Maurer said quietly. "Now we'll see."

Instantly the three operators and Lieutenant Dills were standing, watching their panels intently. White spoke without turning from his panel, reading from a small white card in his hand. "Sir, for the purpose of the drill I confirm a low pressure and level. Spray valve is shut; normal and back-up heaters are on. Level is still dropping."

Dills's body was tense but his voice was steady. "Very well. Turn on your warm-up heaters," he said. Then he spoke into the microphone: "ALL STATIONS, EOS, THIS IS A DRILL. WE HAVE A DECREASING PRESSURE IN THE PRIMARY SYSTEM. UPPER LEVEL CHECK FOR STEAM IN THE REACTOR COMPART-

MENT. LOWER LEVEL TAKE A READING ON THE REACTOR COMPARTMENT BILGES AND SIMULATE LINING UP TO CHARGE WITH THREE CHARGING PUMPS INTO THE PRIMARY SYSTEM."

"The upper-level watch has lead glass windows that allow him to see into the reactor compartment," Maurer whispered to the admiral. "The symptoms indicate a possible primary rupture. A rupture might also increase the water level in the reactor compartment bilges."

The tense silence was shattered by a deafening horn. Quickly the messenger reached over to the steam generator level indicator panel, flipped a toggle switch to silence the alarm, and turned to Dills. "Sir, for the purpose of the drill we have a high-level alarm on the number-three steam generator." He also had a little white card.

"What's the level?" the EOOW asked.

"Forty-three inches and increasing rapidly."

"There's your rupture," Maurer said. "A primary to secondary in number three."

"Is that extremely serious?"

"I'll bet it will be."

Dills acknowledged the messenger's report and turned to White. "Reactor operator, stop the number-three reactor coolant pump."

"Oh-oh," Maurer said.

White threw the EOOW a confused look. "Simulate, sir?"

"That's negative," Dills said sharply. "Stop the pump!"

"We're too close on our power-to-flow," White said.

"Damn!" the EOOW said. "Yes, you're right. Okay, electrical operator, increase pump frequency to achieve one hundred percent flow."

The experienced operator had seen the mistake and was already running the pumps up. "One hundred percent flow," he reported almost immediately.

Dills nodded, regaining his composure. "Reactor operator, stop the number-three reactor coolant pump."

"He's stopping the pump so that he can isolate loop three and the imaginary rupture," Maurer explained.

"Number three is stopped," White said.

"Very well. Messenger, what's the level on number-three steam generator?"

"For the purposes of the drill, increasing, out-of-sight high."

Dills nodded and spoke again into the microphone: "ALL STATIONS. EOS. WE HAVE IDLED LOOP THREE. CONCERNING THE DRILL, WE HAVE INDICATION OF A PRIMARY TO SECONDARY RUPTURE. STAND BY TO ISOLATE LOOP THREE."

He had just opened his mouth to issue the order when the reactor control panel went crazy. Simultaneously there was a blast of horns and a flash of red alarm lights. The rod group position indicators spun in a blur of numbers and then stopped nine inches lower than their earlier position. Almost immediately the temperature meters began to fall in unison, and pressure followed suit, triggering the back-up heaters.

"Full travel partial insertion!" White exclaimed. "Temperature decreasing rapidly."

"Very well," Dills said, his voice rising in pitch. "Throttleman, shut the throttles." Then, into the microphone: "ALL STATIONS. EOS. FULL TRAVEL PARTIAL INSERTION IN THE NUMBER-ONE PLANT. STAND BY TO CROSS-CONNECT."

"The drill supervisor has initiated a full travel P.I. from the control equipment room, simulating the consequences of the loss of pressure. The reactor is essentially shut down but still steaming, so the temperature is dropping and with it the pressure and pressurizer level, this time for real," Maurer said to the admiral, whose face now showed his confusion.

"I don't understand much that's going on," Spencer muttered.

"That's okay, neither do they."

"The P.I. is real. The rupture is simulated. How do they keep it straight?"

"Let's see if they do," Maurer said quietly.

White spoke. "Sir, do you want me to isolate loop three?"

At the same time the electrical operator spoke. "Shall I decrease pump frequency?"

Dills looked bewildered. "Wait a goddamn minute! White, what are you talking about?"

"Loop three, sir. The drill. We have to isolate for the rupture."

"For Christ's sake, let's forget the drill! He whirled toward the EO. "Now what did you want?"

"Never mind," the operator said, shrugging."I've already done it. Pumps are at three-zero hertz."

Dills stared at him blankly.

"He's blowing it," Maurer whispered with a sense of urgency. "His steam demand is still too high. By now he should have transferred pumps off of the TG—turbine generator— and be cross-connected with the aft plant. If he doesn't get on the stick he's going to lose it."

White spoke again, his tone growing sharper. "Temperature is ten degrees below the green band!"

The tension in the room was becoming almost unbearable. The operators glanced nervously between Dills and their panels, waiting for him to act, embarrassed by his silence at first, then worried.

"Twelve degrees below the green band!" White announced.

Then the loudspeaker crackled: "EOS. CONTROL EQUIPMENT. I HAVE MISFIRES ON ALL GROUP-ONE SCRs."

"Well, that tears it," Maurer said.

"Why?"

"I was telling you about the bug in the P.I. system. That's it. Nothing to do now but scram. At least Dills is off the hook."

White looked expectantly toward the platform, but Dills was frantically flipping through the propulsion plant manual, searching for the procedure.

White snarled impatiently, "Sir, I'm scramming the plant."

"No!" Dills blurted, still desperately turning pages. "We can't dump it. I know there's a way to clear the misfire. Bump rods or something. Won't that work?"

"I'll bump rods if you want."

Maurer felt a surge of anger. As if Dills wasn't already in

enough trouble, now White seemed determined to let him commit a disastrous mistake. Maurer could restrain himself no longer. "That's negative," he said sharply to White. "You know damn well that could cause a rod roll-in. Scram it!"

White's response was a snarl. "Fuck off, Maurer, I take my orders from Mr. Dills."

"You'll follow procedure," Maurer said flatly. Then he turned to Dills and spoke in a quiet, firm voice. "Sir, you're ten degrees from a possible restart accident, and you can't move rods. You have to scram."

The officer gave him a shattered look. "You're sure?"

"Yes, sir."

Dills slumped into his chair. "Very well. Reactor operator, scram the plant."

White acknowledged the order, pausing long enough to glare at Maurer before he reached for the switch.

The incident review board lasted nearly an hour. Afterward Maurer and the admiral retired to the quiet of the training office.

"Mind if I ask you a personal question?" the officer said.

Maurer popped the top from a can of Coke. "Shoot."

"Earlier I got the impression you don't think too much of Lieutenant Dills, yet just now you went out of your way to defend him before the board. Why?"

"I figure anyone can get a little rattled."

The admiral's tone was skeptical. "Funny, when it comes to professional competence, I didn't figure you to be very forgiving."

For a moment the technician toyed with his drink. "You're right," he said finally. "Actually, I spoke up for Dills because I was feeling guilty for letting the incident go as far as it did. I should have said something as soon as he started to blow it."

"Why didn't you?"

Maurer grinned. " 'Cause I hate the sonofabitch."

The admiral almost choked on his own drink. "Well, I'll say this for you, Maurer, you're the most candid man I've ever met."

"That's because all you know are officers."

The admiral shook his head. "You never let up, do you?"

"No, sir," Maurer said.

"Why?"

"Sir?"

"Why do you expend so damn much energy fighting the system? You're obviously very bright and very competent. With a little tact you could go as far as you want. Instead—"

"Instead I'm an obnoxious pain in the ass."

"I was going to say . . . instead you seemed determined to alienate the very people who could help you the most. Like Commander Jones. You know what he said to me before he sent me to talk to you? He said, 'Petty Officer Maurer will teach you more in an hour than I could in a week, if you can take his insults.'" The admiral leaned forward, his face intent. "Why are you so negative?"

Maurer rubbed his chin. "Probably because it's fun." The admiral glared at him, exasperated, but Maurer continued. "I'm serious, sir. Don't look too hard for complex motivations when the reality may be a great deal simpler. Your style is ambition and achievement. And for you that's clearly the best choice; you're a hell of a success. But it's not for me. I'll be damned if I'll take any of this seriously. It's *fun* to break the rules, it's fun to stir up shit, it's fun to stick it to all these sanctimonious assholes who would rather die than fart in the wardroom."

He paused to toss the now empty Coke can neatly into a wastebasket ten feet away. "I take my job as an operator seriously because every single thing the manual says to do can be documented as logical and necessary. But as far as the rest of it goes, including your precious naval tradition, there's very little that's necessary and even less that's logical. Mostly it's order for order's sake. I know I can't change any of it, but I sure can make fun of it."

The admiral looked at him with frank amazement. "You sound just like my daughter. Having fun seems to be her first priority these days."

"Sounds like my kind of woman," Maurer said, delighted to

change the subject. "Is she married?"

The admiral laughed. "No, she isn't married."

"Good-looking?"

"A fox, I think the current term is."

Maurer flashed an exaggerated smile. "How would you like to invite a bright, serious, tactful young man home for a Sunday dinner?"

"Well, son," the admiral said, "I would very much like to do that, but there's something you ought to know."

Maurer flinched. "Don't tell me, she hates sailors."

"On the contrary."

"Her boyfriend is nine feet tall and his knuckles drag on the ground?"

"Worse than that."

"Good lord, what's worse than that?"

"She's seventeen."

"Oh," Maurer said quietly.

A little after four p.m., about the time the incident review board was convening aboard the *Bremerton* fifty miles out at sea, Commander Davis C. Stone, OIC Base Security, Long Beach Naval Station, left the security building parking lot and headed out toward the Mole. His timing could not have been worse. The going-home whistle had just sounded, and traffic at the west end of the base was chaotic. Lines of cars carrying impatient shipyard workers converged on the main gate from three different directions, recklessly merging into a single lane to inch past the harried civilian guards. Two blocks farther on groups of teenage dependents marauded back and forth across the main avenue, shuffling to the beat of portable stereo tape players carried on their shoulders, giving the finger to angry, honking motorists. Farther still, in front of the bank, a line of cars was backed up into the street, causing a traffic jam that goaded frustrated drivers into acts of near insanity ˙

The weather only made tempers worse. The temperature was pleasant enough, into the low seventies by mid-afternoon, but the previous night's fog had become a dense, corrosive smog that hung like a yellow-brown cloud of acid in the stagnant air.

But for Stone, both the traffic and the smog were only secondary irritants, like stubbing a toe on the way to the gas chamber; his real problem was waiting for him out on the Mole. He had already spent half the previous night out there, talking with firemen and electricians until he had finally pieced together a story that everyone could buy. He had spent the entire morning drafting the report for Admiral Spencer, only to find out that the CO was off somewhere in the fleet. Now some hot-shot engineers from General Electric were flapping his preliminary findings even before the ink was dry. The more Stone thought about it, the angrier he got. When he finally cleared the mainland, he stomped on the accelerator and sent the big black Chevy speeding at twice the posted limit.

In the four months since Stone had taken over as head of base security, this was the first incident of any real significance. He laughed out loud. What a commentary that was, that a goddamn fire in some goddamn transformer should be the biggest thing going down. Imagine, an ex-star of the naval investigative service writing fire reports.

And he had been that, all right—a star, the brightest of many in a group that was half detective squad and half spy network. In six years he had been involved in a dozen major investigations for the N.I.S. He had spent eleven months undercover at Pearl Harbor to crack a two-million-dollar contractor swindle. He had taken part in three overseas operations, one in cooperation with the C.I.A. He had accumulated a respectable collection of commendations and earned a commander's silver leaf. There were even rumors of a possible appointment as regional chief. Unfortunately he had spent so much time dealing with the harsh realities of crime and espionage that he forgot about the equally harsh realities of service politics. That is, until Operation STOP-VALVE.

Actually, STOPVALVE had been one of his best efforts—a classic example of patient, thorough, relentless undercover investigation. It was also his last.

It began in San Diego when a loose handrail yielded up nearly a pound of 89 percent pure heroin aboard a destroyer just returned from a five-month WestPac tour of Japan, Okinawa, Thailand, Singapore, and the Philippines. Stone took over and allowed the hidden stash to be retrieved by a ship-yard worker who, over a period of a month, made similar connections on six more ships. At that point Stone turned his other cases over to colleagues and settled in for the duration.

Without touching the pipeline, he began following it backwards, first to Hawaii, a port-of-call for virtually every ship crossing the Pacific, and when that failed to pan out, over to the huge naval base at Subic Bay in the Philippines, the only other common port for all seven ships. There he compared lists of shipyard personnel and came up with the names of twenty-two workers who had serviced all seven ships. The slow, painstaking process of checking each one out began. At the same time experts identified the heroin as almost certain-ly coming from Thailand, and a search for couriers was also started. On a hunch, Stone tried correlating passenger lists for MATS flights between Clark AFB and six Thai bases around the dates that the seven ships were in Subic. He drew three pairs, that is, people who correlated on two dates, but no solids. Unhappily, he began the vastly more complicated task of doing the same thing for the commercial carriers be-tween Manila and Bangkok.

Then Stone seemed to get a break. A quiet search of a de-stroyer escort departing for the States turned up nearly two kilograms hidden in the usual manner. But a check of the list of twenty-two names showed that none had worked on the new ship. Instead of helping, the new discovery put Stone back at square one.

Taking a new tack, Stone had the ship brought back to Subic Bay using the phoniest cover story he could think of—suspected transport of "infected" foodstuffs—a story that would let anyone who was interested know that the ship was being searched. For two days, while the crew stewed and the captain appealed his way up to ComPacFleet, Stone maintained a stakeout on the hidden drugs. By the afternoon of the second day he had two possibles—shipyard personnel who had displayed more than casual interest in the out-of-the-way stretch of hand railing—but with a great deal of shipyard activity intentionally scheduled, it was far too little to act on.

Then, just before midnight that night, with Stone himself on duty, the stakeout finally paid off. One of the possibles reappeared with a wrench, and with three taps confirmed that the stash was still there. It was still not evidence enough for a bust, but it was enough to warrant a tail, which in turn yielded a brief rendezvous with a young girl. That meeting proved to be the turning point.

Within hours Stone confirmed that the girl was a frequent passenger on the MATS run to Thailand, one of those he had paired up earlier. He brought her in for questioning at 0800, and by noon he had the four other couriers—all female dependents between sixteen and eighteen—and three enlisted shipyard personnel in custody. He also had three confessions and ten ounces of pure heroin as evidence.

Stone was pleased. The bust had been clean. The case was rock-solid. Under normal circumstances he would have spent three days wrapping it up and left the wheels of justice to grind at their usual snail's pace. But the circumstances were far from normal, at least as far as the suspects were concerned. The three men were just what they appeared: two shipfitters and a machinist's mate, young, greedy, and not particularly bright. The five girls, however, turned out to be the who's who of Subic Bay dependents. The oldest was the daughter of the base's XO. Two sisters were the daughters of the CO of the naval hospital. One was the daughter of the base personnel officer, and the fifth was the daughter of the OIC base operations.

Immediately, a series of unusual "administrative actions" began. The first was an attempt to have the confessions thrown out. Ignoring the advice of his colleagues, Stone fought the effort and won. The next day, over drinks, the base commander delivered what amounted to a warning to leave well enough alone.

Less than twenty-four hours later a move was made to reduce the charges to simple possession. Again Stone fought and won, and this time he drew a lengthy call from Washington reminding him that prosecution was not his area of responsibility. The phone was still warm when a set of leave papers arrived at his door, unrequested.

The pressure bothered Stone, and it angered him, but he considered himself to be a realist, and in that spirit he obligingly made arrangements to fly back to the States. So the goddamn brats only got their hands slapped. At least the pipeline was shut down at both ends, and the stateside confederates, including the money man, were in the hands of civilian authorities. He was not about to jeopardize his career to plug one little hole in a very leaky system.

And he would have left, too, had he not received a tip that responsibility for the entire plan was about to be dumped on the three enlisted men. Angrily Stone cancelled his reservations and marched back to the legal office. Uneven justice was one thing; injustice was something else again.

It took almost two days of relentless argument, but the evidence, carefully arranged and coldly presented, was overwhelming: not only were the five girls clearly *not* the innocent pawns, but, if anything, the opposite was true. Once again Stone had won, but this time he had gone too far. Within ninety-six hours he was out of the N.I.S. and on his way to Long Beach. The rising star had gotten himself eclipsed.

Stone squinted through the dirty windshield into the glaring haze. So here he was at Long Beach, with its occasional drunken brawl, maybe a little dope, a burglary once in a while. He laughed again. Perhaps it wasn't that bad after all. At least here he was never wakened in the middle of the night—or almost never.

He pulled off the road a quarter mile short of the docks and parked next to an electrical service truck that might have been yellow under the heavy layer of oily soot. Before him was the site of last night's conflagration. It was as though he had stopped at the edge of some volcanic crater. Everything within a hundred-yard radius of the transformer was a charred ruin. The device itself was nothing more than a mass of black, twisted wreckage, with water seeping from its ruptured seams. Beside it lay what was left of the power pole, a spindly piece of charcoal still connected by three blackened cables to the one before it. The fence, which had been torn open on the harbor side, lay half down in the mud, black and brittle as an old barbecue grill flocked with a layer of dried foam. Globs of burned plastic hung everywhere like great black cobwebs.

The scene smelled as bad as it looked. The foam used to smother the oil fire had a foul, pungent odor. Added to that were the acridity of burned insulation, the biting sharpness of hot metal, and, most dominant of all, the thick, sweet stench of oil.

Two clean-up crews still labored at the site, one around the nearest standing power pole, attempting to cut away the downed wires, the other down near the ocean edge, working with a small bulldozer to prevent the thousands of gallons of brackish water and foam poured out during the firefight from draining into the ocean.

Stone's assistant, Chief Morton, and another man were waiting for him beside the transformer shell, arms folded, chatting casually. Grumbling to himself, Stone pulled on a pair of rubber fire boots and joined them.

The man from General Electric was a senior electrical engineer by the name of Conklin, a tall, skinny, middle-aged man with a Boston accent. If nothing else he was a diplomat. To avoid the appearance of ganging-up on Stone, he had sent his two colleagues back to the car so that he might face the security chief alone. He got directly to the point. "In most respects, Commander, we concur with your preliminary findings. The explosion and fire was the result of extreme overheating caused by the loss of the transformer's cooling medium. However, we disagree with the conclusion that the failure of the drain valve was the sole cause of that loss."

"The drain valve did fail, didn't it?" Stone asked. His people had been certain on that point.

"Yes sir, no doubt about that. But even a complete failure would not have resulted in the degree of oil loss we're talking about."

"I don't understand."

"If you'll forgive the oversimplification, it would be like trying to pour gasoline out of a good gasoline can without opening the vent. About all you'll get is a trickle because of the vacuum that's inside. It's the same here. Even with the valve wide open, unless the vent was also open, there would be only a very slight coolant loss."

"How much is 'slight'?"

"I'd only be guessing," the engineer said carefully.

"Then guess."

"Well, after an initial gush of four or five gallons, the loss would be, say, a half gallon an hour."

"And how many gallons total?"

"Over a hundred."

"Okay," Stone said after a quick calculation. "So if the valve failed two weeks ago, wouldn't that account for it?"

"No sir," Conklin said quickly. "We considered that, too, but that gradual a loss would have caused a constantly increasing current which would have shown up on the substation monitors. It didn't. In fact, this transient happened so fast that overload devices didn't even have time to react. The oil loss must have been very rapid, which means that the vent must have been open."

"Which it wasn't."

"It wasn't at the time of the fire. But it's possible that it was opened to leak the oil, then shut."

"You mean intentionally?"

"How else can you explain it? The oil pattern on the ground confirms that the source of the leak was the valve. To leak that fast the vent had to have been open, yet it was shut at the time of the fire. It must have been done deliberately. I see no other explanation."

"For what possible motive?" Stone asked impatiently. "This transformer provides nothing but shorepower for ships moored out on the Mole. At the very worst some ships will have to be reassigned to other berths, and a few will have to provide their own power. Hardly what you would call a major strategic impact. I'm sorry, Mr. Conklin, but your theory is ludicrous."

The engineer nodded grimly. "I know, but it's the best I can offer."

"Yes, well, I'll ask my people to check it out and get back to you," Stone said brusquely. He led the man toward his car, thanked him for his trouble, made sure that Morton had his address and telephone number, and assured him again that they would follow up.

"Crap!" Stone said as soon as he had driven away.

Morton looked troubled. "I don't know. He seemed awfully sure that the thing had been sabotaged."

"Yes he did," Stone said sourly. "But doesn't it seem odd that sabotage also happens to be the one explanation that would let the manufacturer, his company, off the hook?"

"So you don't think there's anything to it?"

Stone snorted. "This is Long Beach, not Istanbul, for Christ's sake. I think the man's been watching too much television."

"Should I follow up on it?"

"I'm sure it's nothing that can't wait until Monday," said Stone. Then he flashed a weary smile. "Let's shove off."

"For home?" Morton said hopefully.

"For home."

8

By nightfall the *Bremerton*'s forward reactor was back on the line, and the ship was cruising at flank speed through a calm black sea toward home.

With the passing of the short winter day the air had chilled quickly, and the lookouts sought whatever protection they could find from the cold wind, huddling with the collars of their pea coats pulled up around their ears, glancing resentfully at the radar antennas slowly rotating at the top of the two-hundred-foot mast, knowing full well that those all-seeing metal screens made their suffering pointless. Below, the passing of the day was marked only by the routine announcement to darken ship and a brief flurry of activity as exterior doors were secured and black baffles moved into place. Otherwise, the cool, bright interior was no different than it might have been at twelve noon.

Most of the crew had elected to skip dinner in anticipation of the ship's arrival in Long Beach, so the mess decks were nearly deserted when Hal Maurer cut across to the starboard side and slid down the ladder to the reactor control division office on the third deck. Using the handrails like parallel bars, he swung off six steps from the bottom, landed with a clang on the metal deckplate, and then plunged through the office door, nearly nailing Billy White in the process.

He apologized quickly, but White hardly seemed to notice the clamorous interruption, he was so intent on whatever conversation was in progress. He wore a broad grain that to Maurer seemed almost a smirk. His eyes were flashing and his face was flushed, whether with excitement or anger Maurer couldn't tell.

At the other end of the tiny office, wearing a grim expression, sat Chief Walter Nettles, a wiry little man with fine blond hair carefully combed over a bald spot. His finger had been leveled at White, but with Maurer's arrival he immediately withdrew it and began fumbling for a cigarette.

"Sorry, Chief," Maurer said, retreating toward the doorway. "I didn't mean to bust in."

"That's okay," the chief said, with a great display of nonchalance. "White and I were just shooting the shit. What can I do you for?"

Maurer was puzzled at the obvious lie, but he shrugged and sat down on the Plexiglas top of one of the two small desks, drawing up a chair to use as a footstool. The office, as it was generously known, was hardly bigger than a large walk-in closet, the two desks and a pair of filing cabinets crammed in between ceiling-high racks of test equipment and spare instrument drawers. A half dozen clipboards containing the watchbills and maintenance schedules for each plant hung on hooks along the aft bulkhead. Above them, in a cheap glass frame, was Nettles's love-of-the-month, a color photograph of some innocent-looking blond cut from the pages of a glossy women's magazine. And beside that was a small board to hold the score of special keys used down in the plant.

Near the overhead, on a platform slung by chains from the center beam, sat Nettles' Folly: an ordinary room-style air-conditioner which the chief had installed to cool the usually stifling space. The crew had let him go on for almost a week before someone told him that without the window installation for which it was designed, the damn thing was putting out as much heat at one end as it was cool air at the other. Now, on its useless dangling plug, someone had hung a yellow caution tag with the instructions, "To be operated only during an exercise in futility."

Without asking, Maurer took one of the chief's cigarettes and lit it. "Have you heard?" he asked glumly. "We're getting the shaft again. No shorepower at Long Beach. We're going to have to keep the forward plant on the line all weekend."

"We were just talking about that," the chief said.

White chimed in. "Yeah, I heard they lost their transformer."

"Oh?" Maurer said. "Where'd you get that? When I talked to Jones he didn't know what the screw-up was."

White forced a wink. "I've got friends up in the Com Center."

Maurer nodded and turned to Nettles. "Well, Chief, what are we going to do?"

"Shit, I don't know," Nettles said. "White here offered to stay, and I don't have anything going on so I can stay, but that still leaves us one short." He leaned back and propped his feet up on the desk. "D'you think we could qualify Jameson for shutdown watch in two hours?"

Maurer shook his head. "No way, Chief. I wouldn't trust that idiot to operate a washing machine."

"Well then, I guess I'll have to hold Ditmer from going on leave until Monday. That's all there is to it."

"Yeah, well, I want to see you keep his old lady from going into labor before Monday, too: She's two weeks overdue already."

"What else can I do?" Nettles asked. "This place isn't exactly overrun with volunteers."

"I'll take the goddamn weekend," Maurer said.

"Good!" White said, almost gleefully.

"No!" the chief injected with surprising intensity.

"Why not?" Maurer asked.

"Yeah, why not?" White added. "What a team—Nettles, Maurer, and White, all in the forward plant. This place will never be the same."

Nettles threw the younger man a sharp look and spoke to Maurer. "You can't, Hal, you've had the last three weekends."

"So I'm shooting for the Guinness record. Let's face it, Chief, if you try to draft somebody who is scheduled to get the weekend off, we're going to have to fish your body out of the bay."

White spoke quickly, an odd grin on his face. "He's right, Chief. It'll have to be Maurer. I'm gonna go make up the watchbill." And with that he was out the door.

Maurer looked after him, mystified. "What's with White? He's never volunteered for anything in his life."

Nettles shrugged. "Oh, don't mind him, he's just being his usual fucked-up self."

"I noticed," Maurer said flatly, then laughed as a particularly violent roll of the ship nearly threw him off the desk. "You can sure tell we're headed home. They must have her cranked all the way up."

The chief gave a half-hearted smile and lapsed into a long brooding silence, during which he concentrated on the ribbon of smoke coiling up from the tip of his cigarette.

"What's the matter, Wally?" Maurer asked after a few minutes. "You look lower than a gopher's toenail."

There was a brief smile, then seriousness. "I really don't want you to take the duty this weekend."

Maurer shrugged. "It's no big deal. Once we get some of this new group of trainees qualified, I'll get it back."

"What about what's-her-name, er, Sharon?"

"Sally. She'll be back East until the new semester starts." Maurer laughed. "See, here you thought I was being so noble, and really it's just that I don't have anything better to do."

Nettles remained sober. "I still don't like it."

"What the hell else are you going to do? I don't see anyone trying to bribe their way onto the watchbill." He leaned forward and rested his elbows on his knees. "You know, ol' buddy, I wasn't just kidding when I talked about having to fish your body out of the bay. I live with these guys, and I'm telling you that if we screw up the rotation one more time, we're gonna have a full-scale mutiny on our hands."

"What about White?"

"What about him?"

"Three days together on the same watchbill and you'll be at each other's throats. You and him are worse than a couple of bucks at mating time."

"Are you sure he'd qualify as a buck?"

"That's just what I mean. I'm not going to put up with you two takin' potshots for three days straight."

"You've got a point," Maurer said slyly. "I'll go up and throw him overboard right now."

"Come on, Hal, I'm serious."

"Okay. If it bugs you that much, put him in the aft plant."

"No," Nettles said. Then, quickly explaining, "I want him up forward where I can keep an eye on him."

"Well then, put me back aft."

Nettles chewed thoughtfully on his lower lip. "I guess that would be okay." He dwelt on it for a moment longer, then nodded. "Yeah, that'll work, but only on the condition that we dig up an electrician or somebody to stand in for you tonight so you can at least have a few hours off."

"Fair enough," Maurer said. "But what about you? You haven't set foot off this tub in two weeks."

"Taken care of," Nettles said. "Chief Butler's covering for me until midnight."

"All right!" Maurer said enthusiastically. "Why don't we drop by the Golden Sail, quaff a few beers, and check out the local fauna and flora?"

"Some other time," Nettles said, smiling. "I've got a hot date."

"No shit! A lady, I hope."

"A woman, but no lady."

"Pray tell? Does this mean you're finally done with the late Mrs. Chief Nettles?"

"The divorce became final last week." Nettles's expression was serious again.

Maurer shook his head. "I'm sorry to hear that, Wally. I know it's been a mother."

Nettles shrugged. "It's getting easier."

"Especially tonight," Maurer said, attempting to lighten the mood. "Nothing like a woman to help you forget another woman."

"Yeah," Nettles replied, with a distant smile.

After a moment of awkward silence, Maurer moved to leave. "Then maybe I'll see you at midnight. Stop by the mess if you want, and fill me in on all the graphic details."

The chief straightened up and focused on Maurer. "Maybe I will, if I don't turn into a pumpkin."

"Or a pumpkin eater," Maurer said, and laughed crudely.

◢9

Davis Stone paced slowly back and forth on the carpet in front of his desk, stopping occasionally to gaze out the dirty corner windows at the headlights moving along Seaside Boulevard. Pacing was something Stone did habitually, usually with his hands thrust deep into his trouser pockets and his head bowed in almost prayerful concentration, although sometimes he would gesture his way through an imagined conversation.

He had not planned to return to the office after leaving the Mole. He had intended to catch a bite to eat at the officers' club and then head for his Naples Island apartment, but the conversation with the G.E. engineer had generated just enough doubt to spoil any chance of a decent night on the beach without at least a token follow-up.

A quick check of recent files had produced nothing useful, so he had reluctantly set the duty officer to tracking down his civilian office supervisor. Stone was still pacing when the DO stuck his head in to announce that the man was on the phone.

"Sorry to bother you at home, Pat," Stone said.

"That's okay. Something going on?"

"Around here? You must be kidding. I'm just calling to pick your brain." Pat Cooper was the office's institutional memory. Over a twenty-five-year period he had worked his way up from gate guard to superintendent, mostly through plain tenacity. It was said he could recall the name of every person who had worked in the department during that time span, and more important to Stone at the moment, the details of every significant case, including subjects and dates. He was the poor man's data bank.

"The subject is sabotage," Stone said. "Or maybe just major vandalism. Was there anything noteworthy in that category before I got here, say in the last year?"

There was a moment's pause. "I take it we're talking about more than busted street lights or slashed tires."

"This would involve expensive equipment—generators, pumps, that sort of thing."

A longer pause. "No sir, nothing like that since the rash of incidents during the Vietnam war. Certainly nothing in the last couple of years."

Stone toyed thoughtfully with the telephone cord. "What about at other installations in the area, Seal Beach or Los Alamitos? Have you heard anything? Or maybe at the civilian docks?"

"Nope, nothing I can recall. Oh, there was that bomb thing up on the PCH."

"What was that?"

"Let's see. It was about five months ago. Just before you came. Some kid blew himself up, along with a quarter of a city block up on the Pacific Coast Highway, just west of the City College. Turned out to be plastic explosives, quite a chunk of it as a matter of fact, and some pretty sophisticated detonators, and even a couple of rifles. We were on alert for a while, but nothing ever came of it. Probably just some loony."

"Who handled it?"

"L.B.P.D. at first, and then I think they brought in the F.B.I."

"And they never linked it to any group, or to this base?"

"Not that I know of," Cooper said. "Is there something going on I should know about? Something about that fire?"

"No," Stone said. "I just had some big shot from G.E. trying to tell me it wasn't an accident."

Cooper chuckled. "Sounds like a snow job to me."

"I agree," Stone answered. "I just wanted to make sure I hadn't missed anything."

"Sorry to disappoint you. Right now we're trying to find a gasoline thief and whoever ripped off those yardbird lockers. Those are about the most exciting things I can offer you."

"That's what I figured," Stone said. "Sorry to bother you."

"S'okay. See you Monday?"

"Right," Stone said, and then hung up.

⟋ 10

The nuclear generation began with the birth of a neutron in the center of a tiny pellet of uranium oxide, one of many thousands of identical pellets arranged in a precise matrix within a thin zirconium fuel plate, one of many thousands of fuel plates in the core of the *Bremerton*'s reactor. Even in the solid metal of a fuel plate there was more void than matter. And through that void the neutron hurtled like a subatomic bullet, missing, in accordance with the laws of chance, the matter in its path until it had passed out of the pellet and the fuel plate and into the adjoining coolant channel.

Some of its number would not have survived that far, having collided with particles within the matrix and been absorbed by xenon or one of the other natural neutron poisons present in the fuel. Others would have escaped the plate only to be absorbed by the hafnium control rods which exist for that singular purpose. And a relatively few would have escaped the core altogether, to be slowed and captured in the primary shield surrounding the reactor vessel or, if not there, in the secondary shield which surrounds the perimeter of the reactor compartment.

But this neutron was more typical. Like most of its generation, it penetrated as far as the coolant channel where it collided with a roughly equal-sized hydrogen nucleus in a water molecule, gave up a large portion of its kinetic energy, ricocheted back into the fuel plate, and eventually moved into the vicinity of a uranium atom. The stage had been set for the nuclear process known as fission.

For reasons which are still not clearly understood, the absorption of the neutron by a uranium-235 nucleus destabilizes the forces binding the nucleus together and causes it to split apart; minute quantities of matter are converted into relatively large amounts of energy. In one violent instant the heavy nucleus shatters into two completely different elements, highly ionized because they have left their electrons behind, propelled by the tremendous kinetic force of the mass-energy conversion. These elements, known as fission fragments, tear into the surrounding matter, careening off the heavier nuclei until their enormous energy has been entirely transformed into heat.

Simultaneously the distintegrating nucleus emits gamma rays, alpha and beta particles, and, most important, more high-energy neutrons, 2.47 of them on the average, a new generation of neutrons which will themselves be thermalized and reflected back into the proximity of other uranium atoms and perpetuate the fission reaction.

Even as the new fission cycle began, the heat generated by the last was being put to work powering the *Bremerton* homeward. By conduction and thermal radiation, the heat generated within the fuel plates was transferred to the passing coolant, mixed with the effluent of the thousands of other channels, and carried through the four sixteen-inch-diameter loops to the steam generators. There it passed through hundreds of small tubes, where it was transferred in turn to the secondary water producing the one element basic to marine propulsion—steam.

Much of it went to the two main turbines, which at a flank speed of over thirty-five knots were delivering 150,000 shaft horsepower. Some also went to the lube oil pumps, condensate pumps, main and auxiliary feed pumps, and fire main pumps. Some of it went to the four twenty-five-kilowatt turbine generators that supplied the ship's enormous electrical loads, or to the two evaporators that provided up to 100,000 gallons of fresh water a day. And some of it went to power the two special turbine generators that in turn powered the huge reactor coolant pumps.

The *Bremerton's* two five-hundred-megawatt nuclear cores contained a total of 670 kilograms of uranium fuel, not even three-quarters of a ton. At normal consumption rates they would have lasted for fifteen years.

The *Bremerton* cruised due east until she made the coast off Santa Monica, then south down the San Pedro Channel between Long Point and Santa Catalina Island. The entire eastern horizon was aglow with the lights of seven and a half million people, a dull orange aura punctuated by the bright lights of planes circling into LAX and the closer, sweeping beacons of the numerous light buoys. So continuous was the development that it was impossible to tell where one jurisdiction ended and the next began, as the ship moved down the coast from Santa Monica to Marina del Rey to the airport to the beach cities of Manhattan, Hermosa, and Redondo, to the hillside homes of Palos Verdes Estates.

There was a stretch of relative darkness along the rugged hills of the San Pedro Peninsula, but as the ship rounded Point Fermin, it was met by a second and equally vast expanse of lights stretching from Orange County on the south up to Long Beach itself, the city of 400,000 that sits at the sandy underbelly of the greater Los Angeles area.

A little after seven p.m. the word was passed to set the special sea and anchor detail, and engine speed was reduced to one-third ahead. A few minutes later the *Bremerton* made a slow turn to port and slipped through the middle breakwater into Long Beach Harbor.

Out in the open sea she had seemed so quick and sleek and dagger-thin, over 720 feet long and only 73 feet abeam, but within the confines of the harbor she was just 17,000 tons of hard-to-manuever steel, requiring two tugs to get her around the head of the Mole and into the slip. They did their job well. The first line went over at 7:33; one minute later all engines were ordered stopped. The *Bremerton* was home.

⫷ 11

Chief Walter Nettles Stood at the railing on the 0–2 level aft, already dressed in civilian clothes, watching the final docking procedures being carried out on the floodlit pier below. The *Bremerton* was moored stern-in, port side to Pier 26. The inner harbor and naval base were off her port bow; a mile away, off her starboard bow, were the lights of downtown Long Beach, partially hidden from Nettles's view by the ship's superstructure.

Down on the pier the lines had already been doubled up and fitted with the funnel-like metal rat guards. Up forward a small crane was lowering the officers' gangway into place. The aft gangway still lay on the pier, attended by a contingent of shipyard workers in orange hardhats.

A group of perhaps a hundred people waited restlessly behind a temporary rope barrier, mostly wives with children and young girls in groups of two or three. The ship's two blue vans were parked nearby, and beside them were the black sedans for the admiral and captain. At the foot of the pier was a base laundry truck waiting to collect the first loads for a Monday morning return, and next to it a mobile canteen stood ready to sell ice cream and candy and other junk food to members of the duty section.

Nettles showed little interest in the busy scene. He was a man with a lot on his mind. For one thing he was still bothered by Maurer's presence on the weekend watchbill, a concern born out of genuine affection for the technician, alleviated only slightly by the decision to move him to the aft plant. And then there was White, becoming so difficult to handle that Nettles was nearly ready to fight Maurer for the privilege of throttling him. But mostly he was experiencing a new wave of anger and bitterness triggered by the arrival of the legal-sized envelope which he now carried stuffed in his right hip pocket.

SUPERIOR COURT OF CALIFORNIA, COUNTY OF LOS ANGELES. In re the marriage of Petitioner: Mary Frances Nettles and Respondent: Walter V. Nettles. Case Number 414140. NOTICE OF ENTRY OF JUDGMENT (MARRIAGE)...

God, how he had loved that woman, all five feet, one-half inches of her, her laughing green eyes, her soft auburn hair, her beautiful white ass, and the freckles on her shoulders. She had been the one who had handled the finances and raised their two sons and on two occasions moved the entire household by herself. She was the one who had stayed up until three playing poker with the men, the one who met the ship wearing nothing under a light summer dress, the only woman who really mattered.

Certain differences have arisen between the parties hereto, and they are now living separate and apart, and the parties hereto desire by this Agreement to settle and adjust all rights and claims of each as against their community and jointly owned property, and to liquidate and settle the rights and claims of each in all matters, financial and otherwise, and as well with reference to any rights of inheritance and administration of their respective estates ...

The long separations had never been easy for her. She wrote him every day, long letters in her small, untidy hand. Sometimes they were upbeat letters, sparkling with humor and graphic descriptions of her desire for him and newsy notes scribbled in the margins and clever drawings and four or five postscripts; sometimes morose letters, with rambling diatribes against the Navy that went on for page after page, closing invariably with some sort of vague threat, almost always amended by a conciliatory endearment, by a different pen beneath her signature or on the outside flap of the envelope.

For a long time the in-port periods and, particularly, the two-year stretches of shore duty had made the other tolerable. Those were the days when he sneaked home at noon to make love until the boys got out of school and took four-day skiing weekends and put a new garden in the back yard and a flower bed in front. But with each time together she seemed to dread more and more the coming sailing date or the new set of orders, until a day together meant only that separation was one day nearer, and then there was no joy left at all.

It is the intention of the parties hereto by this Agreement specifically to settle for all times their, and each of their, rights, duties and obligations with respect to each other, and their, and each of their, property rights in respect to the property which either of them may hereafter acquire ...

The joke was that it ended with only two miserable years to go. They had even talked about it before his last reenlistment, sat down and planned it around the kitchen table with the boys in bed and their glasses filled with red Mateus. At that point he had sixteen years in, three and a half short of retirement, and eighteen months left of his tour on the *Bremerton.* After that they could look forward to shore duty in Idaho Falls or Windsor Locks, a two-year head start on a life together. Never again to be separated.

The parties hereto agree that they shall live separate and apart and each be free from the interference, authority and control by the other as fully as if he or she were sole and unmarried ...

Then the rumors began, rumors of extended sea rotations for all nukes. Nettles heard them aboard ship; Mary heard them at home. Nettles went straight to the captain, who assured him that it was only a problem of personnel-flow, just a couple of months while they pushed replacements through training, nothing to get excited about. But Mary was excited—in fact, she was frantic. She had staked everything on his approaching shore rotation. By their original calculation he had 281 days of sea duty left. She told him that when that time was up she was leaving, with or without him.

Within a month the official announcement was issued: all present assignments were extended until further notice. Two weeks later she filed.

You are notified that the following judgment in this cause was entered in Judgment Book No. 252, page 14: Final Judgment of Dissolution of Marriage.

For the first few months after she filed for the interlocutory decree he wandered around in a haze of bitterness and frustration. He hated her for her intransigence. He hated himself even more for not getting out when he had the chance, for not anticipating the screw-job that a sixteen-year veteran should have known was coming. But through it all it had not occurred to him to hate the Navy, at least not beyond the sort of background level of resentment he had always held for the institution that kept them apart. It would have been like hating an alligator for biting off his arm, when biting off arms was part of its nature. How could he expect the damn thing to know any better?

Until the afternoon that Captain Reynolds summoned him to his cabin.

"I was sorry to hear about your divorce," the CO said after a few minutes of shop talk. "If there's anything I can do . . ."

Nettles was not bashful. "You can get me a shore billet," he said flatly.

"I may be able to do just that."

"Really?" Nettles's spirits soared. "Is the extension off?" In his mind he was already writing the letter to Mary.

"The extension is still on, but I've received word that I may be able to get you your shore duty through the reenlistment incentive program."

"The what?" Nettles stammered incredulously.

"The reenlistment incentive program. If you'll agree to sign for another four, I'm pretty sure I can get you orders for Idaho Falls."

Nettles was enraged. "Excuse me for saying so, Captain, but I don't think you've heard a fuckin' thing I've said for the last three months! Being *in* this goddamn navy is what wrecked my marriage. What the hell good would it do to pull a shore billet if it just means that I'm going to be in four more years?" He stared for a moment at the seam of his khaki trousers, gathering his words. "Why is it, sir, that the 'needs of the service' were so great that I couldn't even get a hardship transfer, but now if I re-up, all of a sudden I'm nonessential?"

Reynolds shifted uncomfortably and shrugged. "Well, you know how Washington is."

Nettles rose to his feet. "I know how somebody is, but I'm not sure it's Washington."

"Now take it easy, Chief. I was only trying to help."

"If you say so," Nettles said bitterly. "But next time do me a favor and don't do me any favors."

That was the afternoon Nettles decided to do himself some alligator hunting.

Not long now, Nettles thought as he watched the crane lift the aft gangway and lower it neatly onto its footings on the weather deck directly below him. Then Reynolds can take his orders and his ship and his whole fucking Navy and shove them. In fact they can all shove it, Mary included. From now on he was going to look out for Number One.

He waited until the initial exodus was over, then left the ship and strode slowly up the pier toward the ship's company parking lot. The blue Porsche was parked just to the left of the entrance, facing away from the docks. He walked around to the driver's side and climbed in.

"Welcome home," said the woman in the passenger's seat.

"Thanks," Nettles said with an ironic smile. "They're going to keep the forward plant critical."

"I know."

Nettles laughed softly. "The idiot has already called you?"

"A half hour ago, as soon as they connected the shore phones."

He let his head fall back against the leather headrest. "Well, kiddo, you got your wish."

"*Our* wish," she said, lighting up a thin brown cigarette.

✏ 12

Andrea Doria Einaudi, the revolutionary, and Walter Nettles, the four-hash-mark Navy chief, made love with the lights on and the stereo blaring and a bottle of cheap wine growing warm on the nightstand. In terms of pure technique she was better in bed than Mary: her fingers were more insistent, her tongue more practiced, her thrusts slower and more deliberate. But then she had an advantage; her concentration was not disturbed by any kind of emotional involvement. This was a purely business transaction. Sex had been a central term of their bargain since the beginning, and she knew the importance of living up to a bargain.

"You're good," he said when they were through.

He raised his head and looked down at her. She was curled up beside him with her head cradled in the crook of his arm and her hair cascading over his shoulder and onto the white pillow. Her hand rested lightly on his lower belly, the little finger entwined in the fine curls of his pubic hair. One leg lay heavily on his thigh. A glistening streak of him was drying on her cheek, but she made no effort to wipe it away.

"Thanks." She smiled without opening her eyes.

They rested there until their breathing returned to normal. Then she sat up, drew her feet in so she was cross-legged with her back to him, and reached for a cigarette. He propped himself up against the headboard and poured a glass of wine.

69

"*Andrea Doria* was the name of a ship," he said to fill the silence.

"I know," she answered without looking back, "My parents emigrated from Italy aboard it. In 1954. Third class."

"You were named after her?"

She nodded. "My father was a sentimentalist."

Nettles lit a cigarette and exhaled a cloud of blue smoke. "She sank, you know," he said.

She craned around to look at him. "So a few hundred people have told me."

"I imagine they have." He laughed and let his head fall back so that he was gazing at the ceiling. "Where are your parents now?"

"Dead. My father, at least. Believe it or not, he died of TB." She reached for his wine glass and emptied it in one gulp. "I'll bet you thought nobody died from TB anymore, at least not in the good ol' U.S.A. Well, they still do if they're poor enough, and he was poor enough. I'm afraid his Great American Dream just didn't come true."

"When did he die?"

"Ten years ago," she said. "Ten years ago this month."

"What about your mother?"

"I don't know. Probably dead, too. I took off right after we buried Papa." She threw him a sideways glance. "Why all the questions? You writing a book?"

Nettles laughed. "That might not be a bad idea. One of these days you're going to be famous."

She reached out and patted him on the knee. "Lover, one of these days we're *all* gonna be famous, one way or the other."

A minute later she stood up, slipped on a pair of tight bikini briefs, and began brushing her hair in front of the mirror. Nettles watched her from the bed.

"I suppose now you're going to meet with White," he said after a while.

"That's the plan," she replied, looking at him in the mirror.

"Don't forget to take your whips and chains."

She grinned at him. "You sound jealous."

"Of that faggot? Shhhhit."

She turned around and struck a provocative pose, her hands on her hips, her shoulders thrown back so that her small breasts thrust out proudly. "Now if he were a faggot, why would he be interested in me?"

"'Cause you spank hard," Nettles answered with exaggerated distaste.

"You shouldn't pay any attention to ugly rumors."

He shook his head. "I don't see how you put up with that kinky little bastard."

"We need him. Why do you think I put up with any of these asses?"

"Me included?"

"You I like." She resumed brushing her hair.

"Because I'm such a great lover."

"Right."

"Bullshit."

She laid down the brush and pulled on a pair of tight blue Levi's. "I do like you, Walt. In your own way you're as much of a purist as I am, although in your case it's pure greed. In a world filled with emotional cripples like White and romantic fools like Schmidt, it's nice to deal with someone who knows what he wants and goes for it."

"Another of your snow jobs?"

"It's the truth," she said, straining to fasten the top pants button, then reaching for a gray, high-neck sweater. "Most men think with their hearts, whatever that means, or their testicles. You think with your brain. You're a ruthless, cold-blooded prick, *that's* why I like you."

"The feeling is mutual." Nettles said. He waited for her to pull the sweater over her head. "What's this about Schmidt? I thought you two got along pretty well."

"He's okay."

"But—"

"But he's from the old school. Honor and gallantry and all that crap. I don't think he approves of our methods. He's good when it comes to technique, but I don't think he's tough enough."

"So why keep him around?"

"There are reasons," she said vaguely.

"Like what?"

She flashed him a coy smile. "We are full of questions tonight, aren't we?"

"Sure, why not? I ought to know about the people who're gonna help me get rich." He lit two cigarettes and handed one to her. "Besides, the one thing I've learned about you in the last three months is that you'd rather talk about this scheme of yours than do anything else."

"Anything?"

"Anything," he said flatly. "Let's be honest, sweetheart. You may be the best little piece in town, but it's all programmed in that computer brain of yours. I never flattered myself by thinking different."

"Are you complaining?"

"Shit, no! I said you're good and I meant it." He took a gulp of wine. "But before you succeed in changing the subject, let's get back to Schmidt. What's the skinny on him?"

"Okay," she said, seating herself on the edge of the bed. "Let me put it this way. In the beginning, a certain country agreed to provide funding and some material support for this operation."

"In exchange for?"

She smiled. "Not everyone's as materialistic as you. The country in question has courageously supported the struggle against imperialism for a long time."

"Nice speech."

"Don't be such a cynic. Besides, they're paying for this place."

Nettles thought for a second. "Let's see, a country that finances terrorism. Probably Libya, right?"

She continued without comment. "Unfortunately, in the early stages there was an incident that undermined their confidence in us . . ."

Nettles nodded. "That would be when whats-his-name—Pederson, Peterson—blew himself to smithereens."

"Who told you that?"

"Givens likes to talk about his predecessor."

"Givens talks 'too much and thinks too little."

"Anyway, you were saying . . ."

"Why am I telling you this? If you've talked to Givens he's undoubtedly told you everything."

Nettles shook his head. "The only thing Givens has to say about Schmidt is obscene. Keep going."

"Well, what it comes down to is that Schmidt was sent by this country to, you might say, watch over its investment."

"But he's German?"

"He's a free-lancer."

"Ah," Nettles said, smiling. "So the old guy's from headquarters. Now I understand why you're so attentive."

She bristled. "*I'm* in charge of this operation, and I'm the only one who calls the shots. If I listen to Schmidt more than the rest of you idiots, it's because I respect his experience and knowledge."

"Oh, right, me too!"

Andrea relaxed immediately. "Okay, smart-ass. Anything else you want to know? I've got to get going." She bent down and began to pull on a pair of black boots.

"Does White know about us?"

"What about us? That we're getting it on?"

"Yes. You know he really thinks you two are going to run off together and live happily ever after in some kind of radical Shangri-la."

"Does he?" she said, concentrating more than necessary on her task.

"Encouraged by you, no doubt."

"I hope not discouraged by you."

"I know when to keep my mouth shut. I just hope you're not seriously considering running off with that turkey."

"Would you rather I went with you?"

Nettles laughed heartily. "Sure. I'd be interested to see how your socialist bullshit would go over at a Caribbean resort."

"So that's your plan."

"Sandy beaches by day. Smoky casinos by night. Beautiful

women, fast cars, good booze. You bet that's my plan. You're welcome to come along and see why capitalism will never die."

"You really are hopelessly decadent."

"Damn right I am." He put a half-full glass of wine into her hand and picked up his own. "Here's to decadence."

"To the revolution," she answered and touched her glass to his.

After Andrea left, Nettles took a thirty-minute shower and stretched out naked on the rumpled bed.

Women and their goddamn causes, he thought, as he lay smoking a cigarette. Mary with her hatred of the Navy, this one with her hatred of just about everything, and neither one with any room left in their lives for him. Well, no more of that bullshit. From now on he would buy what he needed in the way of sex and to hell with the rest of it.

At least the evening had been a success in one way. He had planted the tidbit about going to the Caribbean, a good false lead if there was anyone left to hunt for him, but the item about Libya worried him. It confirmed what Givens had told him and meant that he might have to deal with real professionals somewhere along the line. It looked now like he was not only about to shit on the Navy and this bunch of weirdos, but on the damn Arabs to boot. Well, he thought, as he sat up and reached for his clothes, it certainly will be exciting.

When he had finished dressing he poured the last few drops of wine into his glass and raised it in another, private toast.

"To sweet revenge," he said aloud.

✎ 13

At the sound of her knock Billy White cracked open the door, peered out, then threw it open so hard that it bounced off the adjacent wall.

"Where the hell have you been?" he snapped, turning his back and walking into the dingy interior. He crashed on a tattered couch in front of a blaring black-and-white television set.

Andrea stood watching him from the open doorway. Her face was expressionless, her stance relaxed. She had shifted her weight to her right foot, hooked both hands onto the long leather strap of her purse and cocked her head to the side, all to give the impression of passive indulgence. Any second she might start tapping her toe.

After a moment White called out to her. "Well, aren't you coming in?"

"Not if I have to put up with one of your tantrums."

He stared stubbornly at the screen for another full minute until the woman calmly turned to leave; then he bolted for the door.

"Andrea, wait!" he shouted. "I'm sorry. Come in. Please."

Inside, the woman threw her purse on the coffee table, sat down on the couch, and took out a cigarette. "Get me a light, would you please, Billy."

He quickly located a book of matches and struck one for her. "I expected you at ten," he said.

"I was detained."

He waited until it was clear that she would not explain further, then sank down beside her. "I've missed you."

She gave him a stiff smile and patted his thigh. "I've missed you, too."

"Really?" White said, leaning over in an awkward effort to kiss her.

She pulled back and waved her hand at the TV. "Could you turn that damn thing off?"

"Oh, sure," he said, and after switching off the set, "Now, show me that you missed me."

She waited through a long, lingering kiss, allowing him to force his eager tongue between her lips and even permitting him to fondle at her breasts through the thin sweater, but when he tried to slip his hand under the garment she pushed him away.

"What's wrong?" he asked breathlessly, still groping.

"Later," she said firmly, "after we've talked."

His voice was a whine. "You're teasing me."

"I'm not teasing," she snapped. Then less harshly, "I want you as much as you want me, you know I do. Remember how good it was last time. Remember how many times you made me come. My God, it makes me wet just to think about it." With a look of longing on her face she reached out and lightly caressed his arm, only to withdraw abruptly. "But we're soldiers, and we must have a soldier's discipline. After this is all over we can indulge ourselves as much as we like, but for now we must sacrifice our personal desires for the sake of the struggle."

"Yes, of course you're right," White blurted, too quickly to be convincing. He sat up stiffly. "What was it you wanted to talk about?"

"How 'bout getting me a drink first. I suppose all you have is that awful Scotch."

"No," he said, scrambling to serve her. "I got some bourbon, special for you."

"Wonderful." she muttered. She waited for him to bring the drink and reseat himself. "Now, brief me on the situation aboard the *Bremerton*."

"I told you on the phone, your plan worked perfectly. They're going to keep the forward plant critical through the weekend. Chief Nettles and I will both be on the watchbill ..."

"Yes, I talked to Nettles."

"Oh?"

"On the telephone," she said pointedly. "Which reminds me, Nettles said that your . . . er, shall we call it, enthusiasm, nearly resulted in a breach of security."

White looked at her blankly.

"You let slip to somebody about the transformer."

"Oh, that. Some jerk walked in when me and the chief were talking. Don't worry. I covered it, no sweat."

She looked at him sternly. "Are you sure this person didn't overhear more than you think?"

"Maurer? He's so goddamn drifty he wouldn't know shit if he smelled it."

"Nevertheless, from now on keep your mouth shut."

White nodded sourly.

"Do you hear me?"

"Yes, I hear you."

"And no more discussions with Nettles."

"All right, Andrea, give me a break."

The woman let him stew while she slowly sipped her drink. Then she resumed the conversation. "I wish they had kept up the aft plant."

"Yes, that would have been better in one way. It has direct access to the helo deck, but I think the forward plant is going to be a little easier to secure. And besides, I already have all my equipment in the forward plant, and since I work there normally, nobody's going to question my being there. Don't worry, it'll be fine."

"When are you going to make your wiring changes?"

"Some of them I'll do first thing tomorrow morning. I had a chance to test my special controller last week, but I won't install that until the last minute." White proudly launched into a ten-minute technical discussion of his plan, detailing each tiny modification of the plant's system and his reason for it. Throughout the monologue Andrea listened attentively, nodding and injecting approving noises when it seemed appropriate. It was clear by the gleam in his eye and his animated speech that White was dealing in the one secure area of his psyche.

"These things you're going to do tomorrow, you're sure

they won't be noticed?" she asked when he finished.

White's expression clouded with anger. "There's nobody on that goddamn ship that knows the system better than me. Nobody! And nobody's gonna know anything until I want them to."

"Control yourself," she said sharply. "It was only a question."

"I suppose," White said bitterly. "But we've been over this all before. I'm the best there is, Andrea. I won't screw up."

"I know you're the best, Billy, that's why I need you so much. This whole operation depends on you."

Suddenly mollified, White could only mumble his thanks.

The woman laughed to herself. Of all the bullshit compliments she paid him, that one alone was true. When it came to electronics he was the best, or one of the best, a damn genius according to Nettles.

The chief had picked him out according to her specifications: that he be vulnerable enough to be talked into doing the job, and competent enough to do it right. On both accounts White had proven more than adequate.

"He's scared to death that he's queer," the chief had told her. "Prove to him that he's not and you'll have him right in the palm of your hand." As far as it went, Nettles's assessment was right, but it didn't go nearly far enough. Not ony was White a mass of sexual and emotional insecurity, but intellectually as well he was putty ready to be molded by the first forceful mind he encountered. In every respect he was the perfect candidate.

Nettles set them up together one muggy fall night in a Belmont Shores bar; she took it from there. Her strategy was straightforward: a little Marx interspersed with some solid sex—never quite enough of the latter, but enough to keep him coming back. The political indoctrination part of it went smoothly, as she knew it would. Like most Americans, White's political philosophy was infantile. At best he had some vaguely warm feeling about democracy, much the same sort of feeling children have about God, but totally lacking an intellectual base. To White, the economic system and the political system were somehow mystically related, so that justice and equality were directly linked in his mind to private property and free enterprise and the secret ballot. He identified with symbols like the presidency and the flag; he knew virtually nothing of the institutions involved or the processes by which they functioned.

She zeroed in first on that ignorance, painting him a picture of his system that he was totally unequipped to dispute. In heated all-night sessions, she introduced him to the ugly realities of imperialism and classism, overwhelming him with examples of the wanton self-interest and moral decadence that could be perceived to underlie American policymaking. She turned every meal, every walk, every post-coital silence into a discussion, easily demolishing his feeble attempts to dispute her findings, until he gave up trying to argue with her at all. She fed him on a steady diet of critical literature, beginning with respected mainstream analysts of current American policy and graduating him to the more dissident viewpoints and, finally, to radical diatribes.

He soaked it all up like a sponge. In contrast to the chaotic, corrupt, and repressive system which, under her skilled tutelage, he had come to see as the American system, socialism seemed bewitchingly logical, rational, and just—a system that would appreciate his unique genius for what it was without subjecting him to the vagaries of popular acceptance. In the world she was offering, he could have power and prestige because of what he knew, not who he knew.

One of the things that made her so effective was that she believed it herself. America *was* corrupt, repressive, and militaristic; it *was* controlled by the monied interests operating behind a democratic facade. The proof was there for anyone to see. America was in league with the multinational corporations, and it did exploit the world's poor. It had supported murderous regimes in countries like China, Vietnam, Cuba, Chile, and Iran, until one by one they were overthrown, and it was still supporting fascists in places like the Philippines, Turkey, and South Korea. America exploited its own poor through educational, economic, and legal systems operated by and for the upper classes. The American system was evil, capable of destroying whole nations and races in its pursuit of profit. Its victims could be found on battlefields or in coal mines or on Indian reservations or in ghettos. Her own father had been one of those victims. The remedy was a complete redistribution of wealth, power, and justice. The system must be attacked at its military-industrial heart and reduced to rubble. Only then could the rebuilding begin.

All this, reduced to simple terms, she taught to White, skillfully playing off his insecurities and pathetic need for approval, modifying his political and moral precepts a little at a time until she had reshaped them into her own. When he resisted she punished him with devastating attacks of mockery and ridicule, physically rejecting him; when he submitted she rewarded him with respect and extravagant praise, as well as with intense pleasure.

Sex, of course, was the key to his reeducation. For it he suffered her abuses and eventually surrendered his independence. But it was a key that nearly eluded her. Even with Nettles's warning, she underestimated his sexual confusion. For almost half her life she had been manipulating men through their desire for her, but she'd had to deal there with simple lust. In White's case nothing was simple.

She got him to her apartment easily enough, and within a week she had maneuvered him into bed, but no matter what she tried, he proved to be impotent. She was shy, sweet, and patient; she was brazen and demanding; she was sympathetic; she was cruel; nothing seemed to work. And with each frustrating failure, White's humiliation increased, triggering a cycle of anxiety and depression that threatened to break her tenuous hold over him. In desperation she plunged into the literature of sexual dysfunction, but it turned out to be either academic discourse or simplistic drivel. She even went to Nettles, but all he could offer was some weak macho rejoinders.

Then one night, after hours of unsuccessful coaxing and cajoling, her patience gave out. She flew into a savage rage, screaming obscenities and pummeling him with her fists, climbing naked onto his cowering form and physically attacking him, until, to her amazement, she suddenly became aware of his erection pressing against her thigh. On succeeding nights the performance was refined so that the physical brutality was eliminated. But it remained a ritual of domination and submission that tested the limits of perversity. And though the violence was latent, it was never far from the surface.

Even now, sitting beside one another on the couch, they were involved in the script. She had just fed him a small carrot; it was again time for the stick.

She glanced at her watch. "I have to get going."

"Going?" White stammered. "What about me? You said after we finished talking . . ."

"Did I?" she said, in a bored tone.

"Yes, goddamn it, you did! Do you have any idea the risk I'm taking to be here? I have the duty tonight. I'm not even supposed to leave the ship, much less the base. If I get caught my ass is grass!"

She looked at him passively. "Well then, maybe you'd better get back there."

His voice became a whine. "Come on, Andy, you're not being fair!"

"I told you never to call me Andy!"

"Okay, I'm sorry, Andrea." He grabbed her by the shoulders. "Please, I haven't seen you in a week."

Very deliberately she took hold of his wrists and forced his hands down into his lap. Then she spoke in a quiet, patronizing voice. "After Sunday we'll have all the time you could want."

"But I need you now," he pleaded. "Just a little while, please."

Her thoughtful silence encouraged him.

"Please!"

After another moment she stood up. "Wait here," she ordered, then walked in the direction of the bedroom.

Almost ten minutes later, long enough to make White crazy with anticipation, she reappeared, standing feet apart, hands on hips, under the hallway arch. She still wore the gray sweater, but she had shed her jeans and panties so that she stood nude from the waist down, thick black curls on firm white flesh, more provocative than if she had been completely naked.

"Well?" she said impatiently to the entranced White.

He rose slowly, never taking his eyes off her, approaching her with a look that could only be described as reverence.

"I love you," he murmured, as he slid his arms around her narrow waist and aimed his mouth at hers.

At the last minute she turned away. "No!" she said huskily. "Not like that." She told him exactly what she wanted him to do.

He was trembling as he sank to his knees to obey.

The woman was gone when he awoke an hour later. So was every trace of her, her things from the bathroom, from the dresser drawers, from the kitchen cupboards. All there was was a long note lying on the kitchen table. In the main it was a detailed list of instructions for wiping the apartment clean of any trace of the two of them. Only at the end was there a cryptic personal reference. It said:

Sunday. 0730. I'm counting on you. And then a line that made his heart leap:

I have our tickets.

Saturday, January 12

✐ 14

"Thank God!" Cynthia Spencer muttered to herself. It was five-thirty in the morning, and the daughter of the Long Beach base commander was none too steady on her feet. She was celebrating the discovery that the back stewards' door was open. She had a front door key, of course, but if she went in the front door at that time of the morning, she might as well bring along a brass band. Wouldn't her mother love to nail her coming in at dawn, reeking of beer, looking what might generously be called disarrayed, half drunk, more than half ripped? That was the kind of evidence that a father simply could not ignore, not even hers, who could overlook a lot when it came to his only daughter. Jesus Christ! How did it get to be five-thirty?

Actually it got to be five-thirty because she and Gary didn't leave the party until after two, and they didn't get up to the golf course until almost three, and she had to put up at least a token struggle before she let him take off her dress.

She turned the door handle until it clicked softly, lifting up hard on the door so that it would not squeak, and opened it just enough to slip through into the main kitchen area. A little orange night-light let her find her way past the long white tile counters and stainless-steel drainboards, past the baking ovens and butcher-block work table and the swinging door to the narrow back hallway. The commanding officer's official residence had been purposely laid out to permit its small battalion of servants to move about through a separate system of corridors and stairways, without being seen. Cynthia had spent much of her childhood scampering around in such networks in houses just like this one, her own and those of her friends, before she had her own. She knew the pattern well enough: the doors would be unobtrusive, the stairways would be steep and narrow, and best of all, the way would be well carpeted to muffle offending footsteps.

She hadn't meant to get quite so carried away with the young marine; it broke her resolution to be cool on the first date, which she had made after the last first date. But it had felt so good. That was the part that she'd never been told, not by her girlfriends, for whom sex was mostly a social entrance examination, and certainly not by her mother, who only felt comfortable with the subject when she could lecture like a gynecologist. In Sex-Ed it was euphemistically referred to as powerful "urges," when it was referred to at all. Urges, shit! It felt *good*, really good, downright fantastic! She sure as hell didn't need any urging.

Besides, he had been pretty fantastic himself, blond, blue eyes, over six feet. Except, of course, for his ridiculous hair. Marines still weren't allowed to have any hair, not even these days when the sailors were allowed beards and mustaches. Other than that, he was beautiful. And he was nice, too. Macho, but nice. He had seemed as surprised as she at how much had happened, conscientious enough to ask her if it was safe, old-fashioned enough to tell her he loved her when it was over, to jabber nervously all the way home, to object to leaving her off on a corner two blocks from her home.

The stairway was about where she expected it to be. She managed to feel her way up with a minimum of noise to the door that opened out into the upstairs hallway. That put her at the far end, with her father's study on the right and the two extra bedrooms on the left. Her parents' room was farther down on the right, opposite the top of the main staircase; she would have to pass it to get to her room, down the long hallway past old eagle-ears.

Quickly she recomputed her options. Ever since she could remember, she had always made it a habit to have an alternate plan, a fall-back position, just in case the worst came to pass. As a child she kept track of fire exits and emergency hatches and the red lines painted on the decks of cruise ships leading to the lifeboats. On dark streets she picked a house to run to. On buses and beaches she singled out men, usually older and inevitably handsome, to call upon for protection.

By making it upstairs undetected she had improved her options enormously. Earlier, in the kitchen, she had stripped down to her underwear, so that if she were discovered there she'd be able to make a case for having come down to forage. Her mother would be suspicious as hell, but at least she wouldn't be caught flat-footed. Now, safely upstairs, she would be able to claim that she was simply going to the bathroom—not a bad story if her mother didn't notice the smell of beer and the heavy makeup, somewhat smeared, that she still wore.

Poor Gary. What would he do if he knew that his latest conquest was just seventeen, and worse, that she was the CO's daughter? He would shit, that's what. He probably wouldn't stop running until he got to Nevada, and maybe not then. If an officer gets caught screwing an enlisted man's wife, that's an indiscretion; if an enlisted man gets caught screwing an officer's wife, that's rape. What about a daughter, jailbait at that? It'd take him a year to stop shaking.

And his reaction would be nothing compared to the explosion that would occur if her mother found out about him. That she was screwing around was bad enough. That she was doing it at four in the morning in the back seat of an old Ford was absolutely tacky. But that her lover was a lowly marine private—my God! It would be the end of the world. The end of the world and the end of Cynthia Spencer.

She grinned in the darkness. Wouldn't that be the ultimate confrontation, after the stewards had been dismissed, of course. Her mother shrieking and wailing, her father fidgeting in the background, embarrassed by his wife's hysterics, angered by his daughter's insolence, too smart to order a cease-fire that would be ignored. "We used to be so proud of you," her mother would say in a tragic voice, presuming to speak for them both. It was true. For sixteen years Cynthia had been the perfect daughter: cheerful, polite, studious, fair-haired and lithesome, passably talented in sports and music and dance, popular with the group of friends carefully screened by her mother. Even her teeth were naturally straight, a fact which her mother pointed to with pride, as though she were somehow responsible. "Where have we gone wrong?" she would moan.

Then it would be Cynthia's turn. Would she tell them everything? Maybe it was time for that. About the men, or in Gary's case, boys, of whom the marine was only the latest, starting with sweet, lecherous Mr. Evans and the private tennis lessons that ended on the changing room floor, with more than a little encouragement from her. Would she tell them about the cache of birth control pills in her dresser drawer, or the grass rolled up in a plastic bag at the back of her closet shelf? Maybe not then, maybe not until the next time she was asked to serve at one of her mother's interminable weekly teas. "Excuse me, Mrs. Jones," she'd say, nonchalantly affected like her mother. "Would you care for some good Colombian Gold, the very best, thirty dollars a lid?" Or better yet, "Hello, Mrs. Smith. How is your son David? Next time you see him, would you tell him I'd like to ball his socks off?"

She was still grinning when something wet and cold touched her leg. "Muffin!" she squealed before she could check herself, and then she fell to her knees and threw her arms around the prancing spaniel, giggling drunkenly as the long tongue lapped at her ear. "Shush!" she whispered urgently, trying to keep the wagging tail from thumping loudly against the wall. "You're gonna get me hung."

She fought to control forty-five pounds of playful dog, but it was already too late. Her mother appeared at the bedroom door, peering out, a white apparition in the dim light.

"Who's there?" she demanded in a sleepy, bitchy voice.

Cynthia spoke out boldly. "It's Muffin. She was chasing rabbits."

"Chasing rabbits?"

"You know, dreaming. I'm sorry, she woke me up, too."

The woman grunted. "Well, if you have to let that damn dog sleep up here, how about keeping your door closed."

"Yes, Mama," Cynthia said meekly. Then angrily, "Bad dog, Muffin, bad dog!" and at the same time joyfully hugging the bewildered animal.

When his wife returned to bed Robert Spencer turned over and propped himself up on one elbow. "What is it?" he mumbled. "What's the matter?"

"Nothing," his wife said, climbing under the blankets, pulling them over her head. "Just the stupid dog."

"Dog," the admiral muttered, lapsing back into sleep.

⟵ 15

"Who's there?" the patrolman called out nervously. He had jerked his car off the road so that its headlights were aimed at the wrecked transformer site. Now he was out of the car, crouched behind the open door, gun drawn, peering warily into the growing dawn. It was just after six-thirty. The sun was not yet up, but the fog had cleared off during the night and the eastern horizon was ablaze with every shade of blue from purple to white, throwing the charred rubble into sharp silhouette. "Come on out!" he ordered.

"Wainwright?" A figure stepped out from behind the transformer. "Is that you?"

At the sound of his name the patrolman lowered his pistol and stood up. "Who is it?"

"Stone," the figure said, shining a flashlight into his own face to confirm it.

"Commander! What are you doing out here?" The patrolman holstered his gun and walked toward the site.

"Just a little snooping around."

"A little early, ain't it?"

"I couldn't sleep," Stone said with a wry smile. "Since you're here, how about taking a look at something?" He led the younger man around to the ocean side of the enclosure where the fence was still intact. He shined his light toward the top string of barbed wire. "What do you see?"

The patrolman stared up at the wire, a stark black line against the brightening sky. At first he saw nothing unusual, but on closer examination he noticed that three barbs between one set of support struts had been bent almost straight. He pointed it out to the security chief.

"What do you think?" Stone asked.

"I don't know," the patrolman said, puzzled. "Maybe something heavy was leaned up against it, like a big board or something."

"But then it would just twist around out of the way. I don't see how it could have been bent out of shape like that." He reached into his pocket and produced a small shred of stiff, badly charred cloth. "This was caught on one of the barbs."

"What is it?"

"I'm not sure, but I think it's some kind of canvas material."

"How do you figure it."

"I really don't know," Stone said thoughtfully. He returned the shred to his pocket and stared for a moment at the hulk of the transformer. "Wainwright, do you have a hacksaw in your car?"

"I think so, sir. What do you have in mind?"

Stone took off his light jacket. "It's time to take a closer look at that valve."

When Chief Morton arrived at Stone's office forty-five minutes later, the place looked like a home workshop during an engine overhaul. Stone's desk and half the floor were covered with newspapers. Dirty rags and stiff wire brushes were scattered about along with several different sized cans of what looked like paint thinner. In addition to the glaring overhead fluorescent lights, a drafting lamp had been rigged to illuminate the center of the desk. Stone was standing bent over the work area, examining a brass fitting through a large magnifying glass.

"How do you like your new lab?" he asked cheerily.

"Nice," Morton muttered.

"Hope I didn't wake you up."

"I was about to go jogging," the chief said. Along with a pair of rumpled cords he still wore a sweatshirt and sneakers.

"Good, good," Stone mumbled. "Tell me, Chief, I imagine you've polished your share of brass. How long does it take to tarnish?"

It took the man a moment to adjust to the question. "Oh, maybe two, three days. You've probably polished as much brass as me."

Stone nodded. "Take a look at this."

Morton accepted the magnifying glass and a standard, threaded octagonal brass fitting.

While Stone hovered over him he held the object under the light and stared at it, turning it over and over in his fingers. "What is it I'm looking for?" he asked finally.

"Look at the ridges between each face."

"They're a little chewed up" Morton said. "Even a good wrench will do that. . . . What is this from?"

"But look here," Stone said, ignoring the question and using a pencil as a pointer. "See how some of the marks are still shiny?"

"So are these," Morton said, indicating another set of shiny marks right at the edge of the bolt.

"I made those when I took it off the valve, but those first ones were *under* the layer of burned residue."

"This is from the transformer?"

"Right," Stone said excitedly. "And those marks may be proof that those G.E. engineers were right. They have to have been made within the last couple of days."

"Because they're shiny?"

"Right again."

Morton shook his head. "You probably did that when you cleaned it up."

"The cleaner I used had no effect on the tarnish. Look at the older marks."

Morton checked. The others were the same dull color as the body of the fitting, but he was still skeptical. "Shouldn't the heat of the fire have caused these to oxidize, too?"

"Good for you, Chief," Stone said, chuckling happily. "I had the same question. So I did a little experimenting." He dabbed some Brasso on a rag and cleaned off one face of the fitting until it was fairly bright. "Got a lighter, Chief? I'm tired of burning myself with matches."

Morton produced a chrome Zippo and watched as the officer moved the fitting back and forth a few inches above the steady flame. In a short time the polished brass had turned a dull purplish-blue. Wiping it took off some of the darkness, but the tarnish remained.

"See, you're right, it does tarnish," Stone said. "But now watch."

Before repeating the procedure he dipped the fitting in a small dish of oil. This time the brass blackened, but when he wiped it off it was almost as shiny as it had been at the start.

"You see. The valve was down low, in a place that was protected from the worst of the fire. If my theory is right, there was enough oil on this fitting to protect it from complete oxidation, and hence the most recent marks stayed shiny."

"I'll be damned," Morton said. "So it *was* tampered with?"

"I believe so. *Why*, I haven't figured out yet, but it looks like it was."

The chief rubbed his unshaven beard. "What are you gonna do?"

"I don't know. It just doesn't figure. If I could come up with a motive this would be pretty good evidence, but right now nothing fits together." He walked over to the side window, gazed out at the rising sun, and turned back. "I need some time to think about this. Would you be willing to meet with Pat and me late this afternoon? Maybe between the three of us we can psych it out."

Morton squirmed. "What time did you have in mind, sir? I sort of have a lot of money on the playoff game."

Stone laughed. "Ah, football. I almost forgot."

"It's not that important," Morton said quietly.

"That's okay," Stone said, smiling. "I never meddle in a man's religion. What time will the game be over?"

"Certainly by five."

"Okay, then, let's make it eighteen hundred. Here."

"Thanks," the chief said happily.

"Oh, and Chief . . ."

"Yes sir?"

"During the halftime, give this thing some thought."

"Yes sir!" Morton said.

⟍16

"Wake up" whispered a voice from the other side of the curtains. "Time to get up if you want breakfast before you go on watch." The wake-up call was an improvement over the boot-camp system of banging on an empty bucket, but not much of an improvement for a man with a critical hangover.

Hal Maurer groaned miserably, tried to lift his head, and failing in that effort, forced himself to open one eye. He had come awake in heavy seas, instinctively spreading his feet as wide as possible on the narrow mattress to protect against the snap roll. It was several seconds before he realized that all the lurching about was in his head; that, in fact, everything around him was very still. He thought about that for a moment and then fumbled around until he had managed to pull back the curtain.

"Where are we?" he asked in a dry croaking voice.

"Er . . . RC berthing," the messenger answered uncertainly. At best wake-up duty was a miserable job, involving a lot of stumbling around in the dark through unfamiliar sleeping compartments, relying on outdated rack assignment maps, looking for men who didn't want to be found and always facing the possibility that one would come up swinging. It was even worse rousting out men like Maurer, who had spent a long night on the beach.

"No," Maurer grumbled. "I mean the ship."

"Oh, we're in Long Beach. Remember?"

Maurer did, vaguely.

"If you want to skip breakfast I'll come back later," the messenger offered.

"What time is it?"

"Seven o'clock."

"No, I'll get up."

After an awkward silence the messenger spoke again. "Could I get you to initial?" The procedure of initialing wake-up sheets had been adopted to protect messengers from the frequent and usually false accusation that they had failed to wake up a late-relieving watchstander. Nobody liked it, least of all the men trying to sleep while the ritual went on around them, but almost everyone accepted the logic of it.

"Yeah, sure," Maurer muttered, extending his limp hand and groping for the proffered pen.

"You want me to switch on your light?"

"God, no!" Maurer groaned. "Just aim the pen at the right place and go away."

The messenger did, and for a long time afterward Maurer lay very still on his stomach, his head buried in his pillow, reconstructing the events of the preceding night.

He remembered leaving the ship and driving out to the Golden Sail, where he had enough drinks on an empty stomach to make him buzz, danced with a few likely prospects, failed to make a connection. Then . . . then what?

It should have been dinner. That was his intent when he left the Sail and drove down the Pacific Coast Highway, but a few blocks south he came to the El Paso, and that's as far as he got. The band was great, and the place was jammed to the rafters as it was almost every night. Not much chance of scoring, not with a male-to-female ratio of two to one. But there was a girl—he could almost see her sitting beside him at the bar. Or was there? His memory was out of sync, flipping over as if his vertical hold was out of whack. He struggled to remember, and then when he did, when the image of her came into focus, it was like getting hit between the eyes with a wet sponge.

Oh yeah, there *was* a girl, at least that was what she would be called for lack of a better label. She might also be called a dog, except that dogs, both the two- and four-legged type, could be pleasant and likable, and she was neither.

Her face might have been all right, but it was impossible to see beneath the layers of makeup. Of the rest of her, there was simply too much: big thighs, big ass, and worst of all, big mouth. She was a psychology major at Long Beach State and wanted to be a lawyer, or, as she said with her nose in the air, an *attorney*. If she ever made it, which he found hard to imagine, the first thing she should do is sue God and Levi-Strauss, the former for faulty design and the latter for selling size 14 pants to a size 16 butt.

Although in a way it was good that she was overweight, because that was probably the only thing that kept her from drifting away. She was a space cadet, as Denney McGurk liked to say, a lunar brain in earth gravity. Not entirely without cunning—she did not approach him until he had ordered a drink—she was essentially a boring person whose conversation alternated between telling him how much she hated bars because men were constantly trying to put the make on her and inviting him to do just that.

Wide awake now, with the image of her still lingering in his mind, Maurer swung his legs over the edge of his bunk and sat up. He slid open the curtains and peered out into the darkness. To think that instead of this he could be waking up next to her. He smiled ruefully. Had he not been suspended five feet above the deck, he might just have knelt down and kissed it.

He slowly rolled his head to flex the stiffness out of his neck, just barely clearing an overhead airconditioning duct in the process. At least he was able to sit up. The poor wretches in the bottom and middle racks didn't have that much room, with just about three feet from their mattresses to the bottom of the rack above.

Maurer had the choice rack in the compartment, a privilege not unrelated to the fact that he was senior man. It was the top rack in the far back corner, right next to the hull, away from the noise of the clanking metal ladder, closest to the sloshing of the sea which met the side of the ship about two feet above his head. Under way, the constant whisper of the water sliding past the hull together with the *Bremerton*'s characteristic slow, regular roll produced a sleeping aid that was better than any pill; many nights he had fallen asleep with the bright reading light still glaring in his eyes. And there was another significant feature: his rack had the first outlet on the airconditioning line, no small advantage in hot weather when the AC only made it about as far as the fifteenth bunk.

Reactor control division berthing was one of the smaller of the ship's twelve living compartments. At capacity it held thirty occupants, although lately the actual number was more like twenty, all in a room roughly the size of a two-car garage. Most of the space was taken up by the rows of bunks stacked three high. The only common areas were a five-by-five-foot square at the bottom of the ladder, furnished with a tiny table and a few metal chairs, and the three-foot-wide aisles between the bunks. The compartment head, with its one urinal, one toilet, one shower stall, and two washbasins, was just large enough to hold five friendly men.

Maurer grabbed a towel, jumped barefoot onto the cold linoleum deck, and made his way forward through the clutter that was known as "the Pit." Uniforms and parts of uniforms hung everywhere, side by side with civvies carefully protected in plastic bags. The compartment ironing board was a permanent fixture standing outside the door to the head. Clean laundry was piled on the ends of bunks. Spare blankets, pillows, and mattresses were stacked not so neatly in the corners, along with personal items too large to fit into lockers. On top of the partitions that separated the rows of bunks were piles of books and magazines. Nearly every man had his own tape player, yet there were only a few electrical outlets. The result was a tangle of extension cords criss-crossing the overhead like thick cobwebs, draped from pipes and cable brackets, as many as ten of them plugged into a single outlet through a confusion of three-way adapters. And then there were the posters, of almost every size and type, with themes ranging from the religious to the pornographic.

On a Saturday morning in port, the compartment was nearly deserted. The duty section, of course, had slept aboard, but that was just ten men, and half of them were on watch. The cacophony of snoring and wheezing that greeted an early riser at sea was noticeably absent.

The transition from the sleeping compartment, illuminated only by the feeble red glow of two overhead night-lights, to the blinding fluorescent glare of the head was almost too much for Maurer. He shaved and washed as quickly as he could, squinting the whole time, then stumbled gratefully back out to dress in the darkness.

Maurer didn't come into the light again until he stepped through an open watertight door into the bright, spacious crew's dining area on second deck. By then he was feeling almost human again, a status confirmed by the hunger that was growling in his stomach. He paused to glance at the few sailors straggling through the regular chow line, then turned right and walked into the first-class petty officers' mess.

Compared to the drab clutter of the berthing compartment, the *Bremerton*'s first-class mess was downright plush, visible proof of how well first-class petty officers were able to work the system. The walls were wood paneled and hung with muted pastoral prints in hand-finished frames. Acoustical tiles overhead hid the usual ugly maze of ducts, piping, and cables. The forward half of the room was a lounge area, thickly carpeted and furnished with couches and a huge round oak coffee table. The aft half was the dining and recreation area, with not only the usual assortment of tables and chairs but also special tables with tops inlaid with chess or backgammon boards, and one big table particularly suited for seven-man poker games.

The mess was equipped with a large console-style television set and video cassette player, a couple thousand dollars' worth of stereo equipment, and a permanently installed 16-millimeter movie projector. Discreetly stowed behind one of the couches was also an 8-mm projector, for those special movies that didn't come from Hollywood.

Maurer crossed the dining area and walked around a partition into the mess's fully equipped food service area. A young sailor wearing a crisp white cook's apron was perched on a stool beside the grill, reading a paperback novel. When he spotted Maurer he put aside the book and smiled cheerfully. "Mornin', Maurer, what'll it be?"

"Don't bother," Maurer said. "I'll fix my own."

The cook nodded. "Everything's there for you. Mushrooms in the reefer if you want 'em." He sat down and resumed his reading.

Maurer quickly broke four eggs onto the hot grill, tossed in a handful of peppers and tomatoes and some sliced cheese, and, expertly wielding a large spatula, folded it all into an omelet. When it was medium done, he flipped it onto a plate, drew himself a glass of milk, and walked out to the dining area.

The only other man in the mess was Jerry Stubin, the engineering department's lead yeoman and resident busybody—the last person Maurer wanted to see at seven-twenty in the morning. His back was to Maurer, and the technician settled into the first available spot, hoping to go unnoticed. But his luck failed him.

"Hey, nuke," Stubin called out, straining around to beckon to him, "don't be antisocial."

Maurer grudgingly picked up his food and joined the other man. "How you doin'?" he muttered, seating himself across the table.

"Got the duty again, huh? You must really love this place."

"Right," Maurer said curtly.

But the man persisted. "Personally, I think six-section duty is bad enough. Those yeomen up in personnel are on ten section. I don't see how you put up with port 'n' starboard."

"It's rough," Maurer said, concentrating on his food.

"I'll bet. You must be gettin' out when your enlistment's up?"

"Haven't decided."

"You're a short-timer, aren't you?"

"October."

"That's right. I remember seeing a letter from your detailer just the other day. What'd they offer you, prototype?"

"I think so," Maurer mumbled. His vagueness was more than simple evasion; the letter had contained two pages of complicated option formulas.

Stubin shook his head. "The way things are going, if I were a nuke, I wouldn't stay in if they offered me Paris." When Maurer failed to respond, he added, "Are you really thinking about it?"

"Yeah, I'm really thinking about it," Maurer said, openly annoyed. He quit the omelet halfway through, pushed the plate aside, and reached for a cigarette.

Stubin threw up his hand. "Hey, man, don't get pushed out of shape. I was just asking."

Maurer gave him a cool smile. "Kind of a strange question for a guy who just re-upped himself."

"I ain't no nuke."

"Meaning?"

"I like my job."

"I like my job, too. Not some of the people, but the job's okay."

The yeoman missed the sarcasm entirely; his face showed only disbelief. "You like all that nuclear stuff?"

"Sure, it's a kick. You ought to try it."

"Not me," Stubin said hastily. "That stuff scares me."

Maurer knew he was not joking. On his second day aboard, Stubin had reported to sick bay with a mild case of nausea, convinced that he was suffering from radiation poisoning, and even the doctor had a difficult time convincing the man that all he had was a touch of stomach flu. Though he worked for engineering, no one had ever known him to set foot in either of the plants.

"There's nothing to be scared of," Maurer said. "It's just another machine."

"Yeah?" Stubin said skeptically. "What about all that radiation?"

The corners of Maurer's mouth lifted ever so slightly. "Much ado about nothing."

"Then why do you wear that thing?" the yeoman challenged, pointing to the film badge that Maurer wore clipped to his right shirt pocket. It was exactly what its name implied, a small square of photographic film layered with various types of shielding material so that it recorded the wearer's accumulated exposure to alpha, beta, gamma, and neutron radiation. Every month the film from every nuke was processed and the results recorded in the personal files. At least, that was the popular version. In fact, as Maurer had learned while digging through some obscure tech manual, the badges were not sensitive enough to record the extremely low levels of radiation present during normal operations. Their real and more sobering purpose was to provide investigators with exposure data in the event of accident involving the release of large amounts of radioactivity.

"Just a precaution," Maurer said. "Like fire extinguishers."

"Fires don't make you sterile."

"Neither does working around reactors."

"That's not what I hear."

Before Maurer could answer they were joined by a man named Weston, a new RC-type still assigned to the training division. Although he had spent six years in the nuclear power program and had been qualified on three different plants, he was undergoing the same lengthy training program required of a third class just out of prototype, just as Maurer would be required to requalify at his next duty station. In their few encounters, Maurer had found him to be easygoing and droll.

"What do you hear?" Weston said, picking up the thread of the conversation as he placed his breakfast on the table and took a seat next to Stubin.

Maurer answered the question with a sour expression. "Stubin here thinks that working down in the plant makes you sterile." He turned on the yeoman. "Look, Stubin, I don't care what you've heard. The fact is that in order to get enough radiation to make you sterile, you'd have to get more than enough to kill you." He looked at the new man. "Isn't that right?"

Weston pursed his lips thoughtfully; then, as if he had made a decision, he said slowly, "Come on, Maurer, why don't you tell him the truth?"

"The truth," Maurer said. It was a statement more than a question, a stall while he figured out what Weston was up to.

"The truth?" Stubin asked eagerly.

"If you wont' tell him, I will," Weston went on.

"I don't know . . ." Maurer said.

"Tell me!"

"Okay," Weston said, leaning forward and speaking in a hushed, conspiratorial tone. "The truth is that radiation *is* a big problem, especially . . . well, especially in the way you were talking about. That's why we have to keep up on our B shots."

"B shots?" Stubin said. "I've never heard of them."

Weston's mouth fell open in a look of shock, and Maurer, now in on it, contributed his bit. "Stubin here's not a nuke."

"Oh," Weston said with enormous relief. "I was gonna say if you hadn't gotten 'em by now, it's too late anyway."

Stubin was mystified. "Do you mean shot-shots, like in the arm?" He made a gesture as though he were injecting a hypodermic into his shoulder.

Weston looked sheepish. "Well, if you're not a nuke, I really shouldn't be talking . . . "

"Tell me!" the yeoman implored. "What are these shots?"

Weston looked questioningly at Maurer, who shrugged and said, "Why not?"

The new man actually looked around to see if anyone was listening, then leaned close to the yeoman. "It's boron."

"Boron?"

"Shhh!" Weston warned. "Yes, boron. In the form of borontrifluoride, it's a well-known neutron absorber. Every nuke gets a B shot once a month. At least if they want to have kids, they do. And not in the arm, either."

"Oh," Stubin said, squirming. "Who gives 'em?"

"The corpsman, back in sick bay."

Stubin looked worried. "Maybe I should be getting them."

For an instant Weston thought about it, then shook his head. "Naw, you only need it if you work in the plant."

"But I might have to go down there."

"Oh, that's okay," Weston said. "If you only go down occasionally, you'll probably be all right."

"Probably! Look, I want to start getting these shots. I'm not gonna take any chances."

Weston looked dubious. "I don't know if they'll give them to a non-nuke."

"They'll give 'em to me," Stubin said sharply.

"You'd have to put up a hell of a flap."

Stubin snorted, "I'll flap it like you've never seen." He stood up suddenly. "In fact, as soon as it's eight o'clock I'm gonna march right back to sick bay and demand it. I have a right to be protected."

The yeoman threw his plates crashing into the bussing tub and marched determinedly toward the door. As an afterthought, he looked back at the two sober men. "Thanks, guys," he said sincerely. "I just hope it's not too late."

"Don't mention it," Maurer called after him, managing to contain his laughter until the door had shut.

Weston cracked up, and Maurer went to get them both some coffee. When he returned, the new man was still grinning. "What brings you around on a Saturday morning?" Maurer asked after a few minutes.

Weston held up a thick packet of qualification cards. "Training. What else? The Duck has been on my back lately. Anything interesting going on in the plant that might get me a signature or two?"

"Maybe up forward," Maurer said. "I'm not sure. I've got the aft plant this time around."

Weston looked surprised. "According to the watchbill you're the forward RO."

"No," Maurer said with disbelief. "You must be wrong."

"I just checked ten minutes ago."

Maurer was angry. "That damn White."

"Not good, huh?"

"Not good. I was looking forward to four quiet hours of shutdown watch. Instead I've got to put up with a room full of sweaty bodies. Damn!"

Weston smiled lamely. "Sorry about that. I hate to be the bearer of bad news."

"Don't worry. When I get off watch it's going to be worse news for the guy who made out the watchbill," Maurer said. "And speaking of watches, I guess I'd better get down there."

The forward RO was Denney McGurk, Maurer's guitar-playing friend, a stocky, muscular man with a jovial face. Whatever the basis for their friendship, it was certainly not a common love for the program. Overzealousness in the performance of duty was not something McGurk was likely to be accused of, a trait that put him in the majority.

When McGurk saw Maurer enter EOS, he leaped out of his chair and headed for the door. "You've got it," he said.

"Hold it, turkey," Maurer growled. "Come on back here and tell me just what it is I've got."

"You figure it out. I've got places to go and people to see." He performed a quick little two-step.

"I want a turnover," Maurer said impatiently. "Just like I taught you."

McGurk gave an exaggerated shrug. "Steady state, you old fart, what else can I say?"

Maurer sighed. "McGurk, if you don't give me a decent turnover I'm gonna rip your head off and mail it back to Kentucky."

"Oh," said the man, grinning, "since you asked so nice." He sucked in a deep breath and rattled off the information in a machine-gun burst of words. "You've got normal operating temperature and pressure, pumps on fifteen cycles, twenty-five percent flow, twenty percent power, ship's service loads on the forward TG, no alarms, no red tags, caution tags are in the book. 'Kay?"

Maurer laughed in defeat. "Okay, I guess I've got it."

"You sure do, sucker." McGurk beamed and skipped out the door, only to stick his head in a second later. "Oh, yeah, your buddy White was poking around behind the panel earlier, but he's done, I think."

"Doing what?"

"Who knows?" McGurk said. "Jackin' off, probably." And then he vanished noisily up the ladder.

The lead sinker hit with a solid plop and descended rapidly into the murky green water, dragging the nylon leader and two hooks behind it. It was not yet out of sight when the tiny silver perch began zeroing in on the chunks of sardine bait, scores of them competing for the chance to die. The slender tip of the Fiberglas pole dipped sharply once, then twice, as the fingerlings struck with a force many times their weight. Suddenly it bowed down and began to quiver madly.

"Susie's got one! Susie's got a fish!" a curly-headed girl of five shouted, clapping her hands and running off toward her mother, who was standing a few yards down the pier. Susie, an eight-year-old duplicate of her younger sister, was excitedly hauling in the tiny catch under her father's watchful eye.

Grimacing only slightly, the girl retrieved the flopping fish from the dry planking and held it at arm's length with both hands while her father extracted the hook from its mouth. She examined it for a moment, holding it by its tail fin, marveling at the rainbow sheen of its scales. Then she looked up at her father. "Can I give it to the seagull?" she asked.

"Whatever you want." He smiled.

With an excited laugh that brought her sister running back, the girl clambered up onto the middle bar of the railing and shouted down to a huge old gull perched atop a nearby piling. "Here's your lunch, Mr. Seagull," she called in a clear voice and then, with a strong throw, heaved the thrashing perch high into the air.

The old gull swiveled its neck and cocked back its head to follow with one clear black eye the arching bit of silver, watching with seeming indifference as it reached its apex and fell toward the safety of the sea. Suddenly the bird stretched its wings until they extended four feet from tip to tip, issued one joyous cry, and rose straight up. For an instant it hung in mid-air, its tail feathers down and extended, its head cocked to one side, its wings frozen at the top of their swing. Then it banked and wheeled seaward, skimming just inches above the surface, catching the perch a fraction of a second before it reached the water, gobbling it down even as it began a slow, graceful climb.

As the gull made a victory turn and glided in toward its piling perch, Karl Schmidt joined the girls and their parents in a spirited round of applause, then nodded to the strangers and turned from the railing to walk slowly back toward the foot of the pier.

Though it was just ten o'clock, the day was stirring with warmth. A fair number of people were on the Belmont Street pier, many of them tourists from the East, posing in shirtsleeves and smiles for pictures to send back to their snowbound friends. There were locals, too, joggers stretching and flexing before their next lap down the white, newly raked beaches, and a scattering of elderly people in light coats or sweaters.

Schmidt felt relaxed, better than he had in several weeks, youthful and buoyant in the crisp morning air and flooding sunlight, momentarily free of the tension that had become a constant, unwelcome presence. But suddenly, a hundred yards from the foot of the pier, the familiar old signals went off. A man at the right rail had looked around toward him, casually enough at first, but then quickly away. Now he was bringing his camera up, aiming the long lens somewhere off to Schmidt's left, then slowly around until it was leveled right at him. Schmidt experienced an abrupt sinking in the pit of his stomach, an involuntary tightening of his jaw, a slight squint as his focus narrowed to the near range. He could sense the surreptitiousness in the man's movements—no certain malice, but a definite unnatural way about him.

Schmidt made no evaluation, no conscious decision; he simply acted, shifting his weight and turning in mid-stride, a sudden motion that both hid his face and instantly took him to the left, out of the camera's line of sight.

Having his back to the man made the flesh between his shoulder blades crawl. He needed only to glance over his right shoulder to check, to confirm or deny his suspicions, but he kept walking toward the left railing, locked into his course. Only when he reached it did he casually look around. The man was still there with the camera still to his eye, and the lens still aimed at a spot where Schmidt had been. Then Schmidt looked to his left and laughed quietly.

He had not been wrong about the surreptitiousness, only the target. Several meters down the pier, at a spot that put her right in line with his earlier position, a pretty young jogger was absorbed in the task of retying her shoelaces, bent so far over that her shorts failed to cover a portion of her ample white buttocks. With amusement, the German realized he had been holding his breath and let out a long sigh.

"What was that maneuver about?" a voice beside him asked.

The Arab had appeared out of nowhere, smiling broadly, dressed in an obnoxiously loud shirt no doubt acquired at a hotel boutique, light blue double-knit trousers, and new white loafers. Completing the short man's costume were a pair of large-framed sunglasses and not one but two very expensive 35-mm cameras.

"Simply keeping in practice," Schmidt said off-handedly. "By the way, your tailor is to be commended. Can I assume the impersonation is of a Japanese tourist?"

"Don't laugh, my friend. Most people are too embarrassed to even look at me."

"No doubt," Schmidt said mildly. Then, without letting the smile fade from his lips, he reached into his shirt pocket for a pack of cigarettes and offered one to the other man. When the transaction was over, the Arab had in his hand one cigarette and a tiny metal canister about the size of an aspirin tablet. "There is your report," Schmidt said, continuing to smile for the sake of any onlookers.

The Arab nodded and turned to gaze out at the rippled surface of San Pedro Bay. "What are your general impressions?"

"Success is possible but questionable," Schmidt said without inflection. "The plan is a reasonable one. If everything holds together it may work. But there is the real question: Will everything hold together? The replacement man, Givens, is a psychopath; I am not certain he can be controlled. White is nearly as unstable, although in an entirely different way. Nettles is clever and very cool. He may be all right, but I suspect there is more behind his involvement than simple greed. The only ones I trust completely are the two flankers, Leggett and Hall, and they will have relatively minor roles."

He flicked his cigarette into the water and waited for the hiss. "The woman may turn out to be the worst problem. I am certain she has a hidden agenda, perhaps more than one. Periodically she reveals changes in the plans that make no sense at all. What it is leading to, I am not sure. She talks like an ideological purist, but you need only watch her to know that there is more than politics involved." He stopped suddenly. "There is no need to continue. It is all in the report."

"Sounds bleak," the Arab said.

Schmidt shrugged. "Who knows? Everything has gone well enough up to this point."

The Arab was silent for a moment, then turned away from the railing. "Let's walk."

They moved slowly toward the end of the pier, both of

them gazing out toward the open sea. Finally, the Arab spoke. "Shall I call it off?"

Schmidt continued to look off to his right. "I am not sure you could."

"Believe me, I could," the Arab said with cold certainty.

"No. Do not," Schmidt said. "On the whole, these people are no worse than any others. Normalcy is not a prerequisite for this kind of job. If it were, neither of us would be here. I suspect that I am just getting too old for this sort of work."

"But this operation is very important to my superiors," the Arab said. "If it succeeds it would be a major embarrassment for the United States. It would also strengthen the case against nuclear power, which, of course, works to the advantage of the OPEC nations. Not to mention that it would be the most daring terrorist operation ever mounted on U.S. soil."

"All the more reason to proceed," Schmidt reasoned.

"Or to wait until we can find better talent."

"Better talent probably would not attempt it," Schmidt said. "Relax. In less than forty-eight hours your problems will be over."

"*If* it succeeds. If it doesn't, I'll be in the same position you were in five years ago."

Five years before, Schmidt had been in charge of East German intelligence's European sector, until a series of disastrous blunders by top agency officials prompted a swift and thorough "reorganization." He had been about to board a flight from Rome back to Berlin when he was warned of the purge by a member of the opposition, no doubt hoping to turn him around. Most of those that did return never reappeared.

Schmidt looked down at the man. "Whatever happens, I have no doubt you will survive."

"Oh, I'll survive," the Arab said. "But will you?"

Schmidt smiled gently. "Do I look like a man who wants to die?"

The Arab said nothing until they reached the end of the pier and turned to look back at the city. "Okay, Karl, but if you must proceed, at least let me set up an alternative escape plan for you."

"Thank you, my friend, but no. This will either be a spectacular success, or it will be a catastrophic failure. Either way, I would have no use for alternate plans."

The topic was closed. They discussed technical matters for another fifteen minutes, then, with a handshake and a wave, they parted.

From the passenger seat of his rented Monte Carlo, the Arab thoughtfully watched Schmidt moving down the beach in the direction of his apartment building. When the German had diminished to an indistinguishable speck among all the others, he took off his sunglasses and reclined against the headrest. "Back to the hotel," he ordered in Arabic.

The driver cut a tight U-turn on Ocean Boulevard and started back toward town. When the maneuver was completed, he glanced at his superior. "You were not able to dissuade him?"

"Of course not," the Arab said. There was a troubled look on his face as he stared out through the windshield at the joggers running along the wall separating the beach from the stretch of grass known as Bluff Park. "Did I tell you he saved my life once?"

"No sir."

"Two years ago. We were both at a meeting in Marseilles, I with the minister, Schmidt as the bodyguard for some wealthy Italian. That's what he did after he broke with the East Germans, worked as a bodyguard for rich Europeans and sometimes Arabs. It was driving him crazy, the boredom. Anyway, the meeting, of course, dealt with the purchase of a large amount of arms, several million dollars' worth. Enough to attract the attention of the Israeli secret service."

The Arab had closed his eyes to better relive that warm August evening on the Gulf of Lion.

"It was a perfectly executed attack. They hit us just after sunset, as the principals were sitting down for dinner. Two of my men got it before they could get up from their own table.

109

Served them right, the pigs. Schmidt and I were the only security men inside the dining room. Gunfire was pouring in, smashing the chandeliers, the mirrors on the walls, everything higher than six feet above the floor. At the time I thought it was a miracle that none of the principals were killed. There must have been eight or ten weapons shooting constantly into the room for the better part of ten minutes. If they had rushed us we wouldn't have stood a chance, not even with that cannon that Schmidt carries.

"Then, as suddenly as they'd appeared, they were gone. I never actually saw an attacker, and I'm not sure anyone else did either. The Frogs, of course, took credit for driving them off, but, as we soon discovered, there was no truth in it.

"Schmidt was only concerned about his employer. I, like an idiot, went running to check the arms. So did the Frenchman who was selling them. From the house it looked as though they were still there, every box and barrel."

The Arab took out a cigarette and reached to press the lighter on the dashboard.

"I would have reached them first had not Schmidt come after me. 'Don't be a fool!' he shouted at both of us. He said he couldn't believe that they had pinned us down for so long and not destroyed the shipment. I stopped. The Frenchman did not."

The Arab lit his cigarette. "Of course Schmidt was right. With their usual cleverness, the Israelis had set us up. When the Frenchman pulled back the tarp the whole mess went off. As it was, I was hit by the shrapnel, but if it hadn't been for Schmidt I would have been blown apart, right along with the Frenchman." He turned to look at his assistant. "That is why I will try to help this stubborn German, whether he wants it or not."

The driver nodded. "I understand, sir."

"Good, then you won't mind helping me with some unauthorized errands this afternoon."

"I am at your service, of course. What do you have in mind?"

The Arab smiled grimly. "I am going to buy some people."

✒ 18

After checking the beach for the twentieth time Andrea left the sun-drenched balcony and wandered back into the living room of Schmidt's apartment.

"Where the hell is he?" she muttered, more to herself than to Givens, who was seated at the kitchen table.

"Maybe he ain't coming back," the man said. In his hand was the barrel section of a stripped-down Thompson submachine gun. He wiped it once more with an oily rag, then held the muzzle to his eye and peered down the rifling.

"He'll be here. We have a briefing at eleven."

"I could fix it so that he ain't," Givens said with a sneer.

She threw him an acid look. "Just play with your guns and be quiet."

The man shrugged. "It's your show, lady, but if you want my opinion, I think you're bein' stupid. We don't need that no-balls Kraut any more, if we ever did. All he does is preach to us about 'unnecessary bloodshed' and 'innocent civilians.' " He held up the weapon. "If you're worried about all his spook friends, me and Betsy here can handle them. And speakin' of excess baggage, I don't see any reason to keep that chief of yours either. Both of them are just two more ways we gotta split the money."

"When I want your opinion I'll ask for it."

The man gave her a cold, appraising look, letting his gaze linger on her slender body clad in tight shorts and a skimpy halter top. Then his lips curled into a lewd grin. "You know, for such a snotty chick you sure do have a nice ass."

"Is that so?"

Givens continued grinning. "That's so. 'Course I've seen bigger tits on a twelve-year-old, but I guess you can't have everything."

"Givens," she said in an even voice, "shove it!"

111

He laughed crudely. "I've got the eight inches, baby, jus' tell me where you want it."

The woman calmly lit a cigarette, walked over to the table and sat down. "You know," she said, meeting his gaze squarely, "when I was fifteen I ran into a man like you. He lived across the hall, a huge guy with a great big beer belly. A real pig who got his kicks by hassling us girls, me and my friends—talking dirty, grabbing at us, things like that. That was scary enough, but one day he cornered me down in the basement and actually tried to rape me."

"What happened?"

"That time I got away. But he tried again two days later."

"Yeah? And that time?"

"That time I stuck an ice pick into him."

Givens blinked, and his smile faded a bit. "Sweet," he said in a hushed tone.

It was her turn to smile. "Us snotty chicks are like that."

With Givens staring after her, Andrea returned to the balcony. Despite her nonchalance, she was worried about the man's increasing surliness—not so much his crudeness but the growing level of resentment that went with it. The night before, after returning from her session with White, she had consulted Schmidt about it.

The German had thought for a long time, puffing slowly on his pipe. "He does not frighten you," he said finally.

Mistaking his comment for a question, she bristled. "That ape? I could slice him up for fish bait before he could get that silly-assed grin off his face."

Schmidt shook his head. "You misunderstand me. I am saying that is exactly the problem. You are *not* frightened. Givens thinks that all women are stupid, helpless cows, and he is the herd bull. When he encounters one who is in some way superior—brighter, for instance—he is compelled to humiliate her, either through his obscene conduct or, if that fails, by way of violence, as he did with the nurse."

In 1974, Givens, then a marine corporal, was charged with raping a navy nurse. He was acquitted in a court-martial that lasted only four hours because the victim had been too frightened and humiliated to confront her attacker in court. Two days later he was quietly given a general discharge.

A report of the incident had been included in a thick dossier supplied by Schmidt's Arab friends when Andrea was scrambling to fill the spot left by the departed Mr. Peterson. Andrea had gotten three names from her radical contacts, but only Givens was available immediately. At the time he was working off and on as an enforcer for a Las Vegas loan-sharking operation. It was true that his file showed a background of excessive violence, but it also described him as an expert with explosives, a skill acquired in the Marines, and a man utterly without scruples. In the end it came down to having a man with the necessary qualifications available at a time when Andrea was in no position to be choosy. She was able to get him for twenty-five thousand dollars plus one-tenth of the ransom.

"So what am I supposed to do?" she asked. "Play scared? Blush and giggle like a virgin schoolgirl?"

"Would you, even if it would help?"

"No."

"I thought not. It would probably make no difference anyway. He has seen your physical prowess, and unless he is even more stupid than I think, he knows he could not take you with brute strength alone. Unfortunately, he also knows that you are sexually involved with some of the others."

"Meaning what?"

"That he cannot simply write you off as being frigid, which was what he did when you first rejected him."

The woman began to laugh, but Schmidt cut her off. "This man must be taken seriously. I believe you are in great danger. You know only of the one rape, but there is reason to believe that it happened many times in Vietnam, murder as well. He was one of only seventy Americans that the Viet Cong singled out for a bounty. In this country he has been arrested twice for beating up prostitutes, and we can only guess at the number of similar incidents that were not reported. Do not make light of this, Andrea. He is a brutal and violent man."

"I didn't recruit him to sing in the choir."

"True," Schmidt conceded. "But neither did you recruit him to go into a psychotic rage in the middle of your operation."

"You think he will?"

"I would not predict what he might do under stress."

"But we need him, Karl."

"Why? How will the authorities know whether or not we can do what we threaten?"

"I want Givens."

Schmidt looked at her suspiciously. "Are you planning to actually use the explosives?"

The woman's face revealed nothing. "I want Givens," she repeated.

"Very well," Schmidt said. "That is your decision. But at least assign Leggett or Hall to watch him closely. And you might be advised to keep that Beretta of yours handy."

She had made no reply, but she had taken his advice on both counts.

Andrea scanned the beach once more with the binoculars, squinting against the glaring sun reflected off the surf. This time she saw the German, walking slowly along the water's edge, a tall, straight figure looking out toward the open sea, still a half mile away. She put down the glasses and went inside. "Here he comes," she announced.

"Goody," Givens said. He had reassembled the Thompson and was inserting new shells into the long, curved magazine.

She watched from across the table. "Before he gets here I want to know if the air guns are ready."

"They're out in the van. I checked the darts myself. But I think we ought to use this," he said, indicating the dull blue submachine gun.

"Well, stop thinking and run through the plan once more."

Without expression Givens slapped the full clip into its slot in front of the trigger guard and brought the weapon to his shoulder, siting toward the open sliding glass doors. He spoke in a droning recitation. "At oh-six-hundred, Hall and I drive the van to Spencer's house and park it in the service alley. We go in through the basement—Hall has the bolt cutters for the padlock—we cut the telephone and electric lines and move upstairs. If we run into the dog, Hall's got a muzzle . . ." He looked up at her disgustedly. "Now that really *is* stupid. Why don't we just slit the damn thing's throat?"

"Because this way shows more detailed planning," she said impatiently.

"What if it barks?"

"Springer spaniels don't usually bark. Now go on."

"Okay," Givens said, giving the weapon a final wipe with a clean cloth. "The admiral's bedroom is opposite the top of the main stairway. I go straight in, hit the old man with your fuckin' tranquilizer gun, then grab the old lady. In the meantime Hall goes after the daughter, first door on the left. We knock out both the women—Hall has the hypos—carry 'em down through the basement to the van, load them into the boxes, and split. Nothin' to it."

Andrea looked at him angrily. "You forgot the communiqué."

"Oh, yeah," the man said indifferently. "I pin the note to the old man."

"Don't forget it tomorrow."

He looked up and glared at her but said nothing.

"And be cool during the briefing. Do you have your cover story ready?"

"Right. Hall and I are staying here to wire some damn timers or some such bullshit."

The woman nodded and turned away. Givens opened another box of shells and began loading the four spare clips, handling the blunt cartridges by their copper heads to avoid smudging the polished brass casings. As he completed each one he snapped it into the weapon and levered one round through the chamber. Then he carefully wiped each with an oily rag and slid it into the special pockets hidden in the lining of his workman's jacket. Suddenly he stopped and glanced over at the couch where Andrea was bent over a notepad.

"I'm telling you," he said, "it would be a lot safer if we just offed the old man."

The woman looked up from her writing and regarded him with annoyance. "So far you've proposed killing just about everyone. Which particular 'old man' do you mean?"

"Any one you like," Givens sneered. "But I had in mind the admiral. I don't trust your tranquilizers."

"No," she said flatly, "the only thing that would accomplish would be getting us all killed. We want to get their attention, we want them to know we aren't playing games, but we don't want to send them off the deep end." She added another cigarette to an ashtray full of butts and stood up. "Look, who are we actually dealing with here? Not with the Navy. They're just the stooges. The people we're really dealing with are the big industrial corporations who built that piece of nuclear shit and whose profits depend on the average citizen believing that their crap is good for the country. That's whose image will be on the line here—not the Navy but Westinghouse and General Electric and Combustion Engineering."

She paced back and forth, her eyes blazing as she spoke. "As long as those guys think they can get rid of us for a lousy ten million, they'll manage to keep the Navy in line, believe me. But if we screw up and start out by blowing people away, especially important people like Spencer, the Navy isn't going to listen to them or anyone else. They're just going to trip into their John Wayne routine, and then our asses won't be worth a damn."

"I can't believe I'm hearing this," Givens said with a smirk. "Is this the same chick who always lectures us on how cool it is to die for the revolution?"

"And well we may," she said. "But if we do it right we can make our point and still get out in one piece. Ten million dollars will finance a lot of revolution."

"Nine million," he reminded her. "The revolution will

have to get along without my cut."

A tiny smile formed on the corner of her mouth. "Of course."

⟋ 19

As was his habit, Karl Schmidt bypassed the elevators and ran up the twelve flights of stairs, arriving breathless at his apartment. Before he could knock, Andrea opened the door and slipped out into the carpeted hallway.

"I need to talk to you before everyone gets here," she said in a muted voice.

Schmidt was bent over with his hands on his knees, catching his breath. He looked up at her warily. "Not out here."

"Givens is inside."

"Not out here," he repeated firmly.

She gazed at him, first with a look of annoyance, but then she nodded. "Okay, you're right. Go into the bedroom and I'll join you there."

A few minutes later she came in and shut the door behind her. Schmidt was standing shirtless beside the bed, using a hand towel to wipe away the thin sheen of sweat from his face and shoulders. Saying nothing, she stepped up, gently took the towel, and tossed it aside, then slipped her arms around his waist and stretched up to kiss him lightly on the mouth. It was a gesture of such childlike directness that Schmidt was completely enchanted. He gathered her in and returned her kiss with an intensity that surprised them both.

When the moment had passed she pressed her cheek against his hot chest. "I'm glad you're back," she whispered.

"So I see," he said close to her ear. "Is there something wrong?"

She shook her head unconvincingly.

"Givens?" the German guessed. "What is he up to now? Since he is still in one piece, I assume he made no attempt to harm you."

"No, not that," she said, moving away to sit on the edge of the bed. "He just has some very strange ideas."

"Ah," Schmidt smiled knowingly. "Did he finally get around to proposing his hit list?"

When she looked up at him in startled confirmation, he continued. "Of course, I am first. Who else?"

She looked away. "Two others."

"Who?" the German insisted.

"Nettles."

"And?"

"That's all," she said quickly.

"You said *two* others."

"Did I?" she said. "I meant just two, you and Nettles."

"I see," Schmidt said, moving to fetch a clean shirt. "It does not surprise me. As I told you last night, the man is very dangerous. Should we make good our escape, I would expect him to become even more ambitious. Did you assign someone to watch him?"

"Hall. They work together anyway."

"Then you can expect him to approach Hall with a plan to eliminate the rest of us, if he has not already."

Andrea looked doubtful. "He must know that Hall is loyal."

"The word is not in his vocabulary. What were your instructions to Hall?"

"To report any suspicious activities to me. If there isn't time for that, to take whatever actions are necessary to keep him from screwing up the plan or harming another team member."

"He has full discretion?"

"If you mean, can he kill him, yes."

Schmidt nodded approvingly. "For Hall's own protection you might caution him to expect Givens to make such a proposal. If it happens, he must not react negatively. He should appear to be considering it, wrestling with the idea. If he reacts too negatively, Givens will try to stop him from warning you. If he reacts too positively at the outset Givens will suspect a trap with the same results."

"I'll tell him," Andrea said.

For a moment they were silent. They could hear a murmur of voices coming from the other side of the closed door. The team had arrived. The travel clock on the dresser showed five minutes after eleven.

"We should go out," Schmidt said.

He started to walk toward the door, but the woman touched his arm. "I need to talk to you for just another minute."

Her face took on the open look it did when her thoughts were most veiled. The German recognized that they were just now reaching the real purpose of her visit, that her display of affection had been only a ploy to disarm him—softening up the target, as the artillerymen liked to say. He forced himself to smile patiently. "At your disposal," he said with a gallant bow.

Her expression became grave. "We have come to a critical time in the operation. It's very important that you trust me."

He said nothing, waiting for her to continue.

"During the briefing I am going to make one significant change that we have not discussed. You know how much I respect and value your opinion, but any debate at this point would undermine our unity. So I'm asking you to go along with it, as a personal favor to me."

Schmidt waited for her to continue, but she was silent. "May I ask what this change is?" he said finally.

She shifted uncomfortably. "I would prefer to tell everyone."

"I see."

She reached for his hand. "Will you support me, Karl?"

Gently he squeezed her fingers. "As you say, this is a critical time. I will obey orders."

When Schmidt walked out of the bedroom he found Hall and Leggett seated on the couch watching television. They

119

both looked up and nodded at him. Givens was seated at the kitchen table, appraising him with a cool gaze; the ex-marine returned Schmidt's greeting by raising a beer can in a mock toast, swigging down the last few gulps, then crushing it with one hand. Schmidt went past him without comment, took a can of Coke from the refrigerator, and joined the others on the couch.

Like Schmidt, Hall was German, a native of the North Sea city of Bremen and a graduate of one of the numerous small extremist groups that compete with the neo-fascists for weapons and headlines. He was a little over six feet tall and thin to the point of being skinny. Until the day before he had sported a full, neatly trimmed beard and glasses. Now he was clean-shaven and wearing contact lenses.

Leggett was American, an ex-Weatherman and a longtime associate of Andrea's. He had a ruddy complexion, hazel eyes, and a full blond mustache. He was not quite as tall as Hall and considerably stockier. He was fluent in several languages including German, Schmidt suspected, although they had never spoken it. Of the entire team, Leggett was the only one currently married, to a beautiful Cuban woman who had helped out early in the project with securing the apartments and setting up the bank accounts. Thursday afternoon she had flown to Mexico City.

"Football?" Schmidt asked as he sat down.

"Last week's highlights," Leggett answered. "The game isn't on until two. You a fan?"

Before he could answer, Hall whispered to him in German, "Tell him no. Otherwise he will find a way to take your money. I speak from sad experience."

Schmidt laughed and said to Leggett, "No, I prefer association football."

The American looked confused, and Hall broke in with an interpretation. "He means soccer."

"Oh," Leggett said, shaking his head. "Too bad."

The three watched the screen in silence until Andrea entered the room, carrying three large charts rolled up and secured with rubber bands. She moved to the south wall, took down a painting, and called for Givens to help her put up the charts.

"I don't think you ought to do that," Leggett warned with a straight face.

"Do what?"

"Tack those things up like that."

Her glare turned icy. "Why not?"

" 'Cause if you put holes in the wall, it's gonna be hell getting our cleaning deposit back."

Unaware that she had been made the butt of the joke, Andrea just stood there blinking at him. Then the men began to laugh, thinly at first, then heartily as the woman flushed with anger. Her eyes grew dark as she turned around and tried to stare them into silence. Instead she succeeded only in turning a small joke into the cause of much hilarity. Finally she surrendered a weak smile and busied herself with hanging the charts. The laughter quickly died down to winks and smirks.

The first drawing was very familiar to all of them; it consisted of top and side views of the *Bremerton*'s two engine rooms, together with details of each enclosed operating space and the surrounding auxiliary rooms. But for the first time everything relating to the aft plant had been crossed out with big, crude X's.

The other two charts were new, comprised of long horizontal sheets carefully drawn and lettered in Andrea's precise calligraphy, color-coded in the seven colors that represented the seven team members. One was labeled IN, the other OUT. It took Schmidt a few seconds to identify them as some kind of master flow chart for the operation.

"Okay, you clowns," Andrea said when the charts were in place. "Let's get this over with."

Instantly the chatter ended and the television was shut off. The four men listened with respectful attention, some reclining, some leaning forward with their elbows resting on their knees, all watching the woman closely.

She indicated the charts. "These are simply compilations of

the plans we have gone over individually and as teams. This is the first and last time you will see the whole procedure put together." She looked at Schmidt. "Karl, you'll see that they are properly disposed of at the end of the meeting?" The German nodded and she continued. "It's my intent to review the operation straight through from oh-five-hundred tomorrow morning"—using a ruler as a pointer, she indicated a point at the far left end of the IN chart—"to the time when the team members are delivered to their individual destinations. Is that acceptable to everyone?"

The men agreed without comment.

"Okay. Earlier this morning White completed all but the very last modifications to the reactor control system, so that's done. Tonight Nettles will rig a telephone line to number-one control. Leggett, what's the status of the vehicles?"

"The van is here, the car is over on Cerritos Avenue. Both are gassed and ready to go. Both have valid base stickers. I made them dusty enough so that they won't stand out in the ship's company parking lot."

"Thank you," the woman said. "Hall, how's the equipment?"

"Tool boxes and lunch pails are in the appropriate vehicle. All of the weapons and the torch are in the boxes in the van, except for Givens's."

"Good," she said, turning to look at Givens. "As soon as the meeting is over you'll get your stuff to Hall."

"Aye aye, sir," the man answered.

She avoided looking at him and gazed instead at Schmidt. "The work uniforms?" she asked.

"The coveralls are in the closet, ready for everyone to take now. The orange security badges and film badges are on them."

"Now, Givens, what's the status of the explosives?"

The man grinned broadly. "Everything's packed in the van, ready to go."

"Except for the timers you and Hall are setting in the morning?"

"Oh, right," Givens said sullenly.

She went on hurriedly. "Very well. I have left the ransom suitcases at the designated site along with detailed instructions for the form of payment. I think that covers equipment." She looked around at the others. "Any questions so far?"

The men looked at her and said nothing.

Andrea nodded and looked toward Schmidt. "Karl, will you take us from the beginning to the point that we enter control?"

The German delayed long enough to light his pipe, then began speaking in a low, steady voice. "We will assemble here at oh-five-hundred for a full breakfast including vitamins. At that time we will also distribute Benzedrine and protein tablets. Andrea, Leggett, and I will leave here at oh-six-hundred in the car, travel on city streets until we determine that we are not being followed, pick up route four-oh-five northbound to forty-seven, then south to Seaside, west to Gate One, and directly to the ship's company parking lot. At oh-seven-hundred Givens and Hall will join us, and we will transfer the two boxes to hand carts." He stopped and looked at the woman. "I have a question about the boxes."

"Yes?"

"When I saw them yesterday I was surprised by their size. Will not such large boxes only attract more attention?"

Givens interrupted. "Why don't you just take care of your own business?"

But the woman raised her hand for silence. "It's a reasonable question," she said casually. "I was the one who chose the boxes. As you know, our equipment is hidden in the false bottoms. I decided that we should carry something that would be appropriate to our cover, specifically two new steam valves. In fact, you'll be unpleasantly surprised by how heavy they are. What is it, Hall, about a hundred and twenty pounds each?"

Hall nodded grimly.

"Does that answer your question?"

"Yes, thank you," Schmidt said. "To continue, then, we proceed to the aft gangway, go aboard with the boxes, take the first door into the hull to second deck, and proceed forward on the port side to the entrance to the forward auxiliary spaces. Andrea and I will go down first carrying blueprints. Nettles should meet us there. If everything is quiet, Givens and Hall will bring down the boxes one at a time. We will then arm ourselves, and while Givens, Hall, and Nettles guard the equipment, Andrea, Leggett, and I will move around to the starboard side and take the control room."

Andrea walked over to the coffee table, snuffed out a cigarette and returned to the charts. "Thank you, Karl. If everything goes according to schedule we should have the control room secured by oh-seven-thirty." She turned to Hall. "Why don't you go over what you'll be doing in the meantime?"

" 'Kay," the man said. "Givens and I will set the timers like you said, then we'll join you at the parking lot. When the three of you go into control, I will seal off the port side entry hatch, then go down with Nettles and capture the upper and lower level watches and anyone else who might be around. I will take them all to the upper level, handcuff them, and stay there. Givens and Nettles will take the equipment over to control. Right?"

Andrea nodded with satisfaction. "Right," she said. "White will be the reactor operator when we arrive. As soon as the situation in the control room is stabilized, I'll send him out to make his final modifications on the reactor. At the same time Leggett will seal the EOS escape hatch, and Givens and Nettles will go set their charges." She spoke to the ex-marine, "Would you go over those details, please?"

"Booby charges on the two entrance hatches and the engine room access cover. Trips in the bilges, both sides forward and aft. Plastic with four thousand hertz audio triggers on the lead-glass reactor compartment windows and at the four steam pipe penetrations." Givens sounded bored.

The woman pursed her lips. "Okay, that's about it. At oh-eight-hundred I will make my call to the base OOD and then, gentlemen, we will have captured ourselves a nuclear reactor." She was unable to hide her excitement as she glanced around the room. "Any questions?"

There was a moment of silence and then Schmidt spoke up. "Just one. Is it safe for White to leave his station to complete his work on the reactor?"

"Good question," Leggett muttered beside him.

Andrea threw the second man a sour look, then spoke to Schmidt. "According to both White and Nettles there's no problem."

She answered several other questions concerning specific details with terse efficiency and immediately launched into a review of the withdrawal phase. This time she handled most of the recitation herself, moving rapidly through the sequence as if to discourage comment or questions. She began with a discussion of the basic strategy.

"During the OUT phase, the visibility of our detailed planning will pay off. By then the Navy will have seen that we can and will do whatever we threaten." For an instant her eyes seemed to narrow on Givens, as though making a personal point. "They will, of course, have no way of knowing that White and Nettles are any less hostages than the others, and we will have provided them with detailed specifications of how we have wired them with the special charges." She turned to Givens. "Would you explain the theory behind the deadman switch arrangement?"

"It's simple," Givens said. This time he was more animated. "An explosive charge is strapped to the hostage's chest. The electronic trigger is hooked in series to two spring-loaded grip switches held by the men on either side. If sharpshooters should try to take out either of our men, the grip would be released and whammo!"

"Of course the system will not actually be employed," Schmidt said.

"Of course not," the woman agreed, but Schmidt was concentrating on Givens, whose eyes remained carefully veiled.

The woman quickly continued. "We will have demanded that the helicopter with the money touch down at oh-four-hundred Monday morning. At that time—"

It was Hall who interrupted. "Isn't it normal procedure in hostage situations for the pigs to allow at least the first deadline to pass?"

Andrea smiled patiently. "It is normal procedure, but then these people have never been confronted with a situation involving seven million hostages, including themselves. I don't anticipate much resistance if they see a chance to get us away from the reactor."

Hall accepted the point and she continued. "As I was saying, when the chopper lands on the pad, Givens and Hall will take one hostage and retrieve the ransom suitcases. They will also disable the chopper's communications equipment, check out the aircraft, and secure it with one hold-down cable."

She stopped to ask Hall how the rehearsals had gone and he assured her that there was no problem. "When the three have safely returned to control, we will separate out your individual shares for your own packs. Then White and Givens will defuse the reactor, and Leggett will disable the phones."

The woman stopped again and looked hopefully at Schmidt. "From this point we will deviate from the original plan. I have commissioned a second helicopter, a private one, to come in exactly fifteen minutes after the first. It has a specially modified landing assembly so that it can straddle the capstans that are aft and starboard of the helo pad," she said, pointing to the spot on the *Bremerton* drawing. "Schmidt, Hall, Leggett, and Nettles as a hostage will leave control and board that one. You will be taking one of the two ransom suitcases."

Once more she glanced at the German, who was listening expressionlessly. He recognized a certain logic to the new arrangement. Two helicopters instead of one would make tracking and interception that much more difficult. The split of the money, of course, was her way of reassuring them that they were not being set up. But two things concerned him. The first was the unknown pilot, and the second was what he saw as a dangerous combination of people in the second flight—Givens together with White and Andrea. But he asked only about the pilot.

Andrea was pleased to handle a noncontroversial question. "I have worked with this man before. He's both an excellent pilot and an extremely reliable one under stress."

Schmidt nodded, and she returned to her narrative. "Approximately ten minutes after the first chopper is off, Givens, White, and I will board the navy chopper. As we have discussed before, the aircraft, now both aircraft, will fly exactly southwest over the ocean at zero altitude, without lights, until each has rendezvoused with the *Agricola*, where they will hover for three minutes without actually communicating with the ship in any way. Then they will fly southeast until they reach Baja." She looked around the room. "I presume each of you has selected your drop coordinates and made your own arrangements?"

The men nodded except for Schmidt, who was pondering a troublesome detail. His expression revealed nothing until he had made the decision to speak; then a look of perplexity appeared on his face. "I believe I understand your reasons for employing two aircraft, but why do we not depart together?"

The woman shot him an angry look, but her voice was composed. "Because the separate departures will complicate whatever countermeasures they may have devised."

"As would a simultaneous departure on slightly different, or, for that matter, even widely different bearings. Why would you wish to risk an additional ten minutes in the plant?"

From his seat at the kitchen table Givens snarled, "Why don't you keep your nose out of it?"

Andrea's tension increased. "Maybe we should discuss this later," she said soothingly.

Schmidt had turned to study the glaring Givens; now he looked back at Andrea with an unyielding gaze. "No. Let us discuss it now, openly. If you insist on staying in the plant then I shall stay with you. Send Givens with the first group."

"Bullshit!" Givens shouted, starting to rise. But the woman motioned him down.

"I don't see what difference it makes," she said to Schmidt.

"We agreed at the outset that I would be present whenever we were in direct contact with the hostages, including those in the control room and the navy helicopter pilot. Your new plan separates me for ten minutes from the first group and completely from the pilot. That is not in accordance with the plan and in direct conflict with my own orders. I cannot allow it."

Givens was on his feet now and out of the kitchen. "If you don't shut your mouth, Schmidt, you're gonna get separated all right, permanently!"

Instantly Schmidt was up and shoving aside the coffee table, ready to meet the charging giant. Behind him the others scattered.

"Stop!" the woman commanded. To Givens she snarled, "You sit down! I'll handle this."

"Shit!" the man sputtered. "There's only one way to handle this stupid fuckin' Kraut." He lunged forward, swinging his massive right fist directly at the German's head.

But it shattered only empty air. With lightning speed Schmidt had dodged to his left, and as the man's arm passed harmlessly over him, he rose up with the coiled strength of his bent knees and drove the point of his right elbow into Givens's exposed stomach. The startled man doubled up in pain, and as he did, Schmidt rose to his full height, locked both hands into a club and smashed it down onto Givens's kidneys. The man crumpled face-down on the carpet, groaning, and Schmidt leaped to a position that put him beside the downed man's head, his knee poised against the back of Givens's neck just below the base of his skull. Schmidt grabbed a handful of blond hair and jerked the man's head back so that his throat was stretched taut. When the man stirred, Schmidt increased the pressure of his knee.

"Do not move even a finger or I will snap your neck like a piece of dry wood! Do you understand?"

Givens only moaned, and the German yanked harder on his hair. "Do you understand?"

"Yes," the man managed to gasp.

Schmidt looked around. The others were watching the struggle with varying reactions. Hall and Leggett were against the wall to his right, ready to act but passive in their expressions. To his left Andrea was looking on with horror.

"Don't, Karl," she pleaded. "The operation . . ."

The German laughed harshly. "There will be no operation if you do not control this one better."

"I'll take care of him," she promised. She motioned to Hall and Leggett. "Take Givens into the bedroom and keep him there."

The two moved in quickly and held the giant's arms while Schmidt released his death grip. With help Givens struggled to his feet, all the time glaring at the German with an intense hatred.

"Givens," the woman said, "go with Hall and Leggett. That's an order!"

The man spoke to her without taking his eyes off Schmidt. "Okay," he whispered breathlessly. "I'll do like you say for now. But as soon as this thing is over, I'm gonna kill this little piss ant." He coughed sharply and flinched with the pain, but his hateful expression remained. "You hear that, Kraut? I'm gonna step on you like a bug."

Schmidt regarded him with a stiff smile; he was not even breathing hard. "I am sure you will try," he said calmly. "Just be certain that you wait until after this thing is over."

Twenty minutes later, after Schmidt had left to inspect the other apartment, Andrea entered the bedroom. Givens was seated shirtless on the edge of the bed, holding a cold towel to the back of his neck. She ordered Hall and Leggett out, took the towel, and stepped into the bathroom to rinse it out. From the sink she could see Givens in the mirror, and she spoke to him as she wrung out the towel and began folding it neatly into a compress. "I had to promise Schmidt that I would put you on the first flight and let him stay."

He made no reply, electing to watch her in silence as she reemerged and handed him the cold cloth.

"But it won't work," she said, looking at him directly. "There are things I must do in those last ten minutes, things he would not approve of."

"Like?"

"Just things."

"Bullshit! I'm sick of risking my ass without knowing what the hell's going on. Either give me the bottom line or forget the whole thing."

She thought for only a moment. "Okay, Givens, the bottom line, as you call it, is that after we get the money we're going to go ahead and destroy the reactor. I've had White fix it. We'll have a twenty minute head start, then the plant will do its thing."

"Jesus Christ! No wonder you don't want Schmidt around. He'd shit."

"Yes, he would. I'm afraid you were right."

"About what?"

"About having to eliminate him."

"You bet I was," he said bitterly.

"But I think we should wait until just before we start the withdrawal."

His eyes narrowed. "Are you saying now you *want* me to take him out?"

"You're the only one who could," she said softly.

"Yeah?" he muttered with as much shrewdness as he possessed. "What's in it for me?"

"You can have Schmidt's share of the ransom."

"That's a start," Givens said.

"What else do you want?"

"For one thing, I want you to get Hall off my back. I don't like being watched."

"All right, I'll call him off. Anything more?"

"Just one thing."

"What's that?"

A leer formed on his lips. "I think you can figure it out."

She said nothing, but her fingers reached out and touched the angry red mark left just below his breast bone by Schmidt's elbow. "You should let me look at that."

He gave a throaty laugh, cupped his big hands around her firm buttocks, and drew her toward him. "I've got something more interesting for you to look at."

She did not resist as he pulled her down onto the bed.

✐ 20

Davis Stone was pacing again, this time in the presence of Cooper and Morton. Stone's office had been returned to a semblance of order following the morning's experiments. The overhead lights were turned off so that the circle of light cast by the drafting lamps was the only illumination in the room. Chief Morton, dressed in casual civvies, sat in Stone's chair with his feet propped up on the desk, crunching corn nuts and working his way through a six-pack of lukewarm beer. Cooper was seated in the corner, smoking a cigar and occasionally peering out through the venetian blinds. In the center of the room was an easel supporting a large white board covered with clear plastic. On it, in felt-tip pen, Stone had written:

> MARKS ON VALVE
> DAMAGED FENCE (?) = SABOTAGE
> CANVAS SHRED
> CLOSED VENT

and scrawled in big letters the word:

> MOTIVE ???

Now he paced back and forth in front of it, stopping with each pass to stare and bite his lip. When Morton chucked the second empty can noisily into the wastebasket, he turned. "How can you drink that stuff? There's cold in the reefer."

"I like it this way," Morton replied.

Stone looked over at Cooper and shrugged. The supervisor grinned and stood up. "To each his own. Personally I think I'll have a nice frosty one. How 'bout you, boss?"

Stone was considering the offer when the phone rang. He

pounced on it, listened for a moment, mumbled a few terse sentences, and hung up.

"Well, that's it," he said with finality.

"What's it?" Morton asked, popping another corn nut into his mouth.

"This morning I took the brass fitting and the vent cap over to F.B.I. Regional. They got a match between the marks on the fitting and those on the cap. They were made with the same tool—at least they're eighty percent sure of it. I think we can safely say that the transformer was sabotaged."

Cooper handed him a beer and opened his own. "So where does that leave us?"

"That," Stone said with a look of perplexity, "leaves us with a big question—why?" He pulled a chair over to the end of the desk and sat down. "Chief, before you get too bombed, take a shot at it."

Morton chuckled. "Maybe I should be bombed. This doesn't make a damn bit of sense sober." He stared for a moment at Stone's chart. "Okay, what about vandalism? Simple vandalism."

Cooper answered. "It was too slick. I might buy vandalism if they'd shot out the insulators or something like that, but these guys knew what they were doing."

"Guys?" Stone said. "How do you know it was men? These are liberated times."

"Are you kiddin'?" Morton snickered. "You could break a nail at shit like this. Had to be men."

"Okay, that's enough of that," Stone said. "So it wasn't vandalism. What else, Chief?"

"How about a disgruntled employee?" Morton offered.

"Would've had to be an electrician."

"Electricians must get disgruntled, too."

Once more Cooper responded. "I suppose it's possible, but those revenge jobs are usually pretty crude. They want everyone to know they did their thing."

"I agree, Pat," Stone said. "But check it out anyway. It would be someone who's worked on this kind of equipment."

"Gotcha."

Stone looked again at the chief, who was sitting staring off into space. "You still with me?"

"I'm here," Morton said. "I was just wondering if maybe we should rethink this whole thing. So far we've been working on the assumption that wrecking the transformer didn't really accomplish anything. But, in fact, it did. It caused a mess of ships to be moved over to this side of the harbor. Don't we have a list?"

Stone shuffled through a stack of papers on the desk and came up with a hand-written note. "I've got it here," Stone said, holding the paper under the light. "Four destroyers— the *Stewart*, *Francis*, *Aames*, and *Eckhart*—the repair ship *Isle Royale*, and a missile cruiser, the *Cambridge*. The only ship still out there is the *Bremerton*."

"Okay," Morton continued. "So what would be the purpose of getting one of those ships, or all of them, over here instead of out on the Mole? Assume for the time being that whoever did in the transformer knew it would cause the reassignment."

Cooper broke the silence. "Well, it would be a shorter walk to the EM club."

The comment drew a smile from Stone, but Morton shifted impatiently. "Now wait a minute you guys. You've both spent too long on this Mickey Mouse base. You gotta think big." He gazed at Stone. "Commander, if you were still at N.I.S. and something this slick went down, what kinds of schemes would you be looking for?"

"That's a good point, Chief," Stone said. "I might suspect some sort of major theft or possibly an intelligence operation."

"Okay," Morton said. "If they were planning something like that involving one of the six ships, what would be the advantage of getting it berthed over on this side?"

"Access," Stone said, with renewed animation. "Or rather, egress. From the new berths it's only a couple of blocks to Gate Five or Three. From the Mole they'd have to go a couple miles to get off the base."

"With what?" Cooper asked. "What could they take from a ship that would be worth all this trouble?"

"I could think of a couple thousand things, offhand," Stone said. "The destroyers and cruiser carry all the latest cryptography gear, weapons systems, radar and communications equipment. They might even be after one of the *Cambridge*'s missiles, for Christ's sake. Like the chief says, we gotta think big."

"Or something more basic, like money," Morton added. "Tuesday is payday and the *Cambridge* alone is probably carrying more than a hundred thousand in cash."

Cooper lifted his eyebrows. "Not a bad theory, and I gotta admit that sleepy ol' Long Beach Naval Station would be an ideal place to pull it off. But there are still a lot of technical problems, like how would they get aboard the ship? Even with our lax security, you just don't waltz aboard carrying the kind of equipment, maybe guns too, that you'd need to pull off something like you guys are talking about."

"It wouldn't be that hard," Stone argued. "They could disguise themselves as sailors."

"Or yardbirds," said Morton. "A bunch of yardbirds could go just about anywhere they wanted to and carry aboard just about anything they wanted to."

"And nobody actually looks at security badges. It would be a relatively simple matter to forge a set," Stone said.

Morton nodded. "Or steal them."

"That's it!" Cooper exclaimed, jumping up suddenly and leaving the room. A few seconds later he was back, rummaging through a thick sheaf of official-looking papers. He met the others' curious stares and grinned. "Your remark about stolen security badges reminded me." He pulled out a single wrinkled sheet. "Here it is. This is the inventory of items taken during that series of locker break-ins last week. And guess what?"

Stone beamed. "The workers' green badges."

"Better than that. Orange badges. Five of them."

Stone's face clouded with anger. "Are you telling me that

five special access badges are missing, and I wasn't informed?"

"We filed the forms," Cooper said.

"Not with me."

"Sure we did," Cooper protested, pointing at the stack in Stone's in-basket. "It's in there somewhere."

The officer smiled weakly. "Jesus, Pat, you should have called it to my attention."

"Sorry," the man said. "But it looked like a routine rip-off. Check the sheet: a couple of radios, some small change, a lot of tools."

"S'all right," Stone said. "We'll take a look at our procedures later. Right now let's concentrate on what we have here." He walked over, took a cloth from the top of the easel, and wiped the plastic clean. He began to write in rapid, squeaking strokes. A few minutes later he finished and stepped back. The board read:

SABOTAGE OF XFORMER

=

REASSIGNMENT OF SHIPS

=

BETTER ESCAPE ROUTE

+

ORANGE BADGES

=

POSSIBLE THEFT/ESPIONAGE OPERATION

As an afterthought he bent over and wrote:

ACTION?

"Chief," he said over his shoulder, "what's your recommendation?"

"What we have is mostly conjecture," Morton said, after considering for a moment. "But I think there's enough with the confirmed sabotage to call a security alert."

Stone nodded thoughtfully. "Pat?"

Cooper shifted uncomfortably. "I'm not disagreeing, but I can tell you that the admiral will shit if you ask for a security alert. I think I told you last night that we had an alert after that bomb thing downtown. You should have seen what it was like at the gates—there was a two-hour back-up at every shift change, and we had to cancel all days off for our own people. It was just a total mess. I don't think Spencer's gonna be real hot for another one."

"But we have a clear and present danger this time," Stone argued.

Cooper shrugged. "Like I say, I'm not disagreeing with you."

Stone rubbed his chin. "Do you think we could get the exec behind us?"

Morton spoke. "Nope. As soon as Spencer got back, the XO took off on three weeks' leave. He's goin' to the Super Bowl. Remember?"

"Shit. That's right," Stone muttered. "Well, I guess I'm just going to have to flap it with the Old Man." He picked up the telephone and glanced awkwardly at the other two. "Could you men step outside for a minute? This could be bloody."

Twenty minutes later he called them back in from the other office. "Strikeout," he said with a gloomy expression. "The admiral wants to talk about it Monday. Monday, for Christ's sake! By then they could load the damn *Eckhart* on a trailer and push it out the gate. He's concerned that a gate alert would tie up traffic too much and that a color change on the badges would disrupt the shipyard schedules. He's not ruling any of it out, mind you, he just wants to talk about it further."

Cooper tried to calm him. "We do have pretty fertile imaginations, you gotta admit. And I'm sure he has a lot of other things to consider."

"What he's got are family problems," Stone said bitterly. "I just talked to the duty officer, and he says that Spencer called this afternoon and asked that our people keep an eye out for his daughter. Seems that she and the mother had a big blowout this morning, and the girl hasn't been home since. I think we're getting put on hold for personal problems."

"Cheap shot," Morton said. "I know you're frustrated, and I know you've gotten the shaft from some flakey brass before, but give Spencer a break. Would you put your ass on the line for some guy whose only solid evidence consisted of a burnt-up fitting with a couple of mysterious marks on it?"

"And a chief who drinks warm beer," Cooper added, with forced levity.

"Okay," Stone said. "You're right. So what do we have? We can't call an alert, and we can't get the badge colors changed, at least before Monday. What can we do, right now?" He picked up a pencil and tapped it nervously on the desk. "Could we bring our patrols in from the west end and the Mole and concentrate them on this side between the piers and the gates."

"Sure," Cooper said. "We could also notify the quarterdeck watches of those six reassigned ships, give them a list of the stolen badges, and have them double-check anyone who comes aboard."

"Good," Stone said enthusiastically. "Also, see if any of the men would like to volunteer for overtime, and maybe this would be a good time for a weapons drill."

"It's beginning to sound an awful lot like a security alert to me," Cooper mused.

"Coincidence," Stone assured him. "Pure coincidence."

◢ 21

Hal Maurer sat in the engineering department office, talking by telephone to the absent engineering officer. Sitting at the next desk, listening in on the extension, was Lieutenant Paul

Johnson, the senior duty EOOW. "I think we should bring up the number-two plant and shut down number one tonight," Maurer was saying. "The alpha rod control power supply current is running nearly fifteen percent above normal. That misfire we had during yesterday's drill may have damaged a couple of the SCRs. I don't think they'd make it through another P.I."

Jones was silent for a moment. In the background Maurer could hear a television set and the sound of children playing. "What do the biases look like?" Jones asked.

"High."

"In spec?"

"In spec, but at the very high end of the range. They could go over any time."

As the engineer began quizzing Johnson on the condition of the number-two plant, Chief Nettles entered the office. He had the rumpled look of a man who had awakened too quickly. His mouth was set in a grim line, and his eyes were cold. Maurer covered the mouthpiece with his hand and spoke to him.

"I'm recommending we shut down number one. High current on Alpha."

"I heard," Nettles said. "You should have talked to me first."

Maurer dismissed his irritation as a symptom of fatigue. "You were sacked out."

Nettles grunted and walked over to an unoccupied desk. He punched in on the land-line number and listened as Jones and Johnson finished their conversation, then announced his presence.

"Chief, I'm glad you're on," Jones said. "Does RC division have enough people to get number two started up and heated up in case we have to shut down number one?"

"No sir," Nettles said. "We'd have to call at least three men off the beach. But I want to make it clear that I oppose a shutdown." He ignored Maurer's frantic gestures and went on. "I've looked at this thing and I don't think it's all that serious.

We should check it out as soon as we can, but I don't see any reason to drag our people in on a weekend and create a big hassle."

"I disagree," Maurer injected, looking angrily at Nettles.

Jones was quiet. Maurer was aware of his dilemma; he knew his was the more respected professional opinion, but Nettles was senior, and ignoring his strong recommendation would be awkward. The engineer tried first for a compromise. "What if we put the plant into the scram mode so that we don't have to worry about getting a P.I.?"

Nettles said nothing, so Maurer spoke up. "If we do that, the plant may go down anyway. Remember the spurious signal we're getting on Bravo Power-to-Flow. It's only lasting a couple of milliseconds, but if we get it while we're in the scram mode, the rods will wind up on the bottom."

"I forgot about that," Jones said. "How often is that happening?"

"Whenever it feels like it. I'd say about once every forty-eight hours."

"Do you have a spare power-to-flow drawer you could install?"

"It's been cannibalized for the aft plant."

"Great," Jones muttered. "Can you fix the one that's in there now?"

"Well sir, I could try. I think the new man, Weston, is still around. He's a real whiz. Maybe between the two of us we could take another shot at it. The problem is that the failure is so intermittent we really never know whether or not we have it fixed until it screws up again."

"I don't understand this electronics crap." Jones sounded annoyed.

"Neither do I," Maurer said. "These systems are so damn complex they act more like people than machines. I guess this is just one of its idiosyncrasies."

"Well, talk nice to the blasted thing and see if you can get it to stay up for just thirty-six more hours," Jones said, then he directed himself to Nettles. "Is that okay with you, Chief? If

Maurer can get the power-to-flow fixed then we'll go to the scram mode, and if not we'll talk about bringing up the aft plant."

"I guess so," Nettles said, with an uncertainty that baffled Maurer.

"How about you, Maurer, that sound okay?"

"Yes sir," Maurer said. "Can I tell the EOOW that I have your permission to go to test on channel Bravo?"

"You may," Jones said. "And keep me posted."

Once the telephone conversation was over, Lieutenant Johnson left quickly to return to the wardroom movie, leaving Maurer and Nettles to stare suspiciously at one another.

"What the hell was that all about?" Maurer asked. "You haven't even been down into the plant."

"Shit," Nettles said. "Why can't you leave well enough alone? I got the watchbill squared away, and you're nice and cozy now in the aft plant. Why start another flap?" He refused to look at Maurer.

"Because I really think those SCRs are about ready to pop," Maurer snapped back with equal hostility. "If we should get a P.I., God only knows what configuration that thing will wind up in."

"Damn it, Hal, we're at steady-state, we're not gonna get a P.I."

Maurer felt betrayed. "What's the matter with you, Wally? You're usually the one who backs me up on these things."

"Look," Nettles said intensely. "I just want a nice quiet weekend. Let's just keep number one steaming."

Maurer was annoyed by the chief's preoccupation with the forward plant, but he tried to be accommodating. "Okay, if I can get the power-to-flow working, will you go along with switching to the scram mode?"

"I don't know," Nettles said, and he headed for the door, leaving Maurer standing bewildered in the middle of the empty office.

Two hours later Maurer and Weston walked into the deserted first-class mess, drew two cups of coffee, and sat down.

"That was nice," the new man said admiringly.

"What's that?"

Weston grinned and looked around, as if speaking to a non-existent audience. " 'What's that?' he says, like he didn't intentionally suck me into fixing his goddamn equipment for him."

"You mean just 'cause I stood there drinking coffee and watching you do all the work?" Maurer asked. "That, my friend, is called leadership. You fixed it, didn't you? Why should I get in the way of a true artist?"

"Okay, Tom Sawyer," Weston said, laughing. "Now I know how you got the reputation as the hottest tech in the program—you never *touch* the damn gear."

"Haven't for years," Maurer admitted. He leaned back and put his feet up on a nearby chair. "Just to show you how the myth is perpetuated, a couple of weeks ago Ozzie woke me at four in the morning. He's all panicked. 'Can you *please* come down and fix the rod fourteen position indicator? We've been workin' five hours and we jus' can't get it.' So I stagger down, about ten percent awake, get my coffee, and prop myself up against a stanchion. Ozzie, Clark, and Newby are all down there, sweatin' their asses off, bug-eyed because the engineer is making growling noises."

Maurer paused long enough to light a cigarette. "So I asked them what they've tried. 'Such and such,' they tell me. So then I ask them what they think might be wrong. 'Well, we don't know for sure, but it could be the hoo-ha.'

"I ask them if it is the hoo-ha, what would they do. What they tell me sounds reasonable, and I tell them to go ahead and try it, and sure enough it works. And who gets the credit? Me!" Maurer shook his head with amazement. "Honest to God, Weston, I didn't say one thing of substance, all I did was nod at the right moments—I was too sleepy even to know what they were talking about—and they make me a hero."

Weston laughed. "Like you said, that's called leadership."

"Yeah, but some day I'm not going to be able to handle it."

"Never," Weston said. "Once they peg you as an expert, you actually become one."

"I hope you're right," Maurer said.

At eleven-thirty Nettles knocked on the mess door. Weston had gone down to the berthing compartment, and Maurer was watching television, waiting for his mid-watch. When Nettles entered he looked around nervously, seemed to satisfy himself that they were alone, then directed Maurer to the corner table.

"It's okay if we go into the scram mode," he said in a confiding tone.

"Well, thank God for small favors," Maurer replied acidly. "What'd you have to do, go consult with your guru?"

"I just had to think about it," Nettles said defensively.

Maurer sighed. "Okay, Chief, if you want I'll clear it with Jones and inform the forward plant on my way back aft."

"Okay," Nettles said, but he made no move to leave.

After an awkward silence Maurer spoke up. "Is there something else?"

The chief seemed to gird himself. "I just want you to know that I think you did a great job with the power-to-flow," he said, with a gravity that was unusual.

Maurer took it as an attempt to make amends. "It was mostly Weston's doing."

"Maybe so," Nettles muttered. Then he gazed directly at the technician. "I just want you to know that I think you're a good worker and a good friend. I hope if I'm off the wall sometimes you'll still think of me as your drinkin' buddy."

Maurer squirmed a little. "Sure, Wally, I understand. You've been through a lot of shit with your ol' lady and stuff."

"I'm glad you understand," Nettles said. "Can I have your hand on it?" He took Maurer's awkwardly offered hand, gripped it firmly for a few seconds, then suddenly rose and headed for the door.

"I'll see you in the morning?" Maurer called after him.

"Right," Nettles said, without looking back.

After leaving Maurer, Nettles went straight to the forward plant, talking to himself all the way to try to suppress the gloom that was enveloping him. By the time he ran into the control equipment operator lounging under the cool blast of an overhead vent, he was outwardly calm. "Hey, Rocky," he said with a cheery smile, "why don't you go into EOS and cool off for a few minutes? I'll guard the fort."

"Thanks, Chief," the man said, "but my relief will be here in a little while."

"Go ahead," Nettles insisted. "It'll get you cooled down before you go back to the compartment."

It was an attractive offer. Even with the plant at low power, the temperature in the auxiliary was in the high eighties. "Okay, thanks," the man said, vanishing in the direction of the airconditioned control room.

Nettles waited sixty seconds, then moved around to the narrow alley formed by the back of the rod control panels and the reactor compartment bulkhead. Nimbly he climbed up on a six-inch pipe attached to the bulkhead three feet off the deck and ran his hand along the top edge of the large square overhead air duct that fed the room's aft vent. His fingers found the catch and flipped it. A four-foot section of the duct's side wall fell open to reveal a dark, coffin-sized chamber within, six feet long, two feet high, and as wide as the duct, ingeniously constructed so that a small part of the air flowed through it and the rest over the top.

Taking hold of a duct brace with one hand and a nearby armored cable with the other, Nettles jackknifed up, slid his feet into the chamber, eased his slender body in and pulled shut the makeshift door, latching it with a small inside bolt. For a moment there was only darkness, the whistle of passing air, and the thunder of the distant blower. Then his hand found the hidden flashlight and he flicked it on. The sheet metal top of the chamber was only inches from his nose, but by turning partly sideways he was able to create a space large enough to let him look down at his feet and even focus on the two paperback novels he had taped to the opposite wall. There was also a small foam rubber pillow for his head, a canteen of water and a bottle with a soft rubber hose for urine. Most important, at the foot end there was sufficient room for his share of the ransom and even a little extra in case some spare change should happen his way.

It had taken him the better part of three weeks to fabricate this hideaway and its identical counterpart in the aft plant. During a test run he had spent one reasonably comfortable night there. He figured he could go three days or even longer before it became unbearable. By then the feds would be chasing around South America looking for them, and even if it was still too dangerous to slip off the ship, he had keys to places down in stores where he could probably hide for two months. Of course Andrea would be pissed to find herself short one "hostage," but then that was her problem.

Satisfied that everything was in order, Nettles opened the door and quickly climbed out and down. Back on the deck he looked up to assure himself once more that the entrance was virtually invisible in the dim light. Then, with a broad grin, he left to go rig Andrea's shore phone line.

⚞22

The night had grown cold by the time Billy White threw a sloppy salute toward the quarterdeck watch and marched down the aft gangway. A light southern breeze had pushed the day's moderate accumulation of smog inland, so that the coastal skies were clear and starry. Beyond the circles of light surrounding the *Bremerton*'s two gangways, the pier was pitch black. White hurried toward the bright fluorescent glow of the three telephone booths that stood empty at the side of the road. He waited until exactly eleven-fifty-five and then dialed Andrea's number. She answered on the first ring.

"How's it going?" he asked with deliberate casualness.

Andrea's tone was impatient. "Oh, other than the fact that Givens picked this night to vanish on us, everything is just perfect. What about you? Did you get your modifications made?"

"Of course."

"Including the special ones?" Her voice had become low and breathy, as though she were whispering into the mouthpiece. White felt a pang of jealousy.

"Are you alone?" he demanded.

"No, half the seventh fleet is waiting for me in the bedroom," she snapped. Then more softly, "Yes, I'm alone, you idiot. Now tell me about the special modifications before I come down there and kick your ass."

White experienced a flicker of excitement. "I'd like to see you try it."

"Later," she murmured. "What about the special circuit?"

"It's all made up, just like you wanted. Twenty minutes after we pull out, the . . . ah, event will happen. No one will be able to stop it."

"Good," Andrea said. "I knew I could count on you. Remember, this is our secret; no one can know."

"Yes," White said in a hushed tone. "Our secret . . ."

"Very good. Now get some sleep, and I'll see you in seven and a half hours."

"Andrea?" he said hurriedly. "Are you sure you don't want me to sneak over now? I have four hours before my watch."

"Don't be silly. You need your rest. Don't worry, Billy, there'll be plenty of time for that after tomorrow."

"Well, okay," White said unhappily. Then he quickly added, "I love you, Andrea."

"I love you, too."

White felt another joyous flash. "Do you really?" he stammered, but the line was already dead.

23

The odor of decay, of death, blew in from the jungle in a hot, humid wind. Givens stirred, felt his dog tags fall into his armpit, moaned, and stirred again.

Over the shrill buzz of the insects came the thin whistle of a jet engine, a big plane, a 111 or a B-52, coming in low, right on the deck, the sounds of its engines growing into a thundering shriek. Too low. Givens thought groggily, the fucker's comin' down! He tried to scream but only a feeble cry emerged. He tried to move and couldn't. I'm hit, he thought, Holy Christ, I must be hit! Where's the foxhole? Gotta get to the foxhole. All the time the jet plunged toward him, so low now that the ground was quaking. He forced his hand to move, to claw out, expecting to touch warm dirt and sandbags. Instead he touched the satiny coolness of quilted nylon.

He came awake on the hotel room bed, nauseated, squinting against the glare of the bedside lamp, his heart pounding, sweat trickling down his sides. The Vietnamese landscape had vanished, but the roar of the jet was even louder, hammering at his skull. Without thinking, he stumbled to the window and threw back the heavy drapes, just in time to see a 727 touch down smoothly on the runway of the Long Beach Airport. As he watched, uncomprehending, there came the deep rumble of reversed engines, and then the receding whine as the aircraft turned onto a taxiway.

Givens shook his head in bewilderment and yanked the drapes closed. That's when he saw the blood on his arm, a rusty smear from the heel of his palm to his elbow. He staggered backward until he fell sitting on the end of the bed. Was it his? He couldn't tell. He felt nothing, not even the normal sensations, only numbness.

Looking down, he found more blood, mixed with sweat on

his right side, smeared along his naked thigh, and long gouges across his chest and belly, and torn skin on his knuckles. He squeezed his head with both hands and tried to remember. What time? What day? A hotel room, an airport? The pieces were meaningless, as if nothing had existed before this moment. Then he saw her, out of the corner of his eye.

She was dead, certainly dead, pasty white and rigid, face up on the carpet between the bed and the bathroom wall. Trembling, clutching his stomach as if to hold it together he rose up to view her. She lay obscenely exposed, spread-eagled, her torn black panties around one ankle, streaks of blood and dark bruises on her stomach and breasts, her nipples almost purple in death. A pillow covered her face—whether the cause of death or to hide the real cause, he wasn't sure. Beside her, neatly placed, was a pair of beige shoes. At her feet, in a heap, a long tan gown and an expensive leather handbag.

Givens moaned and groped his way toward the bathroom, falling to his knees to vomit into the toilet. But as soon as his stomach was empty, a cold, sweating panic set in. He raced to the door to the hall. It was locked. He stood in the center of the room, not looking at the dead girl, listening. There was nothing beyond the muffled mutterings of television sets and the sounds of plumbing.

He wandered around the room until he found his clothing draped over the TV. He started to dress, remembered the blood, and headed for the bathroom instead. He was sick again in the shower and almost passed out when he bent down to clear the soap wrapper from the drain, but he turned the cold water on full blast, and by the time he emerged he was greatly recovered. Whatever had happened with the woman was still forgotten, but he recalled the place and the date and he remembered about the operation. He dressed quickly, combed his wet hair, checked for his watch and wallet, then sat down on the edge of the toilet and tried to think out his next move.

Fingerprints, he decided, wouldn't make a difference, not after tomorrow. For the same reason there was no need to do anything about the body; by the time anyone discovered it he would be on the *Bremerton*. The only important thing was to get out.

He did that quickly, without looking back, even managing to appear reasonably composed as he opened the door and stepped out into the hallway. For a final touch, Givens hung up the Do Not Disturb card. Then he turned and walked toward the elevators.

Inside the room, the slight stirring of air caused by the closing door lifted two hundred-dollar bills from the dresser and sent them fluttering to the floor at the dead girl's feet.

24

Caroline Spencer stood before her daughter in the upstairs hallway, looking like an old and blurry mirror image; she had the same auburn hair and flashing hazel eyes and slender body, but had gone soft with age. She was so close that Cynthia could see the wrinkles in the corners of her mouth and smell the bourbon on her breath. Against her mother's accusing stare, Cynthia stood tall and collected, overcoming a powerful urge to laugh, to cross her eyes and stick out her tongue at this silly, screaming woman.

"Where were you?" the mother demanded.

"Walking," Cynthia said calmly.

"Walking! Until almost midnight?"

"Yes."

"You're lying." The voice was a screech. "You've been out with those friends of yours, haven't you? Those Hell's Angels. After I expressly forbid it. Doing God knows what just to spite your father and me."

Cynthia flared. "For God's sake, not everybody who rides a bike is a Hell's Angel."

"So you admit it. You were with them."

"No," the girl said through clenched teeth. "I was walking, alone."

"Like that? Half naked?"

Cynthia slumped wearily. "Please, not this again."

The mother smiled viciously. "Are you wearing a bra?"

"You know perfectly well I am *not* wearing a bra."

"Why not just wear a big sign that says 'I sleep around.'"

"Look," Cynthia pleaded. "We went over this whole thing this morning. I'm old enough to decide how I will dress, who my friends will be, and who, if anyone, I'll get it on with. Now I'm very tired, and I just want to go to bed."

"You're disgusting," her mother shouted. "You're a disgusting little—" She stopped abruptly.

"Yes?"

"Whore!" The word was hurtled.

Cynthia smile coldly. "I guess it runs in the family," she said, and turned away.

Almost desperately, her mother grabbed her arm. "Don't you walk away from me."

The girl's gaze turned to ice. "Let go of me," she said.

The mother paled in the face of her daughter's rage. "I'm not through," she said weakly.

Very slowly Cynthia pried the clammy fingers from her arm. "Yes you are."

"I'm—I'm going to—talk to your—father."

Cynthia threw her a look of complete indifference. "Good night, Mother," she said, and walked into her bedroom and closed the door.

For a long time she stood in the dark, leaning heavily against the door, waiting for her mother's voice to stop echoing in her head. Then she switched on a light and began hurriedly throwing an assortment of clothes into a small battered suitcase. She counted her cash—sixty-three dollars—and stuffed it into her purse, along with her bank book and odds and ends from her cosmetic case. Finally she added a photograph of her father, taken when he received his stars, and slammed the case shut.

Throughout the task of packing she moved with grim determination, but after she had placed the suitcase in front of the door and set her alarm for seven, the determination gave way to numb exhaustion. She shed her clothes, rolled a joint from the contents of her hidden stash, and lit it. Then she crashed naked on the bed, a small glass ashtray balanced on her flat stomach. She smoked quickly, without bothering to open the window or lay a towel at the base of the door, sucking in the dry, burning smoke in consecutive breaths until the stub burned her lips. The rush came almost instantly, speeded by her fatigue. She set aside the ashtray and turned out the light. Already starting to drift free, she turned on her side to watch the digits of her clock change with the minutes. Before the third time she was sound asleep.

Sunday, January 13

25

If it hadn't been for the suitcase blocking the bedroom door, Hall would have had the needle in Cynthia Spencer's arm before she knew he was there. The dog had been captured without incident at the bottom of the stairs, and when Hall slipped the lock of Cynthia's door, his only thought was to push through quickly and get to the sleeping girl. The crash of the falling case startled him nearly as much as it did her.

Even given that warning, most people jarred from a fitful sleep would have been immobilized by confusion and fear, but the girl was an athlete by training and a fighter by inclination. She did give a frightened yelp when she saw his dark, looming shape moving toward her, but she also came up scrambling, managing to dart past him and through the open doorway. Had she made for the stairs she might have escaped, at least as far as the first floor where familiarity would have given her an edge—perhaps all the way to the street and the chance of rescue. Instead she ran for the imagined safety of her father's room and straight into Givens.

The collision knocked her backward to the floor, leaving her dazed and gasping for breath. She evaded his first lunge by rolling to her left and even regained her footing, but an instant later she was lifted completely off her feet as the man hooked one huge arm around her and pulled her to him.

"What do we have here?" he grunted as his hand closed around the unmistakable contour of a naked breast. "Going somewhere?"

She fought like a trapped animal in his grasp, hissing

through clenched teeth, kicking and scratching, delivering glancing blows to his shins with the heels of her bare feet and raking his arms with her blunt nails, twisting in a frantic effort to get at his face. Givens responded with an ugly laugh and tightened his hold as if to crush her into submission, but she only increased her desperate struggles until a chance shot sent her elbow crashing into his ear.

He roared with pain and fell back, momentarily releasing his hold. For a split second she was free, looking around in a dazed effort to orient herself. An odd assortment of jumbled images flashed through her mind. She thought in formless questions of her father and Muffin, she thought of Audrey Hepburn in *Wait Until Dark,* of climbing at night on the rocks at Big Sur, and of wrestling with Lloyd Evans. But then there was only terror as Givens was on her again, not laughing now but snarling with rage.

His fingers locked on her throat and he slammed her against the wall, oblivious to her clawing hands. Then he hit her, not with his full, deadly strength, but with a sharp, calculated jab to the stomach that convulsed her and left her writhing and gasping with pain. He waited until her eyes came open, then he hit her again, this time in the lower ribs, knocking the last bit of air from her tortured lungs and flooding her left side with pain. She groaned in agony, no longer able to put up even a token defense, yet he struck her a third time, a savage blow that landed just below her left breast. Her body jerked violently in recoil, but she didn't have the breath this time to even groan. Faintness washed over her, threatening to plunge her into unconsciousness. She was only dimly aware that he had grabbed her by the hair and was drawing back his fist to smash at her face.

"Stop!" Hall's voice commanded out of the darkness. He was in a half crouch behind Givens, aiming a pistol with both hands at the man's back.

"No!" Givens said, breathing heavily. "She's got it coming."

"Let her go or I'll blow your fuckin' head off!"

Givens paused, his fist still poised to strike the girl. "How?" he said thickly. "You ain't got no gun."

In the silence there came the double click of a hammer being cocked.

For Cynthia the conversation was only distant muttering. All she knew was that one minute she was in the man's vicious grasp and the next she was crumpled on the floor with Hall kneeling beside her. There was a slight pricking sensation in her arm, and then the darkness pulled her down.

"What the hell got into you? Hall snapped as he felt for the girl's pulse. "You damn near killed her."

Givens stood above him, dazed and panting. "She deserved it."

"Shit," Hall spat. "What about the old guy? He's nearly dead, too."

"I . . . I had to shoot him twice," Givens answered slowly, as though he were having trouble remembering.

"Two doses?" Hall exclaimed. "Jesus Christ, man, he probably *will* croak!"

"He just kept coming," Givens said in an amazed voice. "I know I got him square in the chest, I heard it hit him, but he just kept coming. There was enough in one of those things to stop an elephant."

"For your sake, I hope he makes it. Herself will shit if this goes wrong," Hall said angrily. "Did you give the needle to the old lady?"

There was a moment before the man answered.

"Yes," he said finally.

"How 'bout the note?"

"The note? No, I forgot."

"Well, damn it, stick it on the guy and let's get out of here."

With Hall taking charge they quickly dressed the two unconscious women in hospital gowns and carried them out to the van. They laid them carefully in the foam padded boxes, checked out the vent holes, and locked down the lids.

The exertion of carrying the women downstairs and loading them into the van had returned Givens to near normal. By the time the men were strapped into their seats and ready to go, he was laughing again. "Not a bad-lookin' piece, that young one, heh?" he said, grinning.

Hall threw him an incredulous look and then, without answering, started the engine and pulled out in the direction of the Mole.

◢ 26

A little after 0700, five shipyard workers straggled along Pier 26 toward the *Bremerton,* obviously in no particular hurry to reach their destination. The four men in the group were engaged in a boisterous exchange, much of which seemed to be directed good-naturedly toward the woman who walked in front. Apparently she was enjoying the banter, because she laughed and turned often to toss them equally boisterous replies.

The five wore gray Shop 51 hardhats festooned with humorous decals and drawings in the current style. Some carried canvas bags slung over their shoulders, others the traditional battered metal lunch pails. The last man pulled a rattling old handcart loaded with two long wooden crates and the workers' five heavy toolboxes.

All also wore the one-piece nylon jumpsuits that were displacing old-fashioned coveralls in popularity. The garment was intended to be loose-fitting and comfortable, a practical design for hot, dirty shipboard work, but to the delight of the quarterdeck watch and his messenger, the woman seemed to have missed the point. Hers had been tailored so that it clung tightly to her body, boldly emphasizing the rippling curves of her ample thighs and buttocks and the bouncing fullness of her big, high breasts.

"Check this out," the messenger whispered, as the work party approached the foot of the gangway.

"Jeeesus!" the other muttered. "That's breakfast, lunch, *and* dinner."

Their watch station was hidden in the shadow of the aft superstructure, still hours away from the sun's rays. Although they could see the steam already beginning to curl up from the glassy surface of the harbor, they stood with their shoulders hunched against the chill. For four uneventful hours they had kept themselves awake by swapping sea stories and consuming cup after cup of scalding coffee. They were tired and bored, primed for Andrea's dramatic appearance. They had no way of knowing that much of what they gawked at was the result of carefully sculptured foam.

Her decision to assume the role of decoy had been hotly debated. Hall and Leggett argued that the boarding sequence should be played perfectly straight, that the team could count on the watch's general laxness and fatigue. But Givens had sided with Andrea. "Bullshit!" was his response to the other two. "Give them a fox and those poor horny bastards will be so busy scoping her out, we could drive a tank past 'em."

Oddly enough, it was the usually conservative Schmidt who supported him. "I agree," he said, suppressing a smile. "It may be the oldest ploy, but I think that old is often best."

The strategy proved itself as soon as she detached herself from the group and walked alone up the steep gangway. The two sailors watched with ill-disguised delight. Only when she was within a step of the landing did they shift their gaze from her body to her face and smile politely. As she had predicted, at close quarter neither of them could bring himself to inspect the I.D. badge brazenly clipped to her breast pocket.

"I have a work order here for the forward reactor plant," she said, with a slight Southern accent.

"Yes, ma'am," said the watch, giving the colored, multipage form a cursory glance. "You waiting for the crane operator?"

Andrea was caught by surprise. "I beg your pardon?" she said.

157

"I notice you've got a couple pretty big boxes there. If you want to wait, it says on my sheet that they're going to have a crane working around eight o'clock."

"No, thank you. We were planning to carry them on."

But he was determined to be gallant. "It's never too early for a coffee break," he said, with a conspiratorial wink. "There's plenty down on the mess decks."

Her mind raced. Not many workers would pass up a break with the excuse he had just provided. He'd know there wasn't a foreman waiting, and there was no URGENT stamp on the work order. She had to come up with something plausible, something that wouldn't raise his suspicions.

"I really appreciate it," she murmured after what seemed an interminable silence, hoping her discomfort would pass for embarrassment. "But, well ... I'm already in trouble for goofing off ..." She lowered her gaze. "You know how it is."

As she hoped, he took her confession in its most suggestive context. He smiled awkwardly. "Oh, sure, I understand. Er ... can my messenger help with the boxes?"

She gave him a grateful look. "I *do* appreciate it, but I think we can get it all right."

Five minutes later the last crate had been wrestled through the door leading to the second deck passageway. With a syrupy smile Andrea waved to the sailors and disappeared inside the ship.

"Honey," the watch sighed wistfully after she was gone, "you can goof off with me *any* time you want."

The messenger added a reverent, "Amen."

At almost the same moment, in the darkness of the second deck passageway, Leggett whispered to Hall, "You gotta admit they were right."

"How do you mean?"

The man grinned. "Nothing succeeds like a big set of knockers."

From somewhere in back Andrea hissed at them to shut up.

27

"Permission to enter EOS?" Maurer requested at the entrance to the forward plant control room.

Lieutenant j.g. Dills was shuffling papers in preparation for the coming turnover. "For what reason?" he asked with stiff formality.

"To speak with the reactor operator," Maurer said sourly. He was in no mood for petty tyrants.

Dills nodded and Maurer ducked under the chain that marked the boundary which none could pass without the EOOW's permission.

White turned and flashed him an exaggerated smile. "Boy, am I glad to see you."

"What do you want?" Maurer's tone was impatient.

"I *really* need a head relief," the man said.

"A head relief," Maurer snorted. "It's twenty after seven. You've only got a fuckin' half hour til you're off watch."

White gave a shrug. "When you gotta go, you gotta go."

Maurer cursed under his breath. "Okay, but don't waste any time playing with yourself. I've gotta relieve back aft."

White gave him a quick turnover, announced to the EOOW that Maurer had the watch, and hurried out.

The technician was reading over the log when he heard a friendly voice behind him. It was Weston, looking amused. "A real dildo, huh?" the new man said.

"Who, White? Yeah, you could say that."

"I told him I had seen his relief on the mess decks, but he insisted on calling for you."

"Figures," Maurer said bitterly. "He's still pissed 'cause the chief switched the watchbill to get me back aft. This is just a chance for him to do a little back-stabbing." He shrugged and changed the subject. "I can't believe you're here on a Sunday morning. Aren't you getting a little radical about this training stuff?"

"There is no such thing as too much training," Weston said loudly for the benefit of Dills, then quietly to Maurer, "Actually, I sweet-talked Fox into paralleling TGs to get me a couple signatures."

Dave Fox, the electrical operator, was a soft-spoken second-class electrician from Alabama. When he heard his name he looked over and tipped his coffee cup. "Mornin' Hal."

"Morning," Maurer answered. "Did our man here do all right?"

Fox grinned. "We're still steamin', ain't we?"

Maurer laughed and whispered to Weston so that Dills could not hear, "How many sigs did he give you?"

"About sixty."

Maurer pretended to choke on his coffee. "What'd you do, buy him a case of whiskey?"

"Showed him a picture of my sister."

"Pretty?"

"Nude."

This time Maurer really did crack up, drawing a stern look from Dills.

"Later." Weston grinned and ducked under Dills's line of vision back to Fox's panel, but he called back, "Oh, by the way, how's our power-to-flow doing?"

"Like the man said," Maurer answered, "we're still steaming."

While Maurer awaited White's return he studied the reactor control panel. Temperature, pressure, and pressurizer level were all normal. Rod height was still up a little to compensate for the xenon buildup that had followed a week of high power operation. The four reactor coolant pumps were on fifteen cycles. Reactor power was hovering right around nineteen percent. The only abnormal sign was the lighted amber indicator in the center of the panel which signified that the plant was in the scram mode. Satisfied, Maurer began to review the previous day's logs, one of his duties as lead RT, examining the hourly readings closely for any significant trends that might go unnoticed from one hour to the next.

Finding none, he initialed the log, set it aside, and glanced up at the clock.

"Looks like you've been abandoned," Weston said, following his gaze. The time was 0733.

Maurer started to answer when out of the corner of his eye he saw Dills stiffen and rise halfway out of his chair. The officer's mouth hung open in shocked surprise. His face was ashen, his eyes huge, staring at the doorway. "What the hell? . . ." he stammered, his jaw flapping.

Maurer leaped out of his chair and spun around toward the door. Inertia carried him a half step, then he froze. Standing in the entryway, just on the other side of the chain, were a man and woman armed with heavy carbines trained into the room.

"Holy shit," Maurer uttered in bewilderment, then his voice caught in his throat. At the sound of his voice the woman had brought the muzzle of her weapon around so that it was leveled right at his chest.

✦ 28

At 0850 Stone's car turned off the road and raced along the pier, squealing to a stop at the foot of the *Bremerton*'s forward gangway. There was little real activity, but the sheer numbers of emergency vehicles on the scene made it clear that something major was happening. Two patrol cars, their blue lights flashing, blocked the head of the pier, and a third car stood empty at the foot of the aft gangway, its occupant nowhere in sight. Two base fire engines and an ambulance were parked nearby, engines idling, radios crackling, their drivers gathered in a group gazing uncertainly toward the ship. The *Bremerton* itself looked quiet. There was a group of officers milling around the forward quarterdeck. A few sailors watched the proceedings from the 0-1 level amidships. A large group of perhaps a hundred crewmen was assembled on the fantail, many wearing only pants or pants and T-shirts.

When Stone stepped out of his car he was met by his duty officer, a lieutenant junior grade by the name of Larson. The young officer appeared grim-faced but composed.

"What's going on?" Stone asked after returning the man's salute. "The call said there had been a terrorist attack."

"Yes sir, I guess that's what you'd call it. About an hour ago the base OOD got a telephone call telling him to send the police out to Admiral Spencer's residence. He called the admiral's house, but there was no answer, so he called me. When I arrived with two patrolmen I found the admiral unconscious on the bedroom floor. This was pinned to his pajamas." He passed Stone a large white envelope, carefully handling it by its edges. Stenciled on the front in huge black letters was the message:

URGENT: *Contains information vital to National Security.* OPEN IMMEDIATELY!

Stone accepted the envelope. "There was no one else in the house?"

"No sir."

"What's the admiral's condition?"

"As soon as we found him I called for an ambulance. We checked for visible injuries but couldn't find any. His pulse and breathing were pretty weak. The corpsman said he thought it looked like a drug overdose. I found two of these in him, one in the chest, one in the abdomen." Larson handed him a plastic evidence bag containing a cylindrical object about an inch long and the diameter of a ballpoint pen. At one end was a shiny half-inch needle, at the other was a flared cone of what looked like nylon bristles.

"A dart?" Stone said, examining the object closely.

"Apparently. One of the patrolmen says he's used something like it in animal control work. It's like a miniature syringe. There's a tiny weight above the plunger which forces the contents of the tube through the needle and into the target upon impact."

"You said there were two. Where's the other?"

"I let the hospital have it so they could try to identify the contents."

"Do they think it was poison?"

"Some kind of drug, they don't know yet. They called a few minutes ago. The admiral's stable but still in a coma."

Without comment Stone returned the bag and carefully lifted the envelope flap and extracted five typed sheets. "Since you're out here, I assume you read it?"

"Yes sir."

Stone nodded grimly. "With a cover like that, who could resist?" Then he began to read.

To whom it may concern:

By the time the communiqué is received an armed force will have captured and secured the number-one nuclear reactor plant of the *USS Bremerton* (CGN–14).

Unless certain political concessions and monetary reparations are promptly delivered, we are fully prepared to destroy the reactor core in such a manner as to effect the release of gross amounts of radioactive fission products to the atmosphere. Our specific demands and timetables will be communicated at the appropriate times.

If our demands are fully and promptly met it is our intention to release all hostages unharmed and return the reactor plant to a safe condition. However, we have both the technical capability and philosophical commitment to meet hostile or uncooperative responses with countermeasures, including those which would result in our own deaths.

Toward that end we have taken the following precautionary measures:

1. All normal, emergency, and maintenance accesses to the number-one reactor spaces have been mechanically sealed and rigged with explosives. At least one of the captured operating personnel has been restrained in the

immediate vicinity of each access. Any attempt to force entry will result in automatic detonation.

2. In addition to at least six crew members, we have abducted and are holding, unharmed, the wife and daughter of the commanding officer, Long Beach Naval Station.

3. We wish to avoid the panic and probable casualties which would result from public disclosure of this action. However, should any action deadline be exceeded, we have made arrangements to deliver copies of this communiqué to all radio and television stations in the Greater Los Angeles area.

To satisfy any doubts concerning the credibility of our threat, the following information is provided:

1. On page 1, following, the technical details of 1 of 21 modifications performed on reactor control instrumentation to permit its destruction.

2. On pages 2 and 3, following, summary analyses of five reactor casualties, any one of which is within our present capability.

3. On page 4, following, an analysis of the radiation dose rates at ranges of one, five, ten, and twenty-five miles, which would accompany various degrees of core meltdown under various meteorological conditions.

4. A small sample of one of the several types of explosive substances at our disposal may be found beneath the change tray in the middle public telephone booth at the head of Pier 26.

We will communicate further via one of those same three telephones at exactly 1000.

Our demands and deadlines are nonnegotiable.

With a sinking feeling of horror Stone flipped through the attached pages, understanding little of the highly technical text and illustrations. Then he read the base document again, twice. It smacked of authenticity: direct, logical, carefully understated, devoid of the inflammatory rhetoric that characterizes the ramblings of a crackpot or the lurid hyperbole that signals a bluff.

When he spoke to Larson his voice was tightly controlled. "Was there any sign of a struggle at Spencer's home?"

"Very little. A suitcase was overturned in the girl's bedroom . . ."

"A suitcase? What was in it?"

"Just the girl's stuff, some pictures, cosmetics, stuff like that."

Stone took out a note pad and scribbled .a few words. "What else did you find?"

"The dog was muzzled and tied to the banister downstairs."

"Muzzled? You mean with an actual dog muzzle?"

"Yes sir."

"Jesus." Stone took off his hat and ran his fingers nervously through his hair. "Anything else?"

"A discarded nightgown, probably the wife's."

"No blood?"

"Not that I saw. I was going to call for a lab team from the F.B.I. . . . but I figured I'd better get over here."

"You did right," Stone reassured him. "I take it the reactor plant is, in fact, sealed off."

"Yes sir, main hatches, escape hatches, every one dogged down tight. The eight o'clock reliefs had already reported it. There were several attempts to call down. No answer. Considering what the message said, I figured we'd better not attempt anything more."

"Good," Stone said. "You called for the fire equipment and ambulances?"

"It was all I could think of to do while I waited for you. Without more information I thought I should assume that the message was legitimate."

"I'm afraid you assumed right. We'll need an expert to take a look at these technical parts, but until we get his opinion we'll have to go on the premise that these people can and will do just what they say."

He glanced at the communiqué one more time, searching for some flaw that wasn't there.

"What about the sample explosive?"

"We found it just as the letter said."

"What did it look like?"

"There was only a very small amount, maybe half an ounce, wrapped in cellophane in an envelope. It was soft-looking, a gray color."

"Like putty?"

"Yes sir."

Stone nodded grimly. He jammed his hat back on his head and gazed up at the looming ship. "Who's running things up there?"

"The OOD until the captain gets here. You want me to introduce you?"

"I'll find him," Stone said. "I have more important things for you to do. You'd better write this down."

Larson flipped to a blank page on his pad and stood ready.

"First, I want you to seal this base completely. No one goes on or off without your personal authorization. Use marines as guards if you need to, and I want their weapons loaded. When people start to bitch just tell them it's a drill and leave it at that." He thought for a few seconds. "In fact, I want you to follow up on the idea of a drill. Get the public affairs officer to whip up a release saying that there's a big operational readiness inspection going on, some deal that Washington has sprung on us. Tell him to let it out only if he gets an inquiry from the press. Tell him to lie his ass off. Understood?"

"Yes sir."

"Okay. Then I want you to draw a second perimeter where the Mole joins the mainland. Put your best men there and tell them to be ready for anything, including an all-out attack. Get some boats to close off the mouth of the harbor and to patrol off the Mole. If you can't get anything else, put some men with rifles on tugs. Get a Coast Guard cutter and tell them I don't want any boats or swimmers within two hundred yards, but don't give them any details. Got it?"

Larson glanced up from his writing and nodded.

"Good," Stone said, pausing to think. "I want the communications van out here. I also want you to call the F.B.I. Ask them for someone who's experienced in hostage negotiations.

Again, as few details as possible. Just tell them we have a potential hostage situation. I'm going to try to get a marine detachment from Seal Beach and more from Camp Pendleton." He chewed on his lip. "Can you think of anything else?"

"Should I notify the Long Beach P.D. or the L.A. Sheriff's Department?"

"Jesus, no. Civilian cops sleep with the press."

Sheepishly Larson struggled to come up with another suggestion. "Isn't there a radiation decon unit on base?"

"Good idea," Stone said. "Get them down here. Call in Cooper and Morton. Work with Cooper, send the chief out here."

"Yes sir," Larson said, closing the notebook.

"No, wait," Stone said, starting to pace in little circles. "Something else. I want the telephone company out here to rig some lines from those phone booths to the van."

"Got it," Larson said. "Anything else?"

"Just one thing," Stone said. "Figure out who the hell's got command of this base and get his ass out here."

Had the issue been a hurricane or a collision or a fire, even the most junior line officer aboard the *Bremerton* would have had some idea what needed to be done. But in the present crisis Stone found that a kind of bewildered paralysis had set in. The OOD, a lieutenant out of the weapons department, the *Bremerton*'s navigator, a commander and the senior man on board, and Lieutenant Johnson representing the engineering department all stood together at the landing of the forward gangway waiting for the arrival of their captain. Their actions up to that point had consisted only of posting armed marines from the cruiser's small detachment at the doors to the forward reactor spaces and evacuating crewmen from the sleeping compartments forward of the plant—the group Stone had spotted on the fantail.

Stone was afforded a polite if somewhat wary welcome. He was briefed on facts surrounding the arrival of the five bogus shipyard workers and permitted to question the aft quarterdeck watches. Johnson in particular was helpful in interpreting the technical parts of the communiqué, but it was obvious no one in the group was willing to commit himself either to the implications of the situation or possible responses.

When Captain Reynolds finally arrived, to the visible relief of everyone, Stone was forced to wait a precious fifteen minutes while the man received the reports of his subordinates and slowly read through the letter. With him was a younger man dressed in a white shirt and tie, curtly introduced as Mr. Saxon from naval reactors. It was Johnson who explained to Stone in a low whisper that Saxon was the local representative of Admiral Hyman G. Rickover, the builder of the first nuclear-powered submarine and still, at eighty years of age, the virtual ruler of the nuclear fleet.

When Reynolds and his silent observer did receive Stone, it was less than cordially, as if Stone were a policeman investigating a domestic quarrel. For his part Stone was not about to assume a secondary role. After briefing Reynolds on his actions, Stone confronted him with the critical question.

"In your opinion, Captain," he asked, "is there any credibility to this threat?"

"None whatsoever," Reynolds said, far too quickly for Stone's comfort. "I assure you, Commander, the design of that reactor is fail-safe. Whatever damage they might inflict could not damage the integrity of the core. These ridiculous casualty scenarios in the letter—a core meltdown, radiation releases, widespread contamination—are pure fantasy. Isn't that correct, Mr. Saxon?"

Saxon was absorbed in reading the attachments to the communiqué; he said nothing.

The captain went on. "My only concern at this point is the safety of Bob Spencer's family and, of course, my men."

Johnson spoke up, visibly nervous. "Excuse me, Captain, but after looking at the letter I don't think we can dismiss the possibility of major core damage."

"Nonsense," Reynolds snapped. "That plant is designed to withstand a worst-case accident."

Johnson fidgeted under the captain's harsh gaze, but he persisted. "Well sir, reactor control isn't my area, but—"

Then Saxon interrupted, his tone matter-of-fact, his voice authoritative. "Unfortunately, Captain Reynolds, the lieutenant is correct. You are right about the core being designed to withstand a worst-case accident, but what we have here is intentional tampering with the core's protective capability. It appears from this drawing that these people have managed to use the battle-short capability to disable the automatic shutdown system."

"Meaning what?" Stone injected.

"Meaning that this reactor is no longer protected by its own instrumentation. Meaning, for all practical purposes, they have taken manual control."

"I don't believe it. It couldn't be that easy," Reynolds argued.

Saxon regarded him calmly. "I didn't say it was easy. This drawing shows a sophisticated understanding of the reactor control systems. Whoever designed this modification had access to the plant schematics and knew what to do with them. At least at first glance, I would have to say this is workable."

"But it's only a drawing," Reynolds sputtered. "It's not proof that anything has actually been modified."

"No sir, it isn't," Saxon agreed. "But if they understand the system well enough to produce this drawing, they probably wouldn't have any great difficulty with the actual modification."

Stone spoke. "Then you would say these people are experts?"

"That's what I will tell the admiral," Saxon said flatly, leaving to search for a telephone.

A uniformed patrolman arrived to end the uneasy silence that followed Saxon's departure. He carried the marble-sized sample of explosive, which he handed to Stone.

"My guess would be that it is some type of plastic, probably C-Four," Stone said.

"But you're not sure?" Reynolds said quickly.

"No sir. I'd have to test it."

"Then test it." The captain scowled. "There's been too much conjecture going on around here already."

"I agree," Stone said. He took the sample from the officer and casually broke off a piece no larger than a BB. "Does anyone have a match?"

One of the navy men produced a match, and Stone pressed the doughlike bead to the headless end.

"What are you doing?" Reynolds demanded.

"Testing it."

"Here?"

"We hardly have time to get very fancy, do we, Captain? If you'll watch from here, I'll take this down to the end of the pier."

Reynolds looked nervously from Stone to the patrolman. "Is this safe?"

"If it's a fake it certainly is," Stone said, as he hustled down the gangway.

The tiny fragment went off with a respectable bang, sending dirt and splinters of wood flying harmlessly into the air at the deserted end of the pier. When Stone returned to the quarterdeck, he found Reynolds looking grim.

"You made your point, Commander," he said.

"Good," Stone said. "How long will it take to evacuate the ship?"

"I have not yet decided on that course of action."

Stone gazed at him angrily. "I'm afraid I must insist on it, Captain."

"You haven't the authority."

"I do, sir. Right now, at least, I am in command of this base. My responsibilities include the ships in port."

"I applaud your sense of responsibility, Commander," Reynolds said sarcastically. "But it's my ship that's under attack, and I will remain in charge. I needn't remind you that I am the senior officer."

"With all due respect, Captain, as acting CO of Long Beach Naval Station, I am ordering you to evacuate the *Bremerton* of all personnel not presently on watch."

Reynolds's voice grew low and menacing. "No, Commander Stone, *I* am ordering *you* to make available all resources at your disposal."

Stone's gaze remained steady. "I will make nothing available without first reviewing the course of action."

"You're exceeding your authority," Reynolds growled.

"I believe you're exceeding yours."

The captain stared at him with growing rage. "Stone, if you refuse to cooperate, I'll have to report this situation to Eleventh Naval District."

Stone calmly turned to look down at the pier. The communications van had arrived, along with a telephone company truck, and under Larson's direction, lines were being rigged to the three booths. Marines armed with carbines had stationed themselves alongside the patrol cars at the head of the pier. Two miles away, where the road joined the mainland, Stone could see the flashing lights that meant a second perimeter had been established.

His eyes followed the line of the ship forward to where, according to his crude calculations, the number-one reactor operated under terrorist control. Finally he looked to the horizon cluttered with palm trees and grimy shipyard buildings and, beyond, the sprawling skyline of the city.

"Then you'd better call," he said quietly.

For twenty-five minutes the calls went back and forth, first to Eleventh Naval District headquarters in San Diego, then to Washington. Everyone along the line was more than ready to provide all the necessary back-up and most wanted to fly in for a personal inspection, but no one was willing to resolve the issue of command responsibility. The same paralysis that had immobilized the men in charge of the *Bremerton's* duty section was now working it s way up through the naval hierarchy, and again it was not so much the severity of the crisis as its stunning political overtones. Men who had grown accustomed to making vital decisions, often involving enormous risks, had also grown accustomed to the two luxuries that characterize high-level decision-making—accurate intelligence and time. Acutely aware that their careers hung in the balance, confronted with little information and no time, the flag officers gratefully referred the question to higher and

171

higher authorities until, with just ten minutes remaining until the scheduled first contact, Washington switchboards were frantically chasing down the chief of naval operations himself.

But the resolution was to come from a different quarter.

"Admiral Rickover wishes to speak to you," Saxon said to Reynolds. He indicated the shore phone located in the small cubbyhole that served as an office for the quarterdeck watches.

The *Bremerton*'s captain spoke in low tones for three or four minutes, occasionally stopping to listen with an intent expression. Then he set the telephone down and called to Stone. "The admiral would like to talk to you."

Stone picked up the phone and fixed his hand over the other ear to block out the surrounding noises. Beyond the rushing sound that signified long-distance, there was only silence. "Davis Stone," he said.

The voice at the other end was devoid of emotion, so quiet that Stone had some difficulty making out the words. "Mr. Saxon has read me the communiqué and briefed me on the situation. Do you have anything to add?"

"Only that we have confirmed that they do have explosives in their possession. Other than that, you know as much as we do."

"What measures have you taken?"

Stone gave him a terse, thorough report.

"Why do you think Captain Reynolds is unqualified to handle this situation?" Rickover asked.

Stone wondered what Reynolds had told him. He felt a flash of frustration at having to deal with this cozy group, but his answer was calmly worded. "I have complete confidence in Captain Reynolds' ability to deal with the *Bremerton*," he said. "But this thing involves a lot more than just one ship. The base and, for that matter, the entire civilian population may be affected. It is a matter of jurisdiction."

The old man's tone sharpened perceptibly. "I don't believe in jurisdiction, Commander Stone, just like I don't believe in rank. I believe in having the most qualified man in charge. Reynolds has nuclear training."

Stone returned the anger. "But he has no experience with terrorists."

"Do you?"

"Two years ago I negotiated the return of the kidnapped naval attaché in Brazil. Before that I worked on a series of terrorist actions in Rota, Spain. In addition I've received anti-terrorist and hostage situation training at Quantico."

"You consider yourself an expert?"

The quiet monotone of the man's voice enraged Stone, but his watch showed that there were now less than two minutes to go. "No sir," he admitted grudgingly.

Rickover muttered unintelligibly and asked to speak again to Reynolds.

Five minutes later Stone was seated in the van in front of a telephone connected to all three lines, appropriately red in color. The call had not yet come in and Larson was anxiously checking with the telephone repairman to make sure that the connection had been properly made.

"Relax," Stone ordered. "They just want us to stew for a while." Then he turned to the technician. "Is the recorder hooked in?"

"Yes, sir, it'll start as soon as you pick up the phone."

Reynolds ducked through the doorway just as Stone was re-reading the communiqué. Without looking at the head of security, he asked the others to step out for a moment. Stone nodded to Larson, and the two ranking officers were alone. When Reynolds spoke it was with the stiff formality of a man carrying out a disagreeable task. "I will cooperate with you fully," he announced quietly. "My men and I are at your disposal."

Stone hid his surprise. "Thank you, Captain Reynolds," he said. Then quickly, "Should *we* decide that an evacuation is in order, what would you propose?"

With Stone's clear signal of cooperation, the captain perked up. "I would evacuate the forward half of the ship entirely, with the exception of guards at the plant entrances, and at the forward magazine—"

Stone interrupted with a sickening thought. "Are you carrying nuclear weapons?" he asked.

"No, thank God," Reynolds said. "We don't load nukes until just before we leave for WestPac." Stone nodded and Reynolds continued. "Relating to the evacuation, I would maintain watches in the aft plant and in the emergency diesel room, also a roving watch for the missile spaces. I would station eight standby fire parties—two each on the forward main deck, port and starboard, two on the mess decks, and two more on the fantail. Carbon dioxide, foam, and fog."

"Hoses pressurized?"

"Yes," Reynolds said. "And I think we should get a bigger crane over here to help empty the forward magazine. In the event of an explosion, I don't want to have that to worry about."

"You'll have your crane," Stone promised, but before he could yell out at Larson the red phone started to ring. It was exactly ten minutes after ten o'clock. Somehow he found the precision in the delay comforting. "Yes?" he said calmly into the mouthpiece. That was when Stone received one of the bigger surprises of an already startling day. At the other end he heard the firm, confident voice of a woman.

⁄ 29

During those first moments of the takeover, when he found himself looking into the muzzle of the woman's rifle, Maurer's mind suddenly became hyperactive. He was aware of Dills's strangled sputterings and the startled movements of the crewmen behind him, but those were only background to the constant stream of images that raced through his head, as though his mind had been switched into fast-forward. For an instant he even considered the possibility that the intruders were part of some kind of bizarre joke, just the sort of thing Turner or Cadman might cook up for a dull Sunday morning. But there was no questioning the deadly authenticity of the guns or the even deadlier iciness of the woman's expression.

Then he flashed on a confidential telex he'd seen during his tour in Idaho, uneven black teletype letters on a yellow tearsheet: "RECENT INTELLIGENCE INDICATES INCREASED ACTIVITY AMONG TERRORIST AND OTHER CLANDESTINE ORGANIZATIONS. AFFECTED SHIPS AND SHORE ACTIVITIES SHOULD BE ALERT TO POSSIBLE ATTEMPTS TO STEAL FISSIONABLE OR RADIOACTIVE MATERIALS OR TO COMMANDEER NUCLEAR FACILITIES . . ."

He stood staring at the weapon, his heart pounding, imagining he could almost see the copper slug nestled in the breach and the gleaming riflings that would send it spinning into his chest. By then he was sure it was the reactor they were after, and his only questions related to how he could stop them. Mentally he measured the distance to the scram switch. Would the first bullet kill him? Surely she couldn't miss, but if he was fast enough she might only get his arm. How much would it hurt? Enough to stop him? Could anything stop him if he had enough will? A bullet in the head, but in the back? Could he pull back the switch cover and keep his focus despite the pain, the sight of his own blood all over the panel? Damn that cover! Without that he could get the switch in one lunge.

The questions were still racing through his brain when some movement or noise behind him caused the woman to aim the muzzle away. Mouthing a silent prayer, Maurer dove for the panel. He virtually climbed up the lower console and tore away the switch cover, ripping the plastic completely from its mounting, tensed for the shock of the bullet in his spine. His fingers locked on the smooth black rotary knob, and he twisted it savagely, glorying in the familiar solid snap of the contacts even as he waited for the sound of the fatal shot. But there was no sound—not of a shot or of the cacophony of horns and bells that normally followed a reactor scram.

He stared at the silent panel, forgetting now the intruders with their guns. The little white line etched into the scram switch pointed squarely at SCRAM, but nothing else had changed. The sixteen rod-bottom lights remained unlit. Power and temperature stood unchanged. The space lights were still on, and beyond the bulkhead there was the steady thunder of spinning turbines. Cursing, Maurer snapped the switch again. Nothing. Desperately he did it again and then again. Still nothing.

Then he heard a familiar mocking laughter behind him. He whirled to find White standing between the intruders, grinning maliciously at him, his arms folded casually across his chest, an automatic pistol held loosely in one hand.

"Nice try," the man said smugly. "Would you care to try the safety injection switch? I believe that's what the procedures would call for."

Maurer did, knowing as he reached for the red-handled knob high on the panel that the effort was futile. When the effort produced no results, he turned to White, his initial bewilderment turning into rage. "You fucking little prick," he snarled. "What the hell is this?"

White only sneered more broadly. "This, Petty Officer Maurer, is a setup, and you're the pigeon."

Maurer calculated desperately. "What do you hope to gain?" he asked, but his attention was elsewhere. Shielding the panel with his body he slid his hand to the rod control switch, eased it to the IN position, and held it there.

White did not notice. He laughed harshly and started to answer, but the woman cut him off.

"No more talk," she commanded, then motioned toward Maurer. "You, move to the back wall, all of you." She waved her weapon toward the standing group of operators.

Maurer held his ground, trying to look as if he were leaning back against the panel for support, cursing the design that limited rod speed to less than two inches a minute.

"You heard me," she said.

"What is this all about?" Maurer asked, almost pleading. "What do you want?"

There was a movement in the entryway and a huge blond man appeared, also armed, this one with a submachine gun. "What's the holdup?" he demanded.

"I think our man Maurer is about to shit his pants," White gloated.

"Don't be a fool," the woman said. "He's not scared, he's stalling. There! What's he doing to make that odometer thing go around?"

White followed her pointing finger to the slowly turning rod group position indicator. "Shit!" he howled. "The fucker's driving in rods. Stop him."

When Maurer saw White and the giant start toward him, he spun around, grabbed the IN-HOLD-OUT switch with both hands, and flung himself across it. There was a furious struggle as White and the giant tried to drag him away, but he hung on desperately, his feet spread wide apart for balance, his shoulders hunched against the panel, twisting his body and head to elude their grasps.

Suddenly he felt a stunning blow at the base of his skull that sent his forehead crashing into the sharp edge of some meter. He looked up, dazed, just in time to see White raise the butt of his pistol and bring it down again, even more viciously. There was an explosion of light and then darkness.

For over two hours Maurer lapsed in and out of consciousness, experiencing brief periods of lucidity only to fade again into swirling darkness. When he finally came to, his head was cradled in the lap of a girl he had never seen before, a slender redhead with a pretty, youthful face marred by an ugly bruise high on her right cheek and another at the point of her chin. She was clad in a loose-fitting garment made from some sort of lightweight green material. She tended Maurer gently, steadying his head with one hand and pressing a damp cloth to his brow with the other. When he blinked his eyes against the harsh glare of the fluorescent lights, he felt the painful sting of a gash above his right eye.

"Who the hell are you?" he asked, brushing away the bloody rag for a better look. His voice was a rasp, and there was still a painful ringing in his ears.

The girl seemed not to hear him. Her face was flushed with excitement, her eyes bright, her shoulders tense as she strained to listen to something over the rattle of the airconditioner directly above them. He could feel the trembling in her body and see the rapid rise and fall of her small breasts outlined beneath the flimsy gown.

He tugged at her elbow and repeated his question. She glanced down at him, an annoyed look on her face. "Florence Nightingale," she whispered. "Now be quiet."

He let his head rest back on her thigh and tried to clear his groggy brain. For the first time he was aware of angry voices coming from the other side of the room. He turned his head, but the EOOW's desk partially blocked his view. He could see the back of one of them, the black-haired woman, and the heavy boots of another. From the voices he could tell there was at least one more.

Again he touched the girl's arm. "What are they talking about?"

"Me," she said, without looking down.

He struggled up and managed to gain a sitting position with his back propped against the hot metal bulkhead. A wave of dizziness washed over him. He felt nauseated, and his skull throbbed, but the worst of it soon passed and by using his sleeve to wipe away the blood and sweat, he managed to clear the blurriness.

Now he could see three of them: the woman, a tall, dark middle-aged man, and the blond giant. He looked around for the other crewmen. Fox was still in his chair at the electrical panel, tight-jawed, watching the intruders. Weston was next to him, equally grim. Dills was standing at his desk, his hands resting palms-down on the Plexiglas top as if they were glued in place, his gaze fixed oddly on the throttleman's wheel directly in front of him.

Suddenly Maurer remembered White and turned to look at the reactor panel. But the chair was empty, and the little bastard was nowhere in sight. Instinctively he ran his eyes over the untended meters, squinting to see the needles. The temperature was well below the operating band, probably the result of his attempt to drive in the rods, but otherwise, as best he could tell, the parameters were holding.

He surveyed the rest of the room and for the first time noticed another woman huddled against the back bulkhead. She was dressed in the same sort of light gown worn by the girl beside him, and had the same auburn hair and fair skin, but she was a good twenty years older. Her face was puffy and ashen, her eyes glazed. She sat still as death with her arms hugging her knees, completely withdrawn from her surroundings. Maurer tried to ask the girl about her, but she shook him off, refusing to turn her attention from the argument that was going on among the armed trio.

The woman was talking excitedly. He could not see her face but he could see the cords in her neck flexing violently and the stabbing gestures of her hands. "Listen to me, Karl," she was saying "It's your turn to be realistic. There're going to be fifty fighter planes sitting up there ready to shoot us down the instant our choppers leave the deck." She jerked her head toward the captive woman. "These two are our insurance."

The tall man showed almost no expression, but his voice was ice cold. "It was unnecessary, Andrea. We have White and Nettles. For that matter, we have all of the crew."

"Shit," the giant blurted, his mouth twisted into a sneer. "No wonder the Krauts shit-canned you. If you really think those brass bastards out there are gonna think twice about wasting a couple of lousy sailors, you're dumber than I thought."

Karl turned on him. "You knew about this?"

"Knew about it? Hell, I thought it up. Do you know who those two are?" He pointed toward the woman who sat unhearing on the deck. "That one is Mrs. Admiral R. W. Spencer. And that sweet young thing over there, that's his only daughter." He gloated. "Now you tell me, Schmidt, which jet jockey is going to shoot down that kind of freight?"

"The one that's ordered to," the tall man answered matter-of-factly. Then he turned back to the woman. "Maybe they will move against us, maybe they will not. But if they do, it is not going to make one iota of difference who the hostages are."

The giant's fingers tightened on his weapon until the knuckles were white. He started to snarl an answer but he never got the chance. There was a sudden movement beside Maurer, and then the Spencer girl was standing, pointing at the huge man and screaming. "You bastard! I hope they do come after you. I hope they blow this whole place to kingdom come. It'd be worth it, just to see you get your ass kicked."

Maurer grabbed for her, trying to pull her down, but she shook him off angrily, her body tall in defiance. The three had turned to stare at her, the woman startled, the man, Karl, strangely amused. But it was the giant that Maurer noticed. A crimson flush had crept up from his neck, and his lips clamped down into a tight white line. Quicker than Maurer thought possible, he brought the muzzle of his gun around until it was leveled directly at the girl's belly.

"Shut up" Maurer urged, clutching at her garment.

"You'd better listen to the hero," the giant snarled menacingly, "before I come over there and kick *your* ass."

Maurer was powerless to stop what came next: it just happened too quickly. He saw the movement of her arm, saw her wrist turn and her fingers tense. In that instant he knew exactly what she was about to do, perhaps because he had seen the gesture a thousand times, perhaps because he would have done the same thing in her place. For whatever reason, he knew, and there was nothing he could do. She brought her left hand up to eye level, palm inward, fingers curled into a loose fist. Then, looking directly at the smirking man with blazing eyes, she carefully and deliberately extended that single middle finger.

For the look on his face she might as well have kicked the giant in the balls. Maurer had never seen such rage in a human being. Had it not been for the massive EOOW's desk between them, he probably would have strangled her before any of them could lift a finger. As it was, Maurer would never understand what kept him from gunning her down where she stood. Perhaps it was that his anger could only be avenged with bare hands. Perhaps in his mindless fury he'd forgotten the weapon altogether.

He started around the desk, shoving the woman aside, his eyes burning red, his mouth working noiselessly. Then came the shot, a deafening explosion within the metal-walled space, and Chief Nettles appeared in the doorway, a pistol in his hand, cocked and ready for a second firing. Maurer's heart leaped, and he started to rise.

"Nobody move!" Nettles screamed. "Freeze, Givens. You too, Hal."

In the wake of the blast everyone obeyed, the giant in mid-stride, a look of rage frozen on his face, Maurer with stunned bewilderment.

"Come on, Givens," Nettles commanded. "Let's go outside and cool off." He glanced at the woman. "Next time keep your boys in line." Then he led the giant out of the room, leaving Maurer standing with his mouth hanging open.

✒ 30

The shot occurred at 10:31. Less than a minute later the news was relayed to Stone outside the communications van. At the time he was huddled with Chief Morton, Reynolds, Jones, and four technicians from the *Bremerton*, amid a blizzard of blueprints and schematics, trying to piece together a strategy to disable the reactor. The pier had been turned into a staging area, and already nearly a hundred marines stood by in full battle dress, with additional reinforcements arriving by helicopter in the parking lot across the road at three-minute intervals. A second landing area had been roped off at the far end of the pier, that one to accommodate the arrival of Westinghouse engineers and naval architects from Mare Island via Los Alamitos Naval Air Station. They were expected within the hour.

Even as a messenger delivered the news of the shot, the red phone began to ring. The woman had anticipated Stone's concern.

"What the hell's going on down there?" he demanded before she could speak.

"There is no cause for alarm," she assured him in a calm voice. "The firing was a planned demonstration. No one was hurt, no damage was done."

"I want to talk to one of the crewmen," Stone shouted. If they're panicky, be calm; if they're calm, bluster—that was the method.

"No," was her flat answer. "We will not deviate from the plan."

"Damn it! If you don't let me talk to someone we're going to come down there like gangbusters."

"Please," she said patiently, "I appreciate your attempted bluff, but it will achieve nothing. Again, I assure you, everything is under absolute control."

The line went dead.

Stone glared at the handset as if it were the offending party. "Damn, she's good."

"What was it?" Morton asked.

"According to her, a 'planned demonstration.' "

"Do you think everything's cool?"

Stone shook his head. "Who the hell knows?"

Forty minutes later the experts from Mare Island arrived, and detailed strategy talks began. At first Stone was optimistic. Earlier discussions had centered around a plan to scram the reactor by cutting the power lines from the operating turbine generator to the rod control power supply. According to the technicians, the power cables passed next to the starboard hull at some point, and it was hoped that the experts could pinpoint the spot where a relatively concentrated explosive charge could penetrate the hull and cut the cables, disabling the reactor and allowing a full-scale assault on the control room. But after two agonizing hours of debate, it became increasingly clear to Stone that the plan was doomed.

One of the architects summed up the problem. "We know *approximately* where the cables approach the side of the ship, but our estimate would be plus or minus ten feet."

"Plus or minus ten feet!" Stone snapped in frustration. "What about all these beautiful blueprints? Are you telling me they're worthless?"

The expert nodded. "They're okay for fixed structures like bulkheads and the generator itself, but there has to be flexibility when it comes to things like cable runs. Adjustments have to be made for turning radii, for access problems the designers couldn't foresee, for unplanned structural changes. God only knows how many change orders went in beween the time this drawing was made and the cables were actually installed."

Stone fought to contain his anger. "So you're saying that the only way we can be sure to cut those cables is to blow a twenty-foot-wide hole in the side."

"That would reasonably insure success."

Are you aware that a blast of that size would probably kill everyone inside and might damn well sink the ship?"

"I'm sorry, Commander, I'm only giving you the best estimate I can."

"Yes," Stone muttered bitterly. "Thank you."

A few minutes later Stone called Reynolds into the van and closed the door. Just after his first contact with the terrorists Stone had received a lengthy call from Washington. At that time he had been given a special telephone number, and now, with Reynolds listening in on another line, he dialed it.

"Please hold for the chief of naval operations," the male operator said. Seconds later a deep voice came over the line. "Commander Stone, what is your status?"

"Unfortunately, Admiral, not good," Stone said. He explained the most recent developments.

"Alternatives?" the CNO asked.

"Very few. Evacuation of any significant part of the civilian population is almost out of the question. There are over a hundred thousand people within a five-mile radius of the ship, nearly half a million within ten miles. The quick calculations we did here show that given the present wind-flow pattern, as many as four million would be in the heavy fallout area. Obviously the only practical procedure would involve some kind of general alert, and the panic that would cause would be catastrophic."

"Do you concur with that evaluation, Captain?" the CNO asked.

"Yes, sir," Reynolds said. "I believe that losses in lives and property would be of the same magnitude as those occurring in the case of an actual meltdown."

"And what are your projected losses for a meltdown?"

"The figures are pretty rough, sir."

"Please, Captain."

"If they actually create the accident described in their scenario, we estimate there could be one thousand to ten thousand civilian fatalities within the first ninety-six hours, assuming an initial dose rate of six hundred rem within a one-mile radius of the ship. The variables are tremendously complex, of course. The actual dose rates could be much lower."

"Or higher?"

"Yes sir."

"What about long-term losses?"

"Virtually impossible to predict," Reynolds said. "It would depend on what specific isotopes were released, the exact meteorological conditions at the time of the release, whether there was an accompanying chemical explosion, how long it took to evacuate the area, a whole range of factors."

"I appreciate the complexity, but I want a number. What is the highest reasonable figure?"

"One million," Reynolds said in a hushed voice.

It was several seconds before the CNO spoke; when he did his voice was subdued. "What other alternatives, Commander Stone?"

"Towing the ship out to sea was considered," Stone said. "But even if we found a way to tap their shore line telephone

so that they wouldn't know it had been cut, it's extremely un-
likely that they would fail to notice some movement regard-
less of how careful we were. As you know, sir, the *Bremerton*
has an extremely narrow beam for its length, giving it a pronounced roll even in the calmest sea. Captain Reynolds and I
agree that the idea is impractical."

"Can you offer any practical ones?"

"Only the one we discussed before, of going in through the
side of the ship and trying to disable the reactor at the same
time. We're still working on that, sir."

"I see."

Stone spoke uneasily. "Might we reconsider the possibility
of meeting their demands, at least until we can get them
away from the reactor?"

"We will not meet their demands," the CNO said. "Not the
so-called reparations or anything else they may come up
with. The president was very clear on that point." From the
sound of his voice, Stone suspected that the CNO might not
agree with the decision, not that it made any difference. The
man continued in a flat tone, "Just in case our activities are
being observed, arrangements are being made to assemble
the ten million as specified in the note you found with the
suitcases, but, I repeat, it will *not* be delivered."

"I understand, sir," Stone said, but only in the sense of an
acknowledgment.

"Have you received any delivery instructions?"

"No sir."

"Any additional demands?"

"No, but as you know we're supposed to get another call at
fifteen hundred our time."

"Yes," the man said. Then, after a long pause, "Commander, we have been studying the situation carefully and, in light
of the difficulty you're having there, we believe there is only
one other realistic course of action open to us."

"Gas?" Stone said heavily. It had been one of the several
possibilities thrown out during the first call—to inject gas into
the forward plant's ventilation system.

"Yes. I have dispatched a jet from Utah to deliver the army's newest type of fast-acting nerve gas and the equipment and personnel to handle it?"

"Nerve gas? As in lethal?"

"Regrettably, yes."

"Isn't there something else we could use, something that would only knock them out? There's seven, possibly eight crewmen down there, plus the two women hostages."

The admiral's tone was patient. "I'm sorry," he said. "I am told that there is no non-lethal gas that acts reliably in less than thirty seconds, which, according to your own experts, might give them enough time to wreck the plant. This stuff acts in less than ten. I assure you, it's not an easy decision, but I believe the trade-offs are obvious."

"Yes sir," Stone and Reynolds said simultaneously.

"Very well. Your orders are as follows: Upon arrival of the gas you will immediately rig the necessary apparatus for its injection into the forward reactor control spaces. From that time on, the injection system will be continuously manned. When, in your opinion, an attempt to destroy the reactor is imminent, you will order the injection. Are there any questions?"

"Just one. If we can come up with a way to disable the reactor and try for a rescue, will you consider approving it?" Stone asked slowly.

There was a long silence. "If you can *guarantee* that the reactor will be disabled, I'll take it to the president. Any other questions?"

"No questions," Stone said.

"Then you have your orders."

"Aye aye, sir."

Stone took Chief Morton aside and spent ten minutes briefing him on the telephone conversation. When he was done, the chief stood silent, gazing out over the harbor.

"That's the shits," he said finally.

Stone laughed tensely. "Well, I guess that's one way to describe it."

"They're right, though, about the trade-off," Morton added."

"Of course they're right." Stone said bitterly.

After an awkward silence, Morton spoke again. "While we're at it, do you want some more bad news?"

"Sure, why not?"

"Larson called me on the radio while you were inside. Guess who's officially CO until the exec can get back?"

"Who?"

"You."

"Bullshit! There must be twenty officers on this base senior to me!"

"Try to find one of 'em," Morton answered. "It looks like you've got it for the duration."

"Thanks. That's just what I needed."

Morton kicked at a splinter in the planking. "I wish to hell we'd been right last night. A simple little payroll heist would look pretty good right about now."

"You know," Stone said quietly. "I've been thinking the same thing all morning."

⟋ 31

"What d'ya think?" Weston whispered out of the corner of his mouth. His words were almost lost to the rattle of the airconditioner overhead.

Maurer sneaked a look around the room. Following the confrontation between the Spencer girl and Givens, the woman had moved all the crewmen to the back corner and brought in a fourth man to watch them. Weston and Maurer sat together along one wall, Fox and Dills along the other. The man, Leggett, was stationed in front of the EOOW's desk, placing himself directly between them and the control panels. The girl had been moved next to her mother and Karl had been assigned to stay with her, probably as much to protect her as to guard her. The woman and White were out in the entryway off to his left, whispering together. Givens and Nettles had not returned to EOS.

"Christ, I don't know," Maurer said. "Even if we could get to the panel, I'm not sure there's anything we could do. That fucker White has everything bypassed, and now that he's shifted control out to control equipment, we couldn't even drive the rods in."

"Why don't we just take these guys?" Weston suggested drolly.

"Sure, you saw how good I did," Maurer replied, letting his head rest back against the bulkhead.

"Yeah," Weston said, suddenly glum. "I'm sorry about leavin' you hangin' out to dry."

Maurer looked at his friend and grinned. "Hey, man, don't be dumb." He nodded toward the control panel. "When it comes to my babies, I'm sorta crazy, that's all. I don't expect anybody else to get suicidal along with me." He held out his open hand. "Okay?"

"Okay," Weston said, slapping it lightly.

Then Fox spoke up for the first time. "I've got an idea, if you're interested."

"We're interested," Maurer said.

The Southerner leaned forward and tried to look as if he were toying with a loose bolt in the deckplate. "The number-one turbine generator is supplying power to the scram magnets, right? So if we tripped the TG output breaker, wouldn't that dump the plant?"

"Yeah, that would do it all right," Maurer said, excited at first, then gloomy. "But White's probably screwed with that, too."

"No, he hasn't," Fox said. "Weston and I were training on both TGs just before you got here, transferring loads back and forth. I know that breaker opens."

"Then, by God, tripping it would work," Maurer whispered. "*If* we can get by Wyatt Earp there."

"One of us could get by," Weston said. "Which switch is it?"

Fox started to speak when Dills interrupted. "No," he said in a hoarse voice. "Don't do anything."

The three turned to look at the pale, sweating man who had sulked in silence since the takeover. They'd almost forgotten he was there.

"For Christ's sake, keep your voice down," Maurer whispered. He glanced toward their guard, but the man was apparently more interested in the conversation going on between White and the woman. "Now if you have a better idea, we'd like to hear it."

Dills's mouth twitched and he avoided Maurer's gaze. "You heard what she said when she was talking on the phone. If we do what they want nobody will get hurt."

"And you believe that?"

"Yes . . . I do."

"You're a fool," Weston grumbled, but Maurer quickly interceded, speaking in a low, calm voice.

"Look, I agree that the chick seems to know her stuff, and the two guys in here now look pretty cool, but White and that big one are crazier than fuckin' loons. I think when push comes to shove it's gonna be a goddamn shooting gallery in here, and we're gonna be right in the middle of it. Face it, Dills, we're dead ducks, and if that's so, we might as well go out in a blaze of glory. Right?"

"Right on," Weston said. Fox nodded, too, although with less enthusiasm.

But Dills only grew more pale. "The people up top will think of something," he mumbled. "All we have to do is sit tight."

"Bullshit," Maurer whispered. "Those people have got a lot more to worry about than my ass or yours. Right now they've got a critical reactor in enemy hands sitting smack in the middle of Long Beach Harbor. If I was them the only thing I'd be worried about was how to shut that fucker down, and fare-thee-well to old Harold T. Maurer. In fact, I'm sorta surprised they haven't chucked a couple of grenades in here already."

"My, my," said Fox, shaking his head. "You do have a way with words."

"A regular silver-tongued little devil, ain't he?" Weston added.

But Dills was trembling. "You all think this is some kind of joke. Well, I don't. The Navy will take care of these hoodlums without any of your heroics. I order you to end this discussion immediately."

Maurer glanced at the other two. "What do you think?" he asked.

Weston did not hesitate. "I think we ought to go for it."

"Me too," Fox said.

"Didn't you hear me?" Dills said loudly. "I ordered you to stop this immediately!"

Dills's outburst brought Leggett from around the desk. "What's going on?"

Dills started to open his mouth but Maurer silenced him with a murderous stare.

"Just a friendly little argument over yesterday's game," Weston said flippantly. "Real football fanatics, these guys."

"That's enough of that crap," Leggett warned. "Knock off the chatter."

"Must not be a sports fan," Weston muttered under his breath as the man walked back to his post.

Leggett whirled around. "I said knock it off!"

Weston flipped him a mock salute and then lapsed into silence. But Maurer was not finished. Resting his forearms on his knees and keeping his head down to conceal his face, he spoke quietly. "We'll hang in here for a while. Maybe we'll get a break. But if it gets crazy we'll all three go for the breaker trip. Second from the left on the bottom row, right, Fox?" He waited for the electrician's confirmation, then whispered at Dills. "And if you try to stop us, Lieutenant, I'll personally break your fuckin' neck."

Dills shrank back in tight-lipped fear and said nothing.

Schmidt watched Leggett's unsuccessful effort to silence the crewmen with keen interest. "It appears your friend has not yet given up," he said in a low voice to Cynthia Spencer.

"Who's that?" she asked indifferently. She had begged one of his cigarettes and was puffing it with the charming awkwardness of a novice.

"The one with the hard head. He and his friends are up to something."

"So take your gun and go shoot them."

Schmidt looked at her with amusement. Her contempt was as real as it was boundless. She referred to Givens as "The Prick," White was "The Wimp," and Andrea was simply "The Bitch." Schmidt himself had been spared a designation, but during her periods of sullen brooding he had caught her looking at him as if he were an insect she wanted to crush.

Her courage fascinated him, the recklessness that had sent Givens into a blind rage as much as the quiet strength. And she had a great deal of the latter. Calmly, without self-pity, she had related to him the events of her abduction, going so far as to gently chide herself for her errors in judgment, as if she were analyzing an athletic contest. Not once did she complain of pain, although several times he saw her touch her left side and grimace.

When she was willing they talked quietly, mostly of the countries they had both visited, he as an intelligence agent, she as an officer's child. At those times she would chatter on with bright-eyed excitement, demonstrating an astonishing memory for details and love of adventure that was at the same time worldly and delightfully romantic.

The only tears he saw her shed were for her father. She was convinced that he had been murdered, not a little because her image of him was so heroic she could conceive of no other reason for him not coming to her rescue. For his part Schmidt found himself unable to lie. As gently as he could, he related exactly what Andrea had told him about the tranquilizers.

"And I'm supposed to believe that?" the girl had asked with growing fury.

"Only because from her perspective it would be a logical strategy," Schmidt said.

"Logical! Logical! Jesus Christ, you're no better than the rest of those shitheads." She was literally trembling with rage. "And I'll tell you something else. If those men did hurt my father, I swear to God I'll cut their balls off!"

What a sweet child she was.

Her response to her mother baffled Schmidt the most. It was a kind of detached concern that seemed no different from what she might show for a stranger. At first she had tried to speak to the woman and had draped one of the crewmen's jackets over her thin shoulders. But when the woman continued to stare dully into space, she turned away and acted as though she no longer existed. "She's probably better off," was her only statement on the subject.

Sometime after Andrea made the three p.m. call to the pier, Givens returned briefly to the control room. It was then that Schmidt saw the real mettle of the girl. There was no fear in her eyes, no trembling in her body. There was not even the hatred he might have expected to find, only a kind of grim determination and a coldness, an extraordinary coldness that he had rarely seen even within the profession. For almost ten minutes, despite the pain it must have caused her, she sat straight and proud, never taking her eyes off Givens, hardly even blinking. Only afterward did she show any emotion, and then just a single tear that trickled down over the bruise on her cheek.

"Listen," Schmidt said quietly, "stay close to me. If there is more trouble I will do what I can to protect you and your mother."

"My hero," she said. But several minutes later she looked over at him. "What you said about helping us, did you mean it?"

"Yes, I meant it," he said.

She managed a weak smile.

Around five o'clock Andrea had sandwiches and coffee distributed to the hostages. Maurer was eating quietly when Weston tapped him. "Here comes Nettles."

The chief walked over to where the crewmen sat and stood there with his hands thrust deep in the pockets of his khaki trousers. There was no sign of the gun. "How's the head?" he asked Maurer with forced casualness.

Maurer kept his head down and continued eating.

"Look, Hal," Nettles said, a trace of pleading in his voice. "I know you don't understand, but I have my reasons, believe me. It's just something I had to do. I tried to keep you out of it . . ."

Maurer took a bite out of the sandwich and set it aside. "Chief, ol' buddy," he said with a mouthful of food.

"Yes?"

"Fuck off."

⟋ 32

By eight o'clock the area around Pier 26 had begun to look like the set of a Hollywood disaster movie. Powerful sodium floodlights mounted on fifty-foot towers cast their eerie orange glow for a hundred yards in every direction. A second communications van had been set up next to the first, and next to that a sixty-foot command trailer had been deposited by a Chinook helicopter. From the top of metal scaffolds a half-dozen closed-circuit television cameras scanned the decks of the *Bremerton*, feeding their images down to a bank of monitors and video recorders housed in the second van. Across the pier were scores of black, snakelike cables, thin ones going out to the lights and cameras, and others, as thick as a man's arm, coming in from the four mobile generators that idled noisily further down the pier.

The force of marines, now numbering over five hundred, had been moved back to the roadway and stood milling around the field kitchen set up earlier in the day. Beyond them, in the parking lot, two helicopters stood with their jet engines whining, ready for instant takeoff.

Four fire engines and two ambulances had been added to the original contingent, and parked beside them were the distinctive pale blue vans belonging to the radiation control units. Eight control teams of six men each—the entire forces from Long Beach and Seal Beach plus reinforcements flown in from Mare Island, San Diego, and Bremerton, Washington—lounged amid neatly arranged rows of radiation counters and containment gear.

Three small boats patrolled in circles just beyond the reach of the floodlights, and in the outer harbor, two hundred yards off the Mole, a white Coast Guard cutter prowled through the waters, sweeping the surface with its powerful searchlights. Still further out, silhouetted against the lights of Orange County, two fireboats cruised slowly back and forth.

Stone arrived one minute late for the eight o'clock briefing in the conference room of the command trailer. He immediately took a seat in the middle of the long table between Morton and Reynolds. Seated across from him from left to right were Jones and Saxon, Admiral Duane Rogers, Commandant of the Eleventh Naval District, Ralph Chambers, Agent-in-Charge of the F.B.I. area office, Lieutenant Commander Bud Turnich, Training Supervisor of the Navy's Underwater Demolition School at Seal Beach, and Major Clark O'Dell, Commander of the Marine Forces.

"Admiral Rogers . . . gentlemen," Stone began. "Before we start I'd like you to hear the tape of the fifteen-hundred telephone call. I think it will give you a better idea of what we're dealing with."

He signaled Morton to start the recorder, then sat back and folded his hands. A slight hissing sound filled the room, followed by a brief, high-pitched cueing tone and then Stone's voice.

Davis Stone.

A woman spoke in a slow, well-modulated voice. *Good day, Commander Stone. The following is a prepared statement of demand. There will be no questions or discussion. Do you understand?*

Yes.

Am I correct in assuming that this call is being recorded?

Yes.

Very well. Then I won't have to repeat any points. By nine o'clock this evening, Pacific Standard Time, the President of the United States is to announce that because of, quote, Israel's continuing policy of aggression against its neighbors, unquote, he is cutting off all military and economic assistance to that nation, effective immediately.

So that the president may save face as well as circumvent his stated policy against personally responding to terrorist demands, we will accept the announcement in the form of a, quote, leak, unquote, to the news media by, quote, top White House sources, unquote.

We will consider our demand to have been met only if news stories concerning the announcement appear on the wire services and broadcast networks no later than the nine p.m. deadline.

Our demand is nonnegotiable.

We will contact you next at midnight tonight.

There was a click and then a dial tone.

Jones spoke up immediately. "Words, that's all they want, goddamn words? My kids could come up with something more substantial than that."

"I'd call the ten million dollars pretty substantial," Morton threw in.

"Any other comments?" Stone quickly asked.

"Yes," Saxon said quietly. "What was the president's response?"

"In keeping with his earlier decision not to concede to any of their demands, the president has refused."

Jones screwed up his face. "I don't want to overdo a point, and I certainly don't want to sound disloyal to my commander-in-chief, but it seems to me that it would be easy enough to make the announcement tonight and simply retract it tomorrow or whenever we get these guys, particularly since it's only a 'leak.' So he catches some political flak, so what? I've got eight men down in the hole."

"It's not that simple," the admiral broke in. "The terrorists know as well as you do that the announcement would be retracted as soon as they gave up control of the reactor. In fact, that's precisely what they want to happen. As quickly as it's retracted the press will start speculating about how the president caved in to the Jews. Not only will they have succeeded in making the president look irresolute on this issue, but they will have driven one more wedge between the Americans and Israelis, with God knows what effect on the stability of the Middle East. Now I'd not only call that substantial, I'd call it damn clever."

He appeared to have finished his speech, but when he glanced down the table and saw the troubled look on Jones's face, he broke into a grin. "And if you want to know how I achieved these brilliant insights, I did it by asking the president's chief-of-staff the very same question you just asked." He leaned back in his chair. "It's been a long time since anyone's called me stupid."

For a moment there were smiles in the room, but Jones stubbornly shook his head. "I'm sorry, Admiral, but I just can't buy this foreign intrigue crap. If the president's staff really believes what they're saying, *they're* the stupid ones." He gestured excitedly, waving a pencil to emphasize his point. "I think *either* this demand is simply a red herring, some political window dressing to cover up plain old extortion and send everyone off looking for a terrorist connection that doesn't exist, *or* it's a little test to see if there's enough softness there to go for something really big. Now, personally, I'm convinced it's the first case—like the chief says, ten million is plenty enough motive—and that's why I say play their goddamn game. Go along with their terrorist ploy, give them their ten mil, and get them the hell outa there."

For several seconds no one spoke. Then Saxon broke the silence. "I fail to see what bearing any of this has on the immediate problem. My chief concern is that the president *has* refused, whether he's correct in that decision or not, and as I read the initial communiqué, when the nine o'clock deadline passes without an announcement the local broadcast stations will automatically be notified of the situation. I can't imagine Washington is going to let that happen."

"No," Stone said soberly, "I'm afraid it isn't."

Saxon looked directly at him. "Does that mean we're going to be expected to use the nerve gas?"

"I hope not," Stone said softly. "We're still working on one alternative we should be able to sell."

Rogers interrupted. "But if you can't 'sell' your alternative, Commander, do you in fact have orders to use the gas before the nine p.m. deadline?"

"Yes, I do, Admiral," Stone said without expression.

"Christ!" Jones snarled, slamming his pencil down on the table. The others simply looked grim.

Stone quickly continued. "But I think the alternative *is* viable." He turned to the F.B.I. representative. "Mr. Chambers, could you summarize what you've been doing?"

The agent-in-charge wasted no time. "Briefly, the situation is this. Early this afternoon we succeeded in tapping the line the group is using to call out on. We found that in addition to the calls they've made to us, they've placed four calls to a Long Beach number. My men traced it down and raided the address. What they found was a device similar to a telephone answering machine, only in this case when a call is received, the circuit is automatically patched in to an AM radio."

"So they can monitor the news," Rogers said.

"Exactly. I'm told the radio is tuned to KBNE, a twenty-four-hour news station."

At that point Major O'Dell broke in. "This may be a stupid question, but why didn't they just bring a radio with them?"

Rogers answered. "It's not a stupid question if you've never served aboard a ship. There's the equivalent of a half foot of steel between those people and the outside. They couldn't pick up a radio signal if the transmitter was sitting on the pier."

O'Dell nodded and the F.B.I. man resumed his commentary. "All right, then, our original plan was to tape a false news report and feed it directly into the monitor beginning at the nine o'clock deadline. KNBE carries the CBS news on the hour and ABC's *World News Round-Up* at the half hour. Both networks agreed to produce a bogus broadcast containing the Israel story."

"How did you manage that?" Jones asked, his frustration again under control.

"We told them a partial truth. That we have a hostage situation and the story is involved in one of the demands."

"Isn't that going to bring the networks crawling all over the place?"

"Except that the place they'll be crawling over is Dallas, Texas. That's the point we asked them to feed to. We'll use our own facilities to feed it here." He paused long enough to allow himself a faint smile. "Unfortunately, whoever did the electronics for this group is very good. Upon examining the device, our technicians determined that it had been fitted with an anti-tampering device. It may even be booby-trapped. At any rate, a direct feed is impossible, so we had to change the plan. As I understand it, Commander Stone has proposed actually broadcasting the bogus news story over the one station."

"That's correct," Stone said, taking up the commentary. "The station has agreed and the F.B.I. technicians are setting up right now. But, of course, the real issue is whether the president will authorize the story to go out even to a limited radio audience."

"How much of an audience could one station have on a Sunday night?" Saxon asked.

"No more than a couple thousand people," Stone said. "But there's no way of knowing who might be listening or how it might snowball if a reporter or public official picks up on it. I'm just hoping the president will see it as an acceptable risk."

"When will you hear?" Saxon inquired.

"By eight-forty-five," Stone said. Everyone in the room glanced up toward the clock. There were fourteen minutes left.

Saxon suddenly stood up and, without explanation, left the room.

Visibly annoyed, Stone waited until the marine guard had closed the door before continuing. He looked at Jones. "Howard, what's the latest on the reactor?"

Jones's tone became businesslike. "We've been able to determine something about the condition of the reactor by watching what little cross-plant instrumentation is available back aft and by analyzing steam samples. The temperature still seems to be a little low, which complicates the accident curves, but because of xenon burnout it is drifting back up. Otherwise, she seems to be hanging right in there. It certainly could be worse."

"Yes, it could." Stone was aware that most of the group was anxiously watching the clock, but he pressed on in an effort to divert their attention. "There is some good news for a change. Commander Turnich thinks he's solved the problem of how to cut the power cables."

"I hope we have," the UDT man said. "Although you might not think it's such good news, Captain Reynolds. It means punching a hole below the waterline."

Reynolds didn't even blink. "Commander," he said slowly, "we've been talking about what we're going to do to that poor ship for so many hours now, it doesn't even faze me anymore. If it means getting my ship back without having to resort to the gas, I'll take a coffee can and bail out the damn thing myself."

"That, at least, won't be necessary. We'd only use the underwater blast to cut the cables you're after, then seal off the penetrations almost immediately afterward." He stood and walked over to an enormous three-view diagram of the *Bremerton* that had been hung on the wall. "Let me explain what we've come up with."

At that moment Saxon reentered the room and took his seat without speaking to anyone. After a moment Turnich continued. "According to the engineers, the power cables lie somewhere between here and here," he said, indicating a twenty-five-foot stretch on the starboard side. "What we propose doing is blowing open about a thirty-foot-long incision just below the waterline at that same spot—below the waterline because we need the mass of the water to direct the full force inward. Ironically, the fact that this part of the hull is heavily armored works to our advantage. When this type of steel shatters, it has a tremendously destructive force. With properly shaped charges and the correct fusing, the shrapnel will slice right through that compartment like a runaway saw blade, cutting the cables and disabling the reactor." He glanced then toward the marine corps officer. "Now, to provide access for your team, Major, we'll simultaneously blow a six-foot hole up here at the third deck level where we believe the hostages are being held." He walked back to his seat. "That's really about all there is to it. Are there any questions?"

"I have one," Saxon said. "In the wake of these explosions, aren't the terrorists likely to kill the hostages?"

Stone answered the question. "That's a possibility, but we have a couple of things working in our favor. First, I understand that because of the reactor scram there will be a great deal of confusion in the control room, alarms, lights flashing, that sort of thing. Isn't that right, Howard?"

"It'll be chaotic," Jones said.

"Second," Stone continued, "Major O'Dell has studied the ship's plans and thinks he can have his men at the control room door within ten seconds. He'll be briefing you on that in a few minutes. The point is, unlike the gas, this plan takes care of the reactor and still gives us some chance at a rescue."

Reynolds spoke next, his tone skeptical. "Commander Turnich, is it really that easy to punch a hole in the side of a ship?"

Turnich answered with complete seriousness. "Captain, given enough plastic and the time to set it, my people could slice up the *Bremerton* like a piece of bologna and have it land in that parking lot out there." Then he added with a little grin, "Now you know why you're not supposed to let anyone get close."

Stone was about to ask for further questions when the

guard stuck his head in the door. "Telephone, Commander Stone. It's the CNO."

Stone looked around uneasily. "Well, I guess this is our answer." He turned to the major. "Why don't you go ahead with your part of the discussion. We might as well be optimistic."

Three minutes later the door opened again and Stone walked through. From the look on his face there was no question what the decision had been. He was beaming from ear to ear, holding both thumbs up in the imperial gesture. "Get going, Chambers," he said. "You've got a news broadcast to make!"

The table exploded with smiles of relief. Jones let out a cheer and tossed his pencil into the air. Morton leaned over and pounded the *Bremerton*'s captain on the back. Even Rogers, while maintaining his composure, seemed to let out a deep sigh.

Stone had to raise his voice to be heard. "Gentlemen, I think we ought to adjourn temporarily. If anyone has a sudden desire to listen to the news, he's welcome to join me."

As the room emptied out, Stone, his face still flushed, pulled Saxon aside. "You know, the CNO told me a funny story just a minute ago," he said. "It seems that just as the president was making up his mind, he got a call from a former skipper of his, an ol' guy by the name of Rickover. Now you wouldn't know anything about that, would you, Saxon?"

"Me?" the man from naval reactors said with a perfectly straight face. "I'm only an observer."

Two hours later Stone ran into trouble from a different quarter. He was seated in the com van listening to the end of one of the phony news broadcasts when Chief Morton burst in. "We've got a problem," Morton said, pointing back over his shoulder to where two marines were literally carrying in a struggling young woman.

When she saw Stone's officer insignia she stopped struggling and stood erect with her jaw jutting out. "I demand that you order these goons to let me go."

"I'm sorry, sir," the chief stammered. "She tried to walk right past the guards down at the head of the pier. I don't know how the hell she got that far."

"I'm a reporter!" the woman stormed. "I've got a press badge that says I can go through police lines. Now if you don't let me go you're going to regret it!"

"Let her go," Stone told the guards. "But don't go away." Then he looked at the woman. She was very tall and a little willowy to be taking on a pair of two-hundred-pound marines. Her hair, which was in a state of disarray, was brown, as were her eyes. She wore an expensive tan suit and carried a huge leather purse looped over one shoulder. He decided that in something other than an attack pose she was probably pretty.

"How the hell did you get out here?" he asked. "You could have gotten yourself shot."

"I walked."

"Through our checkpoints?"

"Some people have more respect for the press," she said, turning to glare caustically at the marines.

"Chief," Stone growled, "find out who let her through, and then kick somebody's ass."

Morton saluted and left. Then Stone turned back to the woman. "I'm sorry, Miss . . ."

"Nolan. Judith Nolan, *Long Beach Press-Telegram*."

"Well, I'm sorry Judith Nolan, *Long Beach Press-Telegram*, but you've gotten yourself in one hell of a bind."

"What's going on out here?"

Stone held himself in check. "A drill, that's all. You should have checked with the public information office."

"Some drill," she said. "I could see all the flashers from the newsroom. It looks like the end of the world."

"The flashers?"

"The flashing lights, on the emergency vehicles. You can see them from all over the city at night."

"Oh, for Christ's sake!" Stone exploded. He yelled for a messenger and told him to have every emergency flasher turned off.

"Tell me what's going on," the woman demanded. "Is it a nuclear accident? Is that what it is?"

Stone did a poor job of concealing his surprise. "What are you talking about?"

"That's it, isn't it? Something's happened on the *Bremerton*. I know it's atomic-powered."

"You know an awful lot," Stone said suspiciously, suddenly remembering that he wasn't supposed to be buying cover stories wholesale.

"I'm a reporter, remember? I've been covering this city for two years now. I probably know more about what goes on on this base than you do."

"Where's your press card?"

He took it from her and passed it to one of the guards. "Ask your sergeant to call the paper and check on this person. And get a description."

"You can't take that!"

He ignored her remark. "As I was saying before, there's a little problem here."

Instantly she pulled out her note pad. "Was I right? Is it an atomic accident? When did it happen?"

"I'm talking about you. You're the problem."

"Look," she said with rehearsed logic, "if you won't talk to me, I'll have to get the story someplace else. Wouldn't you rather I got it straight?"

"There's not going to be any story," Stone said flatly.

"You can't throw me out."

"I'm not throwing you out. I'm arresting you."

"What!"

Stone looked past her at the remaining guard. "I want you to escort Miss Nolan back to the base security office and hold her under constant surveillance. No phone calls, no communication with anyone. And take someone with you." He looked at the furious woman and added, "On second thought, take two men. And use whatever force is necessary. I'll get a matron over there as fast as I can, but until then don't even let her go to the head alone."

"Yes sir," the marine said. He put his hand gently on her elbow, but she jerked it away savagely.

"You can't arrest me," she growled. "I have a perfect right to be here. You have no authority."

Stone spoke in a low voice. "Listen to me, Miss Nolan, because I'm only going to say this once. You have stumbled onto something that's more important than you could possibly imagine. Now you may be right about my authority, but at this moment I could care less. You will, I repeat, *will* do exactly as I tell you to, or I will order you physically restrained."

"You don't scare me," the woman said in a somewhat subdued voice.

"I'm not trying to scare you. I'm just telling you how it is."

Flushing with anger she pulled herself up to her full height. "Whatever's going on around here, it can't be more important than the freedom of the press. You're violating my rights."

Stone looked at her coldly. He was no longer amused. "I'll tell you something, lady. The last thing in the world I'm worried about now is your rights. If I thought it was necessary to keep you from blowing the lid off of this thing, I wouldn't hesitate for one second to have you shot. Dead." He looked at the guard. "Now get her out of here."

But the woman wasn't quite finished. Before the marine could get her out of the door she pulled loose and whirled on Stone. "What's your name?" she demanded.

"Davis Stone," he answered without expression.

"Okay, Davis Stone, now let me tell *you* something. Before I'm finished with you, you'll wish you had shot me."

The corners of his mouth lifted in a weary smile. "Lady, I just hope I'm around to see it."

"Commander Stone, come quick!" the messenger yelled from the steps of the van.

Stone jerked awake in his chair and shot a look at the clock, blinking hard to clear the blurriness. It was 11:43.

"What is it?" he asked, flying out of the doorway.

"The chief, sir, he's down by the after gangway. He said to come quick!"

Stone arrived breathless to find Morton with a group of UDT men talking excitedly over his handie-talkie.

"What's happening?"

"Commander Turnich and a couple of his men are around the other side in a boat, checking out how to rig their charges."

"Yes, so?"

"Evidently the coxswain accidentally bumped the *Bremerton*'s hull."

"Bumped? What does bumped mean? Hard enough for them to hear?"

"Hard, sir. I think he really rammed her."

"Oh, Christ."

⟋ 33

The collision sent a strong tremor reverberating through the ship accompanied by a loud, echoing clang and a series of tiny aftershocks that took several seconds to die out.

"What the hell was that?" Maurer asked Weston in a startled whisper. He had been dozing since eleven o'clock under a rotation system agreed upon by the three of them.

"I don't know. It felt like we got tapped a pretty good one." The alarm in his voice was noticeable.

Their captors were alarmed even more. Leggett had been spelled by the woman and was settled on the deck at her feet, his back resting against the EOOW's desk. White was seated at the reactor control panel poring over a thick binder of schematic diagrams. The man, Karl, was still seated beside the girl along the back bulkhead. At the sudden sound all three leaped to their feet, weapons at the ready, glancing at one another in bewilderment.

Almost immediately the woman started for the door, but

before she could get there Givens raced in.

"What happened?" the woman demanded.

"I'm not sure," he said. "Something hit the ship, something pretty big." He jerked his head in the direction of the starboard side. "I was standing over by the coffeepot. I must have been right next to where it hit. The noise would like to've made me deaf."

"Where's Hall?"

"I dunno, I guess still over on the other side."

"Nettles?"

"With him, I guess."

Her mouth formed into a tight, thin line and she looked around nervously. "I wonder what the hell those bastards are up to?" For a moment she appeared indecisive. Then, indicating that White should follow her, she headed toward the door, stopping when she reached Givens. "White and I will go check things out," she said, talking quickly. "You stay here and help Schmidt and Leggett keep an eye on these people. I want them all moved down to that end, away from the door." She pointed toward the far corner. Then she looked at Fox and Dills. "You two help move the old lady."

As soon as she was gone Givens moved across the room to a spot in front of the electrical panel. "You heard her," he snapped, waving the machine gun. "Let's get going."

Maurer slowly climbed to his feet, silently cursing the luck that had put the armed man directly in the way of the one place they wanted to reach. He used the pretext of wiping his face with his sleeve to whisper to Weston.

"You go ahead, I'll try to hang back. Maybe one of us can get a shot at the breaker trip."

"Check," his friend said, barely moving his lips. "Good luck."

Maurer was concentrating so hard on Givens he didn't notice the trouble Fox was having with the mother until he heard her hysterical screams. Inexplicably, the Southerner's awkward attempt to coax her up had suddenly transformed her from catalepsy to shrieking madness. When Maurer looked over she was already on her feet, clawing at the steel

206

bulkhead and raving unintelligibly. Her eyes, huge with terror, rolled in their sockets, and spittle dribbled from her mouth. Her body shook with uncontrollable spasms. And the more Fox tried to comfort her, the more frightened and panicky she became.

Givens's expression grew ugly, and he roared at them to shut her up. The girl, pale and bewildered herself, took her mother by the shoulders and tried to pull her away from the wall. At that moment, perhaps in response to Givens's voice or even to the touch of her own daughter, the woman went totally berserk. With the strength of a madwoman she twisted free of the girl's grasp and shoved Fox aside, sending him and Karl sprawling to the deck like a pair of dominoes. Then, by blind instinct, she bolted for the door.

"No, stop her!" the girl cried, but before Maurer could move the woman was past him and into the entryway. Then it was Givens who yelled, telling Leggett to get out of the way as he brought the machine gun barrel up in a deadly line with the fleeing woman.

That's when Weston made his move. It wasn't clear to Maurer whether his friend was trying to prevent the giant from shooting the woman or was going for the trip. All he saw was the man lunge in Givens's direction, then jerk horribly as the weapon erupted three times in rapid succession at point-blank range, ripping apart his chest in an explosion of blood.

Even as Weston fell dead to the floor, his slayer was realigning the gun for another shot at the mother, but by then the snarling girl was on him, swinging a heavy red spanner wrench she'd ripped from its bulkhead mountings.

Like the flight recorder of a crashing jetliner, Maurer's brain continued to function despite the numbness that gripped him in the seconds following Weston's murder. It faithfully recorded the girl's movements, as it recorded the specks of blood splattered across the polished top of the EOOW's desk, the smell of human excrement, and the taste of vomit in Maurer's own throat. It even brought up an image of the unguarded breaker trip handle and calculated, almost with a will of its own, his chances of reaching it. But suddenly his rationality gave way to something much deeper, much more primitive and compelling, a rage so complete that any notion of the trip or the girl or even his own vincibility was wiped from his consciousness. With a strangled scream, he leaped for Givens.

He would have reached him had it not been for the desk, but that obstacle allowed Leggett the fraction of a second he needed to tackle him and pull him crashing to the deck.

Maurer fought viciously, half blinded by tears, without any thought of technique or strategy. Leggett was a powerful man in superb condition, but he was no match for the madness that drove Maurer. Within seconds Maurer was on top with his fingers around the man's throat. It was only his consuming preoccupation with Givens that kept him from choking Leggett to death.

Maurer staggered to his feet, leaving Leggett lying on the deck gasping for air. The killing urge had taken over. His breath burned in his lungs. Driven by the wild pounding of his heart, the blood surged through his veins and a deafening roar filled his brain. He felt at that instant that nothing less than death could stop him from avenging Weston's murder. He was so possessed that he didn't hear Fox's frantic warning or see Schmidt's rigid open hand lash out from across the corner of the desk to deliver an expert chop at the base of his skull.

Andrea was cautiously inspecting the lower level when she heard the distant sound of gunfire. Leaving White far behind she dashed up two decks and through the open door of the control room. The sight that greeted her made her skin crawl.

One of the crewmen lay face down in a pool of blood, and sprawled across him was a second crewman, the one who had fought them earlier. Schmidt was bent over that one, his fingers pressed to the side of the man's neck. Givens was nearby, slumped over the front of the desk, holding the back of his head and groaning. She could see the blood seeping between his fingers. Leggett stood near the back wall, visibly shaken, holding a gun on the two remaining crewmen. The mother and daughter were nowhere in sight.

"What happened?" she asked breathlessly.

Schmidt replied without looking up. "This one is okay. Givens killed the other."

"Where are the women?"

"Gone." Schmidt rose to face her. "Both of them got out."

"Jesus Christ! What about you, Givens? What the hell happened to you?"

He lifted his head and looked at her. Hatred burned in his eyes and his face was twisted with pain and rage. "That fuckin' bitch got me," he snarled.

"Who?"

"The girl, she came up behind me."

Andrea slumped into the reactor operator's chair. "God, what a mess. I don't believe you all could be so stupid."

She sat staring silently at the dead man until Givens suddenly lurched away from the desk and staggered toward her. "Are you okay?" she asked, seeing the strange, tortured look on his face.

He continued past her toward the door. "I will be."

"Stop! Where are you going?"

Givens kept walking. "I'm gonna find that cunt."

It was Schmidt who shouted next. "Hold it, Givens. No more. I will shoot!" The .45 automatic came up in his hand.

Schmidt had made his decision. The shell was in the chamber, the hammer was back. He locked his elbows and exhaled half a breath and chose the spot between Givens's shoulder blades. When the man got one step from the door his finger slowly began to squeeze the trigger. The well-oiled mechanism moved smoothly; he could almost feel it approaching the release point. Another fraction of a millimeter more.

But suddenly Andrea was standing, screaming, directly in his line of fire. Had the woman leaped up a hundredth of a second later, he would have blown her head off. Had Schmidt been less steady, her cry might have caused him to jerk that last tiny bit. Had he been only slightly more committed to the act of killing . . .

"No, Karl, don't!" she screamed, and somehow, with a feat of muscular control so great it caused him physical pain, he stopped his finger in that final instant.

Monday, January 14

34

The second hand of the wall clock swept past the twelve, and then Monday was nine minutes old. There were less than sixty seconds until the moment Stone had determined would be the decision point—ten after midnight—exactly fifteen minutes since the shots had been fired. The red phone sat squarely in the center of the tiny desk; beside it the recorder stood threaded and ready. But Stone had no hope left. In his guts he knew that this time there would be no telephone calls, no calm reassurances. Whatever had happened down there after the collision had irreversibly altered the situation.

During the first minutes of chaos following the gunfire, the order to inject the gas hung on Stone's lips like bitter hemlock. The reports from the two listening posts situated in the spaces directly above and forward of the reactor control room had told of a woman's screams, a burst of shots, then more yelling and finally silence. Immediately Stone had put the injection teams on alert. Only the constant reports that there was no change in the reactor's status, received from Jones who'd rushed down to the aft plant, kept him from issuing the command.

He told himself over and over during those minutes that his hesitation was justified, that the CNO's condition of "imminent destruction" was not satisfied, that the rescue was still a realistic option. To assuage his conscience he invented a list of decision rules—one more shot, more screaming, the first hint of change in the condition of the reactor—if any of those occurred *then* he would give the signal. But the cold, rational part of him knew that he'd already violated the spirit, if not the exact letter, of his orders.

"Your men in position, Major?" he asked quietly as the second hand crossed the three. In the com van with him were Major O'Dell, Saxon, and Morton. Captain Reynolds had chosen to return to the *Bremerton* for the final act.

"They're loaded onto the tugs and ready to go," O'Dell said.

"Chief, what's the status of the UDTs?"

"Commander Turnich says they're in the water," Morton replied.

Since nine o'clock the rescue plan had been revised and discussed and revised again, but there had not been time for a rehearsal. Turnich, O'Dell, the rad com teams and corpsmen volunteers were all working from a plan that had never gotten beyond the chalk board in the command trailer conference room.

Stone waited until the second hand moved past the six, then spoke again. "I am assuming full responsibility for this decision and all its consequences, but I feel obligated to formally advise you all that this plan has not been approved by a higher authority and could, in fact, be construed as violating prior instructions."

It was a fact of which everyone in the van was profoundly aware. O'Dell answered for the others. "Noted," he said simply.

The red phone remained mute as the second hand once more touched the twelve. Stone breathed deeply and reached for the open line to Jones.

"This is Stone. What is the status of the reactor?"

"Still no change."

"Okay," Stone said calmly. "We're going in."

"Understood," Jones answered.

Stone stood up in the cramped quarters and the others followed suit. "Major O'Dell," he said in a clear voice, "commence the rescue operation."

"Aye aye, sir," O'Dell responded.

"And good luck."

"Thank you, Commander. Good luck to you."

⟋ 35

It was as if there were two Cynthia Spencers, a confused and terrified one for whom the labyrinth of pipes and machinery was a steamy hell, and a watchful and calculating one for whom it was a deadly but somehow fascinating puzzle.

The latter Cynthia knew something of ships, assorted bits of knowledge accumulated during dependents' cruises and aboard navy transports, even something of engine rooms—little more than faint recollections of dirty white lagging and rusted metal flanges, but a starting point, a recognizable piece with which to begin putting the puzzle together. More important, she knew something of the *Bremerton*, a rudimentary knowledge gained by studying the damage-control diagrams mounted on the wall of the control room and listening to the discussions of her captors.

The first Cynthia felt as though she'd fled into a nightmare. Everything around her was hot—the walls, the railings, the deck beneath her bare feet; the air itself was like the blast from a furnace. The noise was deafening, a confusion of shrieking turbines from someplace below her, the roar of the main steam lines just overhead and all around the infernal hiss of escaping steam. The pain in her side had grown until each breath was a greater agony than the one before, and there were times when it seemed that it would be better not to breathe at all. The sweat that soaked her flimsy gown into near transparency stank of fear, and she had to keep her fists constantly clenched to control the trembling.

The latter Cynthia went on plotting and replotting her options. The first searched frantically for some dark hole in which to hide. And ironically, it was she, the frightened and bewildered seventeen-year-old, who found her mother—partially by luck, but more because a common panic had led them along similar paths in their flight.

The woman was lying face-down on the hot steel deck, half hidden behind some huge piece of silent machinery. Over the awful noise Cynthia could not hear her sobs, but she could see the spasms that racked her body. At that instant the battle between the two Cynthias reached its climax.

For a moment it seemed that the pain and hopelessness would prevail. She sank to her knees, gently shifted the woman until her head lay in her lap, and began to cry. But at the sound of her own sobbing, felt rather than heard over the ceaseless roar, she was gripped by a rage that overwhelmed even the pain. Suddenly, as quickly as they had started, the tears stopped and her eyes filled with a look of defiance. They might die, she and her mother, but they would not die this way, mewing like a pair of helpless kittens. It was on that basis, perhaps nothing more than pride, that the battle was decided. The other Cynthia, the father's daughter, had won.

"Mother!" she shouted, taking the woman by the shoulders and shaking her roughly. "Can you hear me, Mother?"

The woman's eyes came open, and she looked around in wild confusion, her mouth moving soundlessly.

"It's Cynthia, Mother. Can you hear me?"

"Cynthia?" the woman moaned, "What? . . ."

"Listen to me. We have to get out of here. Do you think you can walk?" She spoke slowly, exaggerating the movements of her mouth as if she were talking to a deaf woman.

The mother struggled weakly onto one elbow. "Where are we?" she asked, her voice rasping and thick with fear.

"I can't explain now, but we have to move. We have to find a better place to hide until I can figure a way out. Can you walk?"

The authority in Cynthia's voice seemed to penetrate the woman's bewilderment. "I . . . I think so."

Cynthia nodded and then carefully raised her head to survey the room. If her earlier calculations were correct they were on the third deck, port side. On her right was the door through which she had come, the only door, as it appeared. The sloping steel wall across the room was the hull of the ship. The reactor lay beyond the wall directly behind her. Some of the machinery she recognized—the piping and valves, of course, and to her left three machines that looked like giant air compressors. The huge machine beside her bore a brass label identifying it as the #1 M-G Set, but she had no idea of its purpose.

And if her earlier calculations were correct they were also trapped there. Beyond the doorway there were three ways to go. One ladder went up to the hatch leading to second deck; it was sealed off. Another ladder went down to the so-called upper level, which, from what she had overheard, was occupied by still more terrorists. The third alternative, a narrow passage to the right, led directly back to the control room. For the time being, at least, the only thing she could think of was to find a hiding place, and so she searched until she spotted one, in the back corner next to the hull—a tall gray double door cabinet big enough to hold both of them.

Glancing one last time in the direction of the doorway she hauled the woman to her feet and half dragged her toward the cabinet. The distance couldn't have been more than thirty feet, but in that suffocating noise and heat the move seemed to take an eternity. At one point the woman smashed her foot against a machinery mount and fell to the deck, clutching her bloodied toe and writhing in pain. A few feet further on she managed to grab hold of an overhead pipe and refused to let go until Cynthia literally pried her fingers free.

When they finally arrived, breathless and soaked with sweat, the woman was barely conscious. Cynthia let her crumple to the floor and reached for the cabinet handle. It turned a quarter of an inch and stuck. She tried it again, swearing violently, but it refused to budge.

"My God, it's locked!" she cried aloud. She'd anticipated finding it full of equipment, but never had she considered the

217

possibility that it might be locked.

Fighting to control her panic she carefully inspected the smooth metal sides and ran her hand along the grimy top edge, praying that she would find a key, knowing with sick certainty that she would not. Then she spotted the laminated card that was neatly taped above the handle.

!!! HANDS OFF !!!

it said in red typed letters,

> These tools are for the use of B Division personnel. All others must obtain the key from the Plant LPO.

"Shit!" she blurted, savagely jerking at the unyielding handle with both hands. "Shit, shit, shit!"

Then, from somewhere behind her, she heard a laugh that made her sick with horror. She whirled around and uttered a strangled little cry. Standing three feet away with an obscene sneer spread across his face was Givens.

"Too bad," he mocked. "You just can't seem to do anything right today, can you?" His face was pasty white and dripping sweat; the pupils of his eyes were narrowed into burning black points, and there was a slurring in his speech, as if one side of his mouth had been shot full of Novocain. But his hand was steady enough as it brought the gun into line with her body.

"You . . . how? . . ." The words stuck in her parched throat.

"What's the matter, little girl? Surprised to see me? You didn't really think it would be this easy, did you?" He pointed to a mat of blood and hair at the back of his head. "It'll take more than some sneaky little cunt to wipe me out."

She answered him in a voice totally devoid of emotion. "So now you're going to kill me."

"Maybe, eventually. It depends on what you're worth to me alive."

She stared at him blankly.

"First I'm gonna collect for this." He again pointed to his head. "Then we'll go from there. If you're good enough maybe I won't kill you after all, maybe I'll keep you for a pet." The last statement seemed to strike him as being somehow uproariously funny.

She shuddered at the sound of his laughter. "Collect?"

"That's right, honey. Collect. You owe me, real big. And we both know there's only one thing a little girl like you has that's worth having, don't we?"

She blinked uncomprehendingly. "What are you talking about?"

"Pussy!" he shouted. "That's what I'm talking about, you stupid bitch. Good ol'-fashion pussy! If you don't know what it is you'd better learn fast, 'cause right now yours is the only thing that's keeping me from blowing your head off."

She stared at him with a rage that started in her guts and grew until she could not contain it. "Go ahead and kill me!" she screamed. "Prove what a big man you are. I'd rather be dead than have you touch me. Come on, shoot, before I puke all over you!"

For an instant it seemed as if he would. His eyes jerked in their sockets; his sneer became a twisted snarl that showed his white gums. But then the moment passed, and to her astonishment he began to laugh again.

"Nice try, honey, but it ain't gonna be that easy." The sneer returned to his face. "So you're not gonna let me touch you, huh? I'll tell you something. Before I get through with you, you're gonna be touched in places you never even thought of."

"I'll see you in hell first," she screamed, slowly backing away, coiling herself up for one last desperate flight.

"Go ahead, run," he sneered. "But first you'd better say goodbye to your mama here." He moved the gun so fast the motion was a blur. One instant it was pointed at her, the next it was pointed at her mother's head.

Cynthia froze, too horrified to speak.

"Go ahead," he taunted. "I won't stop you." He inched the weapon forward until its muzzle was pressing against the woman's temple.

"My God," Cynthia gasped. "Don't!"

"No? Why not? I thought you wanted me to shoot."

"Please," she begged. "For God's sake!"

"Come on, smart mouth. You can do better than 'please.' Tell me why I shouldn't blow your mama's brains out."

"What do you want?" she screamed, tears streaming down her face.

His sneer broadened into the ugliest expression she had ever seen, the face of the devil himself. "You know what I want," he snarled. "The question is, are you gonna deliver?"

She shook so badly she could hardly control it, not out of fear, but out of a revulsion more powerful than any feeling she'd ever known. She wanted to piss and vomit at the same time. She wanted to scream out the words that clogged her throat. *Sick vile ugly freak pig prick!* She wanted to tear out those mocking eyes and squeeze them until they burst. But then she looked at her mother lying moaning on the floor, too mad to know that her life hung in the balance, too weak to care even if she knew. A final tear rolled down to the corner of her mouth. "All right," she rasped, "I'll do whatever you want."

From that moment on she was numb, without sensation, without emotion, and without will. She endured his insults and submitted to his touch, and when he ordered her to kneel before him she obeyed. "Now," she heard him say, "let's see if that big mouth of yours is good for anything else." And when she saw his hand move to the zipper of his bulging fly, she knew she would do even that. But then the room exploded.

It was Givens's left hand that had torn away the girl's garment and fondled her breasts and groped between her legs. His right hand continued to hold the machine gun against the woman's head. And it was that right hand that Schmidt watched, oblivious to all else, patient in the knowledge that it would move.

It did, at the moment Givens fumbled with his zipper—not much, but enough to pull the weapon off line. And when it moved, Schmidt blew it off, as simply as that, without warning and without compunction. One instant the hand was there, the next instant it was not.

The girl screamed and Givens spun around, flinging blood everywhere, his eyes popping, his face a mask of rage. Snarling like a wounded animal he charged at Schmidt, but he got only two steps before the German calmly checked to be sure the girl was safely out of his line of fire and then shot him squarely in the midde of the chest.

From beginning to end the violence lasted ten seconds. When it was over Schmidt ran to the girl and lifted her to her feet. For a long moment she just stared at him without recognition, her eyes glazed over, her body limp in his arms. Then suddenly she tensed and her eyes grew wide. "That man. He ... he ... " Her jaw began to tremble and she sobbed uncontrollably.

For a long time he stood there stroking her hair and murmuring assurances while she cried in his arms. When she finally quieted he brushed the hair from her face and kissed her on the forehead. Then he spoke to her in a quiet voice.

"Cynthia, listen to me. We have to get you and your mother to a safe place. Do you think you can do that?"

"My God! Mother! Is she okay?" she tried to twist free but he held her firmly.

"She is all right," he said, "Please, there is no time. The others may come. I want you to put your dress on and help me get your mother to safety. Now can you do that?"

The girl brushed away her tears with the back of her hand and nodded.

Schmidt squeezed her arm affectionately and bent down to retrieve the torn gown. It was that tiny act of gallantry that saved his life.

The bullet from the dying Givens's hidden pistol was

meant for the middle of Schmidt's back. Instead, because he moved in that final second, it entered at a point just above his right hip, deflected off his bottom rib, shattering the bone, and exited below his shoulder blade. Schmidt pitched forward, whirling and firing as he fell, getting off two shots before he crashed, groaning, on the deck. He need not have bothered. Givens was dead before the first bullet reached him.

The girl saw the blood soaking through the back of Schmidt's coveralls and fell on him, sobbing.

"No!" the German said, grimacing in pain. "I am not hurt badly. You must take your mother and hide yourselves. There is a space between the ship's side and the back of the cabinet. It will be safe there."

"I won't leave you," the girl said, shaking her head.

"They must not find you. I will be okay."

"No!" she said, stubbornly. "I won't go unless you come, too. You need me to take care of you."

Schmidt looked up and saw the determined set of her jaw. "All right," he said, "I will come in a moment, but only if you go right now."

"Promise?"

The grimace softened a bit. "I promise."

36

The door of the communications van flew open and Admiral Rogers burst in, followed by his marine orderly and one of Stone's own flustered guards.

"What the devil's going on?" Rogers demanded. "It looks like the Inchon Landing out there."

Stone sat at the desk holding a telephone in each hand. One linked him to Jones in the aft plant, the other to the leader of the injection team. In front of him was a hastily rigged television monitor providing pictures of the activities out on the pier. Without taking his eyes from the screen he waved his guard away and spoke to Rogers.

"We've begun the rescue operation."

"You knew I wanted to be informed when Washington approved the plan. Why didn't you call me?"

Stone shook his head. "Washington didn't approve it."

The admiral's mouth fell open. "Have you lost your mind? You can't do this!"

"I am doing it," Stone said calmly. "In my opinion the situation warrants it." He quickly summarized the events of the past twenty minutes.

When he was finished Rogers dismissed his orderly, pulled a chair close, and sat down. "Look, Stone," he said in a hurried, quiet voice, "I've been a naval officer for over thirty years. I tell you that only because I want you to know I've had to do my share of shitty things. Believe me, I know what you're going through, but you don't have any choice, man. Your orders are clear. And what's more, they make sense. Any second those people down there could set off that damn reactor. An hour ago maybe we could second-guess them, but now we don't know what they might do.

"To save twelve lives you're risking twelve thousand, or even ten times that many. I know it's a crappy deal, but you *have* to use the gas." In a gentler tone he added, "If you want, I'll give the order."

"No sir," Stone said respectfully. "It's been over twenty minutes since the shooting. If they haven't screwed with the plant by now, there's no reason to believe they will before we can get to it."

"And what happens if you're wrong?"

"I'm not."

"Okay," Rogers persisted, "suppose you are right. Suppose your men do get in. Chances are you're going to lose as many men as you rescue—maybe more. Remember the *Mayaguez* incident? Thirty-eight marines died to save thirty-nine crewmen."

"Major O'Dell thinks he can pull it off."

"Okay," Rogers sighed, "this has gone on long enough. Commander Stone, I'm ordering you to call off the rescue and immediately issue the injection order."

Stone continued to watch the monitor. "I acknowledge your order, sir, but I must refuse to obey it."

There was neither surprise nor rancor in Rogers's reply. "Very well, then, I relieve you of your command." He called over his shoulder. "Corporal Hastings, Commander Stone is under arrest. Please escort him to the command trailer and await my instructions."

But instead of the orderly, Chief Morton appeared in the doorway. "Sorry, Admiral," he said with a great show of nervousness, "I had to send your orderly over to the trailer. That's what I came to tell you. You have a phone call in the conference room."

"Not now!" Rogers snapped.

"It's the White House, sir."

"The White House? All right, then, have it transferred over here."

"I'm sorry, Admiral, it's on the special line."

"Christ!" Rogers grumbled. "Very well, Chief, I'll be right there." Then to Stone, "For your sake I hope this call is to approve the rescue plan."

"I'll be here," Stone said calmly.

It was Morton who reappeared two minutes later.

"Where's Rogers?" Stone asked.

"I'm afraid he's been detained," Morton answered.

"Okay, Chief, what's this bullshit about calls from the White House and special lines?"

"No call," Morton said. "For that matter, no line."

Stone threw him a glance. "Where is he, Chief?"

"The conference room. His orderly, too."

"Can I expect him back?"

"Not unless he has an extra one of these in his pocket." Morton placed a heavy brass doorknob on the desktop.

Stone shook his head. "Morton, you're as crazy as I am. I just hope they give us adjoining cells at Leavenworth."

"Maybe I should call for reservations."

The long silence that followed was ended by a beeping noise on Morton's handi-talkie.

"Turnich reports that the charges are set," Morton announced. "He says he's ready to go."

"Very well," Stone answered. "Tell him I'm sending the boats now, and that I will give him a mark when they're in position."

Morton relayed the message. "Turnich acknowledges."

"Oookay," Stone said, taking a deep breath and leaning back in his chair. "Are you ready for this?"

"Ready," Morton replied.

◢ 37

"It's all over," Nettles announced. He had the tone of a man who, deep down, had never expected to succeed. He was standing with his elbows resting on the front edge of the EOOW's desk. The butt of a pistol hung casually out of his back pocket like a mechanic's wrench. A makeshift sweatband was fixed around his head. The zipper of his jumpsuit was open down to his navel, revealing his hairy chest glistening with sweat.

"It's not over," Andrea answered angrily. "We've still got the reactor. It's only seventeen after twelve. I'll call for the chopper just like nothing happened and we'll still be out of here by four o'clock."

"Just like nothing happened?" Nettles said incredulously. "In the first place those people out there aren't likely to agree to anything after all the fireworks that've gone on." A gray wool blanket had been used to cover Weston's body. He nodded toward it, unable to bring himself to actually look.

"In the second place, you wouldn't be able to produce the two hostages that were supposed to be your secret ace in the hole. And in the third place, your powder man, Givens, the key to this whole fucked-up mess, is missing in action."

"Givens will be back after he finds the women."

"Finds 'em? From what Leggett here tells me, Givens wasn't exactly going out on a search and rescue mission."

"He knows how important they are to this operation. He'll be all right."

"Not if Schmidt finds him."

"Givens can take care of himself."

"Yeah? So can Schmidt. Between those two I wouldn't be so quick to pick a winner."

"It'll be Givens," she pronounced. "I told you once, Schmidt's just not tough enough."

"Okay, lady," Nettles said, shaking his head. "Keep on dreamin'." He headed for the door.

"Where are you going?"

"I'm gonna go take a body count, do you mind? When I'm standing in shit, I like to know how deep it is."

Andrea knew better than to try to stop him. "All right, but get Hall to go with you. He's still on the upper level. And if you don't find anything in fifteen minutes, get back here."

"Sure," Nettles answered on his way out the door.

He did hunt down Hall and tell him to check the port side while he checked the starboard, but then he headed straight back to control equipment.

Poor, stupid broad, he thought, as he hefted himself up on the pipe and snapped down the door to his hidden chamber. She really believes she can still pull it off. And elephants can fly.

But then he smiled. In a way he wished, by some miracle, they would make it, just so they'd get his little surprise.

He climbed inside, pulled closed the door and lay in the dark, letting the cool air flow over his sweaty body. He tried to feel regret over Weston's death, over Maurer's injury, over the Spencer women, but somehow his thoughts kept returning to the two women who'd fucked him over, each in her own thorough way, and the one million dollars that would have set things right.

"Shit," he said aloud as a final comment.

At the end of the dream there was a grisly reality, so Maurer clung to the dream, as a child lingers in the warmth of his bed on a cold morning. Weston was sitting with a big grin on his face and his thumbs hooked under his belt and an old-style white hat pushed back on his head, tossing off one-liners like a stand-up comedian.

"Did I die good, or did I die good?"

"You died real good," Maurer heard himself say. "A fuckin' hero, you were."

"It's the training." Weston nodded with mock gravity. "There's no such thing as too much training."

Maurer started to answer when the dead man suddenly leaned forward and whispered conspiratorially, "You want to know something else?"

"What?" Maurer asked in a hushed voice, hypnotized by the blazing black eyes.

"Givens is dead."

Weston vanished and Maurer awoke to find himself sprawled out face-down in the corner of EOS. But the words were still there.

"Givens is dead," said a voice that he'd never heard before.

"Was it Schmidt?" It was the woman speaking.

"I don't know, I didn't see anyone. But I didn't look real hard either."

Maurer heard the woman reply with a barrage of questions. He tried to focus on her words but they were lost amid the painful hammering in his skull. He lay there without moving, trying to put the pieces together, wishing he could get back to the dream but knowing that it was gone forever.

He remembered with startling detail the moments before he had lost consciousness: the mother's flight, Weston's murder, the girl's assault on Givens, and his own violent spree. He remembered, too, the rage that had consumed him, but only reflectively, like the memory of some past pain; the feeling had gone like the dream.

He feigned unconsciousness and waited for the pounding in his head to subside. Eventually he was able to make out the four voices: the woman, White, Leggett, and the unknown man who had announced Givens's death. They were heatedly debating what to do next, with Leggett and the other man in favor of attempting some kind of escape and the woman and White arguing to stay with the plan. The three men were clearly agitated, their voices loud and sharp with anger, but the woman continued to speak with unnerving calm. It was she who finally proposed a compromise.

"Let's do this," Maurer heard her say. "Let's get all the crewmen moved down to upper level. Leggett, you and Hall can do that. White and I will call for the helicopter just as we planned. If they buy it, then we'll go ahead. If not, we'll try to get out through the bilges. Is that agreeable?"

There was a round of muttering which Maurer took as meaning assent.

"Okay," the woman said, "go ahead and get those two out of here."

"What about this one?" Leggett asked. Maurer fought the urge to stop breathing. Obviously he was "this one." The voice had come from directly above him. He lay perfectly still.

"Is he still out?"

A boot jammed into Maurer's ribs in an effort to turn him over. Maurer willed himself to remain completely limp, as heavy as a corpse, unfeeling even when his arm flopped over in the wake of his body to slam painfully against the bulkhead.

"Yeah, he's still out," was the verdict.

"Then leave him."

There was scuffling nearby as the crewmen, presumably Fox and Dills, were led away. Then he was alone with White and the woman.

After a long silence he heard White speak in a high, tense

voice. "Are you thinking about what you're going to say?"

"Say to whom?" The woman's voice seemed distant.

"When you call."

"I'm not going to call."

"What? But you said . . ."

"What I said was bullshit, to get Leggett and Hall out of here. There's no point in calling, there's no chance of going ahead with the plan. Givens is dead. Schmidt and the women are gone. Apparently that fucker Nettles, too. Just the four of us could never pull it off."

"Christ, Andrea, you're not going to give up?"

"Give up?" she yelled. "Did I say anything about giving up?"

"No, but . . ."

"Do you want to give up, Billy? Do you want to let those fascist bastards beat us?"

"Andrea, I . . ."

"We came here for one primary purpose, to strike a blow against imperialism so devastating that they'll never be able to recover. We can still do that, Billy. *You* can still do that!"

"The reactor." White's voice was strained with emotion.

"Exactly. The reactor. You must do it quickly, before the others come back!"

"Yes. Quickly."

Maurer, his heart pounding, could wait no longer. He lifted his head and looked. The woman was standing near the door. White was already out in the entryway, moving toward control equipment.

The woman called to White. "How will I know when to set off the explosives?"

White stopped and looked back. His face was a sickly white color. "There'll be all kinds of alarms, that's when. When you hear the horns." He started to turn back, but then, out of the corner of his eye, he saw Maurer watching. He grabbed the woman and pointed frantically. "He's awake! He knows!"

Instantly Maurer was on his feet, shaking off the wooziness and lunging toward the electrical panel. His hip smashed into the side of the EOOW's desk, and he crashed sideways into the empty operator's chair, but then he recovered and pulled himself back, groping now for the breaker trip that was only inches from his outstretched fingers.

Suddenly there was an explosion and it felt like a truck had slammed into his left shoulder, lifting him off his feet and flinging him back against the bulkhead. He couldn't breathe. There was no feeling at all in his left arm. He tried to grab the edge of the panel to drag himself up but it was slippery with blood. The room started to spin and everything went out of focus. He felt himself falling crazily. The last thing he saw was the woman's face grimacing over the barrel of her gun.

White quickly made the final hookup, working neatly despite the trembling of his hands and the sweat that stung his eyes and dripped off the end of his nose. When he finished he checked each connection twice, standing on a wooden stool so that he could see down into the top drawer of the rod control panel. Then he stepped down and took up the small aluminum control box.

He cradled the box in one arm and used his shirttail to wipe off the sweat and smudges, inspecting the array of dials and switches with intense pride. The components inside were the Navy's—a high-speed drive motor, a photo pulse generator, switches, cables, and connectors—all stolen at cautious intervals from the spare rod control drawers. Even the precision timer had been cannibalized from a piece of test gear. But the design was strictly his own.

Deftly he worked through the bank of switches, rearranging them to bypass the timer and go to the manual mode. Now only a single, small toggle switch was needed to begin the sequence.

White paused with his thumb poised against the lever, savoring the moment. His mind was filled with many thoughts, but nowhere among them was the concern that his device might not work. In a few seconds he would throw the switch and trigger what amounted to a reverse partial insertion. Instead of moving in, the control rods would move out of the core at a speed of nearly one hundred fifty inches per minute.

The results would be catastrophic. The rate of reactivity addition would exceed anything ever seen in a power reactor. The water in the coolant channels would almost instantly flash to steam, creating a water hammer that might well blow the top off the pressurizer and a pressure transient that would burst the tubes in the steam generators. Then the fuel plates would buckle and begin to melt, spewing their accumulations of deadly radioactive isotopes into the escaping steam and water. At two thousand degrees a zirconium-water explosion would rupture the pressure vessel itself. Within a matter of minutes the atmosphere would be poisioned with an ever-growing cloud of the most toxic substances known to man.

White's thumb tensed, ready, almost eager, but before it could move the ship was rocked by a tremendous explosion that jarred the box from his hands and sent him staggering back against one of the power supply cabinets. The blast had occurred directly below him, leaving him completely deaf, but it made no difference; the only thought in his mind was that single little switch. Frantically he scrambled on his hands and knees toward the dangling box.

He reached it and his thumb found the lever. He felt the resistance of the tiny spring. He pressed harder, to the release point, past it. And then, with an exquisite sense of victory, he felt the solid snap as it sprang closed.

But that was the last thing he felt. At that instant a second explosion blew open a six-foot hole in the side of the ship, not twenty feet from where he stood. The next instant a four-inch piece of the shattered hull pierced his brain.

The first explosion produced exactly the effect that had been predicted. A sheet of fragmented steel thirty feet long and six inches thick literally sliced across the fourth deck a foot from the overhead, cutting cables, air lines, steam pipes, nearly everything in its swath. By every rule of logic it should have cut the cables running from the number-one turbine generator to the rod control power supplies. And it would have, except that, for some reason long forgotten, those cables had been anchored to one of the few vertical stanchions in the compartment. Though the stanchion was badly damaged, the cables were untouched. The number-one reactor plant remained critical.

It wasn't until he saw the flakes of paint falling from the overhead that Maurer realized the explosions were not just in his mind. The first had shocked him into consciousness. By the second he had managed to grab hold of the electrical operator's chair and drag himself to his knees. When it came, he was barely able to keep from being thrown back down to the deck. His left shoulder was a mass of pain, his vision was blurred, and he felt too weak to even lift his head.

But then the alarms went off, and six years' worth of conditioned responses took over. He glanced at the reactor control panel and gasped in disbelief. Virtually every meter was pegged at the high end. Pressures were above twenty-five hundred pounds, temperatures were over six hundred degrees, and the needle on the power meter had risen past the end of the scale. Alarm lights flashed red all across the panel: high power, high rate, high temperature, high pressure, power-to-flow, primary reliefs.

The woman was standing nearby, staring at the chaotic panel with an expression that was at once terrified and enraptured. In one hand she held some kind of small transmitter; in the other she cradled the carbine, but both were forgotten as she gazed open-mouthed at the bewildering display.

Suddenly he remembered the breaker trip. With the last of his strength he began dragging himself to his feet. His left arm was useless. He would have to reach across with his right. It was his last chance. If he fell he knew he wouldn't have the strength to try again. He willed his right knee up onto the chair and leaned forward, trying desperately to focus on the correct switch, fighting to keep his balance.

Then, out of the corner of his eyes he saw the woman whirl around and raise her weapon. He was still too far from the trip, he wouldn't make it. He squeezed his eyes shut and braced himself for the shock, but the shots that came weren't from her gun. From out of nowhere a soldier burst into the room, firing as he came, spinning the woman around with his first shot and knocking her backwards with two more in the center of her chest.

She was dead before the sound of the gunfire stopped echoing in the control room. But by that time Maurer had made his final, desperate lunge, twisting the trip handle until he saw the little OPEN flag pop up. Then he slid unconscious to the deck.

Friday, January 18

✒ 38

Just after lunch on Friday, Commander Jones breezed into Maurer's hospital room, pulled a chair up to the head of the bed, and sat down. "It's official," he announced with a fat grin.

Maurer answered with a scowl. He was sitting up with his left arm sticking straight out in a bulky cast that covered half his left side. Before dawn on Monday the surgeons had spent four hours removing a .30-caliber bullet from his shoulder and repairing his shattered collarbone. Afterward they concluded that, except for a slight loss of mobility in the joint, he would suffer no permanent disability. They had failed to mention short-term suffering, which, at the moment, included a good deal of pain and itching. He was in no mood for riddles. "What's official?" he asked.

Jones refused to lose his good humor. "You're a hero, my boy, I've got it in writing." He pulled several pages from his briefcase and flipped to the last one. "These are the preliminary findings of the Naval Reactors investigating team. The details of this thing are still classified, by the way, so officially you haven't heard any of this."

"If we just skip it, I really won't have heard it," Maurer said.

Jones ignored him and began to read. " 'Pending a detailed physical inspection of the core, it is our opinion that the operator's quick and innovative response prevented core damage of a far more serious nature than that which occurred. While it is true that the roll-in of control rods 1, 2, 5, and 6 significantly mitigated the severity of the transient—' "

Maurer perked up. "Four rods rolled in? What the hell caused that?"

"Their SCRs blew out as soon as the high-speed drive came on."

"Ah ha!" Maurer said. "Didn't I tell you those suckers were gonna pop?"

"And thank God they did," Jones said. "Now be quiet and listen to this, we're getting to the good part. 'While it is true that the roll-in of control rods 1, 2, 5, and 6 significantly mitigated the severity of the transient, the rapid rate of withdrawal of the remaining group-one control rods generated a net positive reactivity addition of extreme magnitude. Had the operator not acted when he did to interrupt power to the scram magnets, it is unquestionable that there would have followed an accident with the gravest consequences. The operator is to be most highly commended.' " Jones was beaming. "Now what do you think of that, Spiffo?"

Maurer frowned. "I think the credit should go to Fox, who thought of tripping the TG breaker, and to Weston who died trying to do it." Maurer had pretty much reconciled himself to the events of those sixteen hours, but Weston's death continued to intrude into his thoughts like a cold, dense fog.

Jones was undeterred. "They deserve a share of the credit, that's for sure, but you, my boy, you're the one who got the job done. And I'll be damned if I'll let you weasel out of an awards ceremony."

Maurer was both pleased and embarrassed. To change the subject, he asked for the latest word on the reactor.

"Still a mess," Jones said. "When did we talk last?"

"Wednesday."

"Okay, well, now they think the meltdown was between ten and fifteen percent. That's down some from the initial estimates. The bubble in the pressure vessel is still giving us fits but we may get it collapsed by late tonight. That leak in the primary is apparently a ruptured D-P cell sensing line. It's got the reactor compartment so contaminated it'll be a month before we can start cleaning up. The last radiation reading I saw for the compartment was two thousand REM. In addition to all that, we've got hydrogen coming out of the woodwork; more than half our steam generator tubes were blown out, and most of the secondary system is crapped up." Jones sighed wearily. "Basically, it's the shits."

Maurer nodded sympathetically. "I read a little about it in the papers, as much as you can trust them to keep their facts straight. So it looks like she didn't do so good, huh?"

"Who?"

"The reactor."

"Are you kidding? The engineers are having orgasms over how well it held up. The best guess is that some design specs were exceeded by a factor of ten. They estimate the pressure hit thirty-nine hundred pounds—that's eleven hundred *psi* above hydro pressure. I think you could say that was doing good."

"I guess you could," Maurer said, and he went on to question Jones about details for the better part of an hour. It was nearly two o'clock before the engineer rose to leave.

"Oh, by the way," Maurer said, "Davis Stone tells me you took on the big brass to keep them from doing the nerve gas number."

Jones gave an awkward shrug. "Stone's the one who really put his ass on the line. And now they're taking turns kicking it."

"So I hear," Maurer said. "But getting back to you, according to Stone you made some pretty gooey speeches."

"All I remember is mentioning that it would be inconvenient to have to replace you guys on such short notice," Jones said, grinning.

"Thanks," Maurer said.

The engineer winked at him. "Any time."

It had been an exhausting week for Maurer. Debriefing sessions had started Tuesday morning and continued off and on, mostly on, until Thursday afternoon. Sometimes there were as many as fifteen people jammed into the room: engineers, officers, representatives from Naval Reactors, and always, at

Jones's insistence, a legal officer to protect Maurer's interests. "Right now the brass are trying to figure out how many medals they can pin on you," Jones had said before the first session. "But you can never tell when they might decide to pin something else on you, like part of the blame, especially if this flap gets as big as I think it will. So when this guy I'm putting in here tells you not to answer something, you do like he says, you hear?" Maurer heard and obeyed, although the issue came up only twice, once when he was questioned about his activities on the evening preceding the attack, and again when he was asked to judge the conduct of the other crew members.

In addition to the debriefing there had been two press conferences, choreographed by a public information officer. Wednesday night there was an emotional reunion with a group of his shipmates, led by Denney McGurk. And his girlfriend Sally arrived on Thursday morning, flown in from Boston on a navy jet. There had also been two long telephone conversations with Rickover, who wanted to hear his account first-hand, and even the president called to wish him well.

Through conversations with Stone and Jones he pieced together most of the story. Weston had been the only fatality among the hostages and their rescuers. The eight crewmen held on the upper level, including Fox and Dills, were rescued unharmed when Leggett and Hall surrendered without resistance. Cynthia Spencer and her mother were found hiding in the AMR; the girl was treated for three broken ribs suffered during her abduction, and her mother was hospitalized for emotional and physical exhaustion.

The terrorists were not as lucky. Leggett and Hall escaped injury, but Schmidt received a serious back wound and was hospitalized under heavy guard; his condition was reported to be good. Givens and the woman, Andrea, were killed outright. White died seven hours later on the operating table. Chief Nettles was still missing.

Throughout the week Maurer had found himself growing more and more confused about his feelings toward Nettles. At one extreme he felt contempt for the man who had betrayed his shipmates and plotted against so many innocent people. Yet he also felt a certain fascination, even a grudging admiration for the man who continued to elude what had become an international dragnet. Nettles himself had added to that confusion. On Monday morning a letter from the chief had shown up in Captain Reynolds's personal mail. In part it was a bitter attack on both the skipper and the Navy in general, but it also contained a section detailing the escape routes the terrorists were supposed to have followed, information which the C.I.A. was able to substantiate.

The letter generated a couple of opposing theories. The minority opinion was that its intent had been to make amends. The more prevalent theory was that it was an out-and-out double-cross. Maurer's own view alternated between the two, depending on how bitter he felt at the time. By Friday afternoon Maurer was becoming convinced that the question would never be resolved, at least not by asking Nettles. The man had literally vanished, and the investigators didn't have the slightest idea how he got out, much less where he was headed.

Maurer was still dwelling on the subject when Stone arrived at three o'clock; he was glad for the interruption. They exchanged friendly greetings as the officer flopped into a chair and hoisted his feet onto the end of Maurer's bed. Immediately Maurer raised a question he'd been waiting all day to ask. "Who's this reporter, Judith Nolan?"

Stone shifted uneasily. "Why do you ask?"

"Because I'm basically nosy. Last night I read the exclusive interview you gave her—all two hundred column inches. She starts out trying to shit all over you, but by the end you'd think she was writing about Richard the Lionhearted. What gives?"

"I guess she liked my answers."

Maurer eyed him suspiciously. "She certainly liked something about you. Anyway, how come you gave her the interview? I thought we were supposed to stay low."

"Let's just say I owed her a favor," Stone said.

"Yeah?"

"Besides, I needed the good press."

Maurer sobered at the gloominess of the man's voice. "The brass are really raking you over the coals, aren't they?"

Stone smiled weakly. "They have this thing about people who disobey orders."

"I like people who disobey orders, especially when it saves my ass," Maurer said; and after a moment, "Are they going to hang you?"

"No," Stone said. "They won't hang me. But they'll help me pack."

"You're resigning?"

"Effective thirty-one January."

"Well," Maurer said, "at least they're getting theirs too. Jones tells me there were about five thousand demonstrators outside the main gate last night."

Stone nodded. "Here and at half the naval bases across the country. For the past twenty-five years nuke ships have been merrily steaming in and out of most of our major harbors, but from all the yelling that's going on you'd think they arrived for the first time last Monday."

"I guess no one's really thought of them as a hazard before now. All the attention has been focused on commercial plants."

"Not any more," Stone said. "By the time this flap is over, nukes will be lucky if they're allowed to park up in the Aleutians."

"If there," Maurer said. "Jones mentioned Guantanamo Bay as a possibility."

"It's a thought," Stone said, smiling.

There was a long silence, then Maurer spoke. "Well, enough frivolity. What brings you to the mausoleum during working hours?"

"Besides your pleasant company, I wanted to drop in on the admiral."

"Spencer? How's he doing?"

"Fine, he's going home tomorrow."

"And his wife?"

Stone made a so-so gesture. "She was doing pretty well until this latest thing."

Maurer's eyes narrowed. "What latest thing?"

"You haven't heard? Last night the Spencer girl and two men busted Schmidt out of his hospital room. They got away slick as a whistle."

"You're shittin' me!"

"No shit. The girl stood in the hallway and started screaming to draw out the guards and when they came up she pulled a gun on them. She and her accomplices took Schmidt out and there hasn't been a trace of any of them since."

"Well I'll be damned," Maurer said with a chuckle. "Any idea who helped her?"

"Witnesses said they looked foreign, maybe Arab. That's all they know."

Maurer shook his head. "How do you figure it?"

"I've given up trying to figure any of this," Stone said.

"It *is* getting pretty weird," Maurer said. "And speaking of weird, anything new on Nettles?"

"Zip."

"First the chief, now Schmidt and the girl. You guys are really slipping."

"Uh-uh," Stone grunted, standing up and jamming his hat on his head. "*Those* guys. I'm out of it, and fucking glad to be!"

"Right, Dave. Whatever you say," Maurer said. "Where are you off to now?"

Stone's smile returned. "To have coffee with a certain reporter."

"Business, no doubt."

Stone paused in the doorway. "Not if I can help it."

✐ Epilogue

Three weeks after the raid on the *Bremerton*, the body of Chief Walter Nettles was discovered in a sealed-off section of a ventilation duct. Death had occurred as the result of a self-inflicted gunshot wound in the head.

Initial decontamination of the forward propulsion spaces was completed, and the plant was sealed on March 3. One week later, under her own power, the *Bremerton* proceeded to Mare Island Naval Shipyard in Vallejo, California, for replacement of her number-one reactor.

A routine intelligence summary dated June 9 reported Karl Schmidt and Cynthia Spencer to be living together in the coastal town of Paranagua, Brazil.

On October 21, Petty Officer First Class Harold T. Maurer reenlisted for another four years.